"You're early," she said, her arms full of folded linen. "Let me put this on the bed."

He watched her as she moved past him toward the bed, and he caught a fleeting scent of cinnamon. Desire washed over him so abruptly and strongly that he caught his breath. "Never mind the sheets."

She turned to face him, surprised. "For heaven's sake, Tyrone—" It was a breathless protest without strength.

He stepped to her, taking the sheets and dropping them to the floor. His hands pulled the pins from her hair and cast them aside until her hair fell about her shoulders in a shining dark brown mass. The heat of an inner fire was rising in her cheeks.

Tyrone thought she was beautiful. He always had, even before seeing this hidden part of her. He reached for buttons and began unfastening them slowly, one by one, beginning at her throat. It took a tremendous effort to keep from crushing her in his arms, but he held on to his control with all his will.

When the dress was unbuttoned to her waist, he drew the edges apart, leaving her barely veiled in her shift, her pale, soft skin gleaming in the half-light.

"This is how I think of you," he muttered roughly. "Wanting me as I want you, until nothing else matters." He yanked her against him suddenly, and he kissed her with a driving, punishing hunger, taking, demanding everything.

And his lady, her mind and senses whirling, refused nothing. Her heart was pounding, and she was burning . . . burning for him. . . .

The Thirteen Books in the Delaney Dynasty Series
Ask your bookseller for the books you have missed

THE DELANEYS, THE UNTAMED YEARS
II

Velvet Lightning

Kay Hooper

BANTAM BOOKS
TORONTO · NEW YORK · LONDON · SYDNEY · AUCKLAND

VELVET LIGHTNING
A Bantam Book / November 1988

ISBN 0-553-21980-4

Published simultaneously in the United States and Canada

Bantam Books are published by Bantam Books, a division of
Bantam Doubleday Dell Publishing Group, Inc. Its trademark,
consisting of the words "Bantam Books" and the portrayal of a
rooster, is Registered in U.S. Patent and Trademark Office and
in other countries. Marca Registrada. Bantam Books, 666 Fifth
Avenue, New York, New York 10103.

PRINTED IN THE UNITED STATES OF AMERICA

O   0 9 8 7 6 5 4 3 2 1

Author's Note

The *Delaney* saga has spanned nearly three years of my life. It began as a fun challenge, a change of pace; it began as a project with interesting possibilities. Thirteen books later, I can honestly say that our project brought with it innumerable joys and frustrations—and I wouldn't have missed it for the world.

I wish here to thank my two collaborators. My experiences with them have taught me more about writing and about myself than I could have learned alone in a decade. Their patience, generosity, and understanding made the tricky business of collaboration possible, and their friendship is a gift I treasure.

I wish also to thank everyone at Bantam. Carolyn Nichols in particular, who worked above and beyond the call of duty on the project. Each of our agents managed to hang on to her sense of humor despite being forced to cope with contracts that boggled the mind, and for that, I thank them all.

And, finally, regarding this final Delaney book of mine, I would like to apologize to those who may feel affronted by the liberties I have taken with history as we know it. In my defense, I can only say it was all done in the pursuit of a good story.

THE DELANEY DYNASTY

Shamus Delaney m. 1828 Malvina Kelly

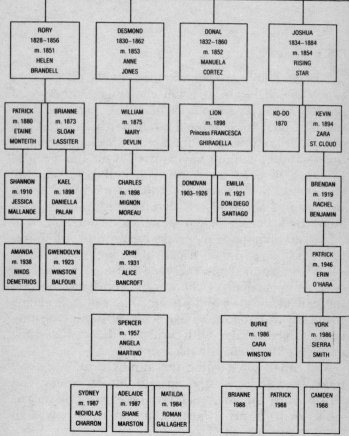

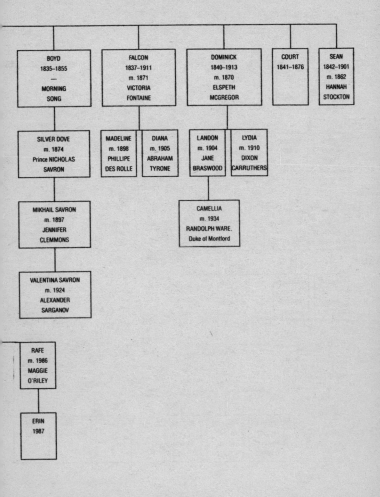

Prologue

Aboard *The Raven*
New York Harbor, November 1871

Captain Marcus Tyrone stood on the captain's deck and absently watched his unusually small crew scurrying about the ship. He had taken on volunteers this trip, explaining that *The Raven* would be at anchor for an extended period, and that those accompanying him would be expected to behave themselves.

His men took the mild warning to heart. Twenty of those who had been to Port Elizabeth on previous trips had elected to sail this time, knowing there would be rest and ease, and that they would be well paid. Bored, most likely, but well paid.

Tyrone gazed briefly back at the city, then sighed and looked ahead. He had left instructions in his office for Jesse, as he had on past occasions, and smiled a little as he thought of that young man's probable reaction. Jesse Beaumont had developed a strong liking for the sea these last years, and hated being forced to remain on dry land for any length of time. Still, he would take good care of Tyrone's business during this trip.

He was the only man Tyrone trusted to do so.

Tyrone hoped that business affairs were all Jesse would be forced to cope with. However, since Jesse had gone west to find his long-lost sister, Tyrone had had time to think everything through, time to curse the vagaries of fate. When he had received Jesse's telegram saying that all was well and that he was returning to New York, Tyrone had swiftly made his own plans to slip away.

Falcon Delaney wouldn't be stopped, Tyrone knew. That man had been on the trail of stolen gold for too many years to abandon the search no matter how obscure and tangled the path had become. And there had been too many deaths tied to the gold, the most jarring to Tyrone being the man to whom he owed so much.

REGRETS—MORGAN FONTAINE IS DEAD.

Jesse's telegram, the statement made baldly. Tyrone shook off the memory, but he couldn't help thinking of how two separate webs of intrigue and deceit spun so many years before had somehow overlapped, catching both himself and Falcon Delaney in the sticky strands. And now neither could escape.

It would be over soon. Tyrone could only hope that there was enough time yet to see his plans to their completion.

But for now he was going home.

1

The discovery of Morgan Fontaine's hiding place for the gold shipment stolen from the Union by him and his conspirators should have ended my long search at last. Unfortunately, that is not the case.

The grave had been undisturbed for years, of that I am sure. Victoria is certain Fontaine never returned to the old mission after he had buried the gold there eight years ago. The group of conspirators he betrayed are all dead; only two, in fact, survived the war, and those two were killed while still searching for the gold.

It seems obvious that no member of the group could have found and recovered the gold in the years immediately after it was secreted. That trail has ended, and I know of only one other.

Victoria and I arrived back in New York yesterday to find that *The Raven* had sailed south with Captain Tyrone aboard and in command himself. I can only believe that, as in the

3

past, he will sail to some point between Florida and the Bahamas.

Though I cannot as yet know what lay behind it all, and though I find myself reluctant to accept it, the conclusion seems inescapable. Marcus Tyrone was Fontaine's friend; he delivered the gold to Fontaine rather than to the group that had commissioned its transport. And I have discovered that back in 1865 while *The Raven* was anchored in Charleston harbor for a period of several weeks Tyrone journeyed inland alone. I can find no witnesses to his return. *The Raven* raised anchor and left the harbor with a midnight tide. She did not return to any port along the coast for six months.

A simple theft by Tyrone of the gold seems to me incredible and unbelievable. Still, I must discover the truth. I have been too long on the trail of the gold to stop now.

Victoria's brother, Jesse, was almost continually aboard *The Raven* in those days, and could doubtless provide me with at least some of the answers I seek. He, however, refuses to discuss the matter at all, and how can I press him to forget his natural and understandable loyalty to Tyrone?

I am in the unhappy position of requiring information from the man who, yesterday afternoon, stood witness to my marriage to his sister.

Camelot

Falcon, bending over a desk in a dark and silent office near the waterfront, squinted in the faint light of the desk lamp and frowned. He was staring down at a ledger which for the most part seemed to detail business transactions during the year of 1863. He had found the ledgers stacked neatly on a shelf behind the desk, with this particular year on top.

The heading on the page he stared down at was simple: only the month—*April.* There was no mention of gold. There was no explanation of a business transaction. There was only the word *Camelot* beneath the month. It was heavily underscored and followed by a list of names.

After a brief hesitation, Falcon drew a notebook from his pocket and copied the list neatly. He thumbed through the remaining pages of the ledger but found nothing of interest. He returned the ledger to its place and put out the lamp, then, soft-footed, went to the door.

Minutes later he was striding soundlessly through the dark, dangerous streets of the waterfront. Behind him, the business offices of Marcus Tyrone were left undisturbed, as though he had never been there. Tyrone wouldn't discover the illegal visit, of course, since he had left New York. But Jesse—reluctantly and with a great deal of swearing—was occupying the office in Tyrone's place, and Falcon had no intention of further upsetting his new brother-in-law.

Entering an uptown hotel a considerable time later, Falcon nodded briefly at the sleepy desk clerk and went straight upstairs. She was waiting for him, dressed for bed but awake, and relief eased her delicate features as he came into their room.

"You've been such a long time. I was beginning to worry."

Falcon pulled her into his arms and kissed her lingeringly. "Nice to have someone to worry about my hide," he murmured, then grimaced faintly. "A poor honeymoon for you, sweet."

Victoria Delaney smiled broadly at her husband. "I believe I can bear it." Then she sobered. "You won't be content until you find out what happened to that gold, and neither will I. The job has to be finished."

"Yes. The trail's getting hellishly tangled though."

"You found something."

"I'm damned if I know." He pulled her down on the bed beside him and showed her the list he had copied into his notebook. "Look at this. You'll probably recognize at least a few of these names. James Sheridan and Ryan Stewart are senators; Steven Franks is a judge; Paul Anderson is a cabinet member. And you remember Leon Hamilton."

"Yes, of course. But what's this? Camelot?"

Falcon shook his head and hesitated, then said slowly, "It sounds to me like a code name."

"And you found this in Captain Tyrone's office?"

"Um. Yes. In a ledger dated 1863."

"What does it mean?"

"It means—have you ever been to Washington, sweet?"

Washington

Victoria was amused two days later to find that the visit to the nation's capital consisted of a whirl of social events. Falcon, it emerged, believed more strongly in casual approaches to those he sought to question than in formal interviews. Victoria was learning more about her husband with each passing hour, and her respect for his intelligence and instincts grew enormously.

That he was a strong man with a powerful sense of right and wrong she knew; his persistence in the years-long search for a stolen shipment of Union gold made that obvious. He was sensitive enough to be highly aware of loyalties that couldn't be interfered with, and so refused to press her brother, Jesse, with questions about Captain Tyrone. His devotion to his forceful family was strong despite his infrequent visits home, yet he could, with a dry amusement, send a laconic telegram to Killara that stated: Lawfully wed. Falcon. And he was independent enough to subsequently ignore wires from his incensed father demanding more details.

Victoria, who had a keen desire to meet the family that had helped shape her man, cultivated her own brand of Delaney stamina and claimed her place at Falcon's side, ready at an instant's notice to go wherever his trail would lead.

Not that Falcon complained. In fact, one of her greatest joys lay in the understanding that once a woman won her place at the side of a Delaney man she belonged there always in his view. His past warning to the contrary, she discovered very early in their marriage that Falcon wasn't the kind of man to send his wife home to his family while he cheerfully went on with his job.

And since the last months had shown him quite clearly that she was a strong, intelligent woman with an innate sense of justice and the will to take matters into her own hands, he never hesitated to share the baffling questions and discuss possibilities with her.

He had made it clear that the ranch in New Mexico, left to her by her first husband, Morgan, was hers. If, when this job was completed, she wanted that to be their home, fine; he would help her in the running of it, and it would be left, in due course, to their children. It wasn't, he had said with a secret amusement, a part of the Delaney spread in Arizona, and his father wouldn't be allowed to annex it to add to the already vast family holdings.

When she was told that, Victoria was conscious of an even more intense interest in meeting the Delaney patriarch, realizing Falcon anticipated an argument with his father. More, she believed, Falcon looked forward to it.

Strong men, she thought in amusement, bred strong sons. And in Falcon, Shamus Delaney had bred a maverick, as stubborn and fiery as he was himself. He had passed stubborn Delaney traits to all his sons to varying degrees, Falcon had told her wryly.

Victoria foresaw an engaging meeting with her new in-laws and was untroubled by it. In the meantime, she had sent a telegram to the ranch saying that all was well, and that she would be returning in time. A more private communication in the shape of a long letter went to Morgan's manservant and friend, Galen, in which she told him everything that had happened these last weeks.

She was content to be with Falcon, grateful that they had found each other, that their love had survived much that could so easily have destroyed it. And she had found that her second marriage, a real and complete one, was all she had ever hoped for.

"You look beautiful tonight, sweet."

She smiled at the murmured words, her loving eyes resting on the tall, handsome figure of her husband. "I thought wives had to learn to do without compliments," she said, amused.

Falcon carried the hand he was holding to his lips, his green eyes warm and steady. "My love, they'll be putting me in the ground before you stop hearing them."

Recognizing the look in his eyes, she tucked her hand firmly in the crook of his arm and said, "We came here tonight so that you could talk to those men on the list. They're all here, and there will never be a better time. That's what you said."

Falcon sighed as they strolled through the warm, gleaming lobby of the Willard Hotel. "I meant it, at the time," he said with a touch of wistfulness. "But then your gowns came from the ranch, and you chose this black one to wear tonight. It brings back several—interesting—memories, sweet."

Victoria felt her cheeks warm, and smothered a laugh. A great deal had happened the night she had first worn the black gown, and not all were happy memories. But she knew very well which memory Falcon was referring to. "You must ask your questions," she told him serenely.

"For some time now I've been wishing that gold was in hell," he said dryly, and though both knew he half meant it, they also knew it wouldn't stop him from asking questions and seeking long-elusive answers.

"There are Mary and Leon," Victoria said as they entered the ballroom to find a glittering assemblage of Washington society enjoying themselves. She gestured slightly, indicating a couple standing near the doorway.

"Umm. I need to talk to Leon alone," Falcon murmured, "before I approach the other men."

"He'll be expecting a report, won't he?" Victoria asked as they made their way toward the other couple, knowing now that Leon Hamilton was the man who had assigned Falcon the task of finding the gold years before.

"Yes. And since he wasn't in New York when we returned, he won't be surprised to see me here. However, he may well be surprised to learn I've married since he last saw me." Falcon sounded amused.

And Leon was, though his wife, Mary, sent Victoria a look that was far less surprised. "I knew it," she said happily, embracing Victoria and kissing Falcon's cheek. "I told Leon after you both left New York that it was just a matter of time."

Falcon, thinking of everything that had happened since, grinned faintly. "That's what it was, all right. I had to chase her all the way to Texas."

"Texas!" Leon looked at him narrowly. "You told Andrew you were heading for New Mexico."

"Yes, well, things happened." Falcon shook his head, remembering. "I needed to talk to you in person, but this is the first chance I've had."

Leon nodded, his gaze revealing his curiosity. "Fine. Ladies, if you'll be so kind as to excuse us?"

"We always do," Mary said with a long-suffering sigh.

Victoria smiled at her husband. "We'll be fine."

Falcon kissed her cheek and said for her ears only, "Don't dance with anyone under seventy, or it'll be pistols at dawn." She laughed as he winked, then watched him leave with the older man.

"Well?" Mary Hamilton demanded.

Victoria looked at her innocently. "Well, what?"

Mary laughed.

In a small room down the hall from the ballroom, a frowning Leon faced Falcon. "You told Andrew you were going into New Mexico with a warrant for Morgan Fontaine's arrest. As far as I can determine, the warrant was never served. Now you say you went to Texas—and you show up here married."

"To," Falcon said softly, "Morgan Fontaine's widow."

Leon Blinked. After a moment he said, "So Fontaine's dead. Was he the one we were after?"

"Yes and no."

"Would you care to explain that?"

"It's simple enough, as far as it goes. Fontaine and those with whom he conspired did commission the transport of the gold via Captain Tyrone's blockade runner. But then something happened; my best guess is that neither Fontaine nor Tyrone could stomach what was apparently an assassination plot against Lincoln. Instead of that group of men getting the gold, Tyrone apparently delivered it directly to Fontaine, who took it all the way to Texas and buried the chests in the graveyard of an old mission."

"You found the grave?"

"Thanks to Victoria, yes."

"But . . . no gold?"

"That," Falcon said ironically, "would have been too easy, wouldn't it? No gold. The chests were there, but empty. And as far as I could tell, the grave hadn't been disturbed in years."

"Fontaine must have gone back—"

"No, Victoria's certain he didn't, and I agree with her. Fontaine didn't need the money, and once he buried the chests he never went back."

Leon was frowning even more heavily now. "Then one of the others."

"Of that list of men only three survived the war. Morgan Fontaine was killed—tortured to death—by the other two. Obviously, they didn't know where the gold was hidden. Both were later killed before the grave was found."

Leaning back in his chair, Leon lighted a cigar and brooded for a moment. "Tyrone," he said at last.

"It's the only trail left. About two years after the gold was stolen, Tyrone anchored his ship in Charleston Harbor and went inland. I don't know how far inland, but I believe he had time to go to Texas. Did he get the gold? I have no idea."

"Where is he now?"

"*The Raven* left New York a few days ago and headed south."

"Destination?"

"I haven't been able to find that out." Falcon decided not to mention Jesse; Leon was single-minded when it came to getting answers and was unlikely to appreciate the niceties of behavior that had kept Falcon from questioning his new brother-in-law.

"You'll have to find him."

"Yes." Falcon studied the older man, then said slowly, "I had a look inside Tyrone's office at the waterfront a few days ago."

"Don't," Leon said, "tell me how you got in."

"Right." Falcon grinned, then sobered. "Anyway, I found a ledger dated 1863. On a page headed by the month of April, there was a word, heavily underlined, and a list of names."

"What word?"

"Camelot."

Leon went very still, his eyes narrowing. After a moment he said slowly, "That's interesting."

"Your name was on the list, Leon." Falcon had been following no more than a hunch, but now he felt an odd leap of his senses as he took in the older man's blank expression and the guarded look in his eyes.

Leon smoked in silence, then shook his head. "You're on the wrong track, Falcon. That can have nothing to do with the stolen gold shipment. Nothing at all."

"I think it does."

"No. You're wrong."

"Was Camelot a code name?"

Leon ignored the question. In a slow, careful tone, he said, "Something happened, something Tyrone took part in. But it was before the gold was stolen, and there's no connection."

Aware that Leon would dig in his heels and refuse to say a word if he was pushed too far, Falcon probed cautiously. "Why did Tyrone write down the names of those involved?"

"He shouldn't have done that. It was reckless of him."

Falcon, who thought privately that Marc Tyrone was one of the least reckless men on earth, saw a different answer. "Was it? Or was it, perhaps, Tyrone's way of safeguarding himself—because something went wrong?"

Leon's mouth tightened. "You're guessing."

"I have the other names, Leon."

"You won't question them." Perhaps realizing that Falcon had stiffened, Leon went on more calmly. "Look, Falcon, you'll have to trust me. Camelot is not connected to the gold. It was, however, a . . . a sensitive issue at the time, and still is. If you go poking around and asking questions, you're going to disturb the men involved for no reason. *No reason.* It's a closed book, and I mean it to stay that way."

"I don't like this, Leon."

"No, I don't expect you do. But facts are facts.

There's no sense stirring up a hornet's nest when it would bring you no closer to finding the gold."

After a moment Falcon relaxed and smiled. "Well, it wouldn't be the first time I've been wrong."

Leon felt uneasy, and tried to read those enigmatic green eyes. For the first time, he questioned his own wisdom in setting a determined Delaney on the trail of lost gold. "You won't question the others?" he asked a bit sharply.

Falcon absently adjusted the leg of his trousers, his eyes veiled. "As you said. There's no sense in stirring up a hornet's nest."

"Good. Good." He hesitated. Still uneasy, he tried to project casualness into his voice. "I suppose you'll be trying to track down Tyrone now?"

"He's the only one left."

Leon nodded slowly. "Yes. Still, I can't see what use he would have had for the gold. He was a wealthy man even then."

"I know. Interesting, isn't it? The only man who couldn't possibly have needed the gold was likely the man who got it." He was watching Leon intently, saw unease and worry.

Abruptly, Leon said, "If I took you off the case, you wouldn't stop, would you?"

"No," Falcon said quietly. "I wouldn't stop."

Leon said nothing more.

Much later that night Victoria sat brushing her hair while she watched her husband pace. "It's really bothering you," she said softly.

Falcon sighed. "It wouldn't be if Leon had been less bothered himself. He's so sure this Camelot has nothing to do with the gold, but whatever it is, he's worried to death about it. I think he was shocked to find out that Tyrone had kept a list of names, had written down that code word. It's almost as if . . ."

"What?" she prompted after several seconds of silence.

"As if Leon were afraid. I've never seen him like that. As if this Camelot had the power to destroy his life."

"What if it does?"

Falcon paced a moment longer, then came to the bed and sat beside her. "I have to talk to Jesse," he said reluctantly. "I have to find Tyrone. If there *is* a connection to the gold, then he's it."

"Which are you after?" she asked him. "The gold? Or Camelot?"

"Both now. Victoria, I've always trusted my instincts. And my instincts are telling me that if I find out what this Camelot is, I'll know what happened to the gold."

After a moment she nodded. "Then you'll have to talk to Jesse. He's the only one who knows where Captain Tyrone is."

"I don't want to do it," Falcon said.

She smiled. "I know. But you don't have a choice."

"I hope Jesse sees it that way," Falcon said dryly.

2

Port Elizabeth

Flicking the thong of his whip lightly over his horse's gleaming chestnut rump, Marcus Tyrone was conscious of an unusual impatience within himself. The horse trotted more quickly, hooves rapping sharply against the hard-packed dirt of the drive. Behind the buggy, a large and imposing house loomed among tall trees draped in Spanish moss; it was almost lost in the shadows, left insubstantial, as the horse, buggy, and man moved away from it.

The horse turned automatically north toward town as it left the drive, and Tyrone shook the reins lightly to encourage a faster pace. The buggy was well-sprung and comfortable, but he hardly noticed. He glanced to the west sometime later as they topped a rise, seeing his ship, *The Raven*, at anchor in the snug little harbor. She was a neat, fast little ship, and had, during the war, made him his fortune. She had been his first ship, bought more than ten years before with a loan from Morgan Fontaine.

The loan had been repaid in full exactly one year later.

Following the road as it curved eastward, the buggy moved on, and Tyrone lost sight of the harbor. The only town on the island had been built some distance from the harbor at the northern end of the island, an inconvenience the merchants despised; they tolerated it because the settlers on Port Elizabeth had made it clear they remembered only too well the congested port cities of England and would not repeat their forebears' mistakes.

They were an odd sort of people to have settled here, Tyrone thought idly. Though far closer to American shores than to their own England, they considered themselves British subjects and had been known to fight about it when challenged. Tyrone, who didn't much care whether English or American law ruled, kept his amusement to himself and got on with the islanders quite well. Regarded with suspicion when he had built his house nearly eight years before, he was now accepted. Even if they still referred to him as "that American, Captain Tyrone."

They were, for the most part, wealthy people who had chosen to settle here, which was just as well. Port Elizabeth, named grandly for England's Virgin Queen, hadn't much to recommend it as a thriving center of agriculture or industry. The fishing was fair, but the soil refused to support crops, and all foodstuffs had to be imported. There was a severely limited supply of fresh water originating with a small wellspring, and any idea of mining was a dream. Lacking good soil, fresh water, and valuable mineral deposits, the settlers of Port Elizabeth had opted for civilization. And they were very good at it.

Tyrone, called a rogue by his own people, found the settlers of the island amusing in their careful surface courtesy and extreme refinement of manner. Amusing enough, at any rate, to be willing to be polite and civilized himself.

In general, he spent at least a week out of every month in Port Elizabeth, returning between visits to his shipping business based in New York City. He planned to remain considerably longer this time. He had arrived late the night before and had gone directly to his house without stopping in town. The middle-aged couple who kept house for him had greeted him without surprise, having grown accustomed to his comings and goings.

He suspected he was an enigma to them; if so, they never mentioned it. To them, as to the settlers of the island, Marc Tyrone was a wealthy businessman who kept a second home there, and who could be counted on not to disgrace himself with drunkenness or with compromising unmarried daughters. (A daughter or two had been heard to complain about that, but only amongst themselves.)

He was a tall, loose-limbed man with powerful shoulders and a way of moving that was like a big, lazy cat. He had black hair lightly silvered at the temples, a handsome face, and rather cold and impersonal gray eyes. His smile, which he rarely offered, was surprisingly charming.

A few female heads turned as his buggy swept briskly down the main and only street of the little town, and polite nods of welcome were sent his way. Tyrone returned the gestures with exact courtesy, giving only what he received and neither asking nor offering more. He stopped the buggy before the mercantile and got out, moving forward to tether his horse.

He felt again the unaccustomed flash of impatience, a touch of eagerness that was alien to him. He was, for the most part, a patient man, given to observing, to reflecting cynically, and this unusual mood surprised him. He was, he decided finally, merely tense and restless from having worked hard since his last visit. It would do him good to relax.

That settled to his satisfaction, he stepped up onto the wooden sidewalk, and promptly cannoned into a tall lady burdened with packages who was leaving the store briskly. The packages, of course, scattered wildly, and Tyrone quickly grasped her upper arms to keep them both on their feet. He could feel her stiffen instantly, and wasn't surprised when she stepped back the moment balance was regained.

"Pardon me, Miss Waltrip," he said politely, and bent to gather the packages at her feet. At her feet . . . the thought was secretly amusing to him.

She waited in silent disdain, a tall, slender woman not yet irrevocably "on the shelf" at twenty-eight, but fast approaching the status of spinster. It didn't appear to trouble her. Nothing, in fact, appeared to trouble Miss Catherine Waltrip. The unattached men of Port Elizabeth tended to eye her warily; the women treated her with the same frigid politeness she offered them; and her charming rogue of a father often seemed her child rather than her parent when he quailed visibly before her ironic gaze.

She had dark hair worn always in a braided coronet, the milky pale complexion of old porcelain, and frosty blue eyes. Her voice was calm, her posture straight, her gaze direct and impersonal. A genuine smile might have made her beautiful, but even her meaningless public smile was rare and brief.

She wasn't smiling now.

Tyrone got to his feet, holding her packages and inclining his head politely. "May I carry them for you, Miss Waltrip?"

"No, thank you. Sir."

The "sir," he thought, had definitely been tacked on as a pointed afterthought. He bore the subtle insult like a gentleman. "My pleasure," he insisted.

With an economy of movement she reclaimed her packages, never once touching him with her neatly gloved hands. She nodded briefly in spurious courtesy and walked past him.

Tyrone turned to watch her, absently admiring the straightness of her carriage, her brisk, almost mannish stride. She went a short distance down the street and stowed her packages in the back of a buggy like his own, then climbed in with grace and without help, showing no more that a fleeting glimpse of a neatly turned ankle. She picked up the reins and moved away down the street, looking straight ahead. She would, Tyrone knew, drive to the big weathered house just outside town, where she and her father had lived for slightly more than two years.

"That woman!"

Tyrone turned back toward the store, correctly guessing that the explosive comment had been intended to gain his attention. "Good morning, Mrs. Symington," he said cordially, greeting the self-elected guardian of manners, morals, and gossip on Port Elizabeth.

She simpered a bit, a stout, middle-aged lady, tightly corsetted and sporting an impressive hat of French ancestry. "How nice to have you back among us, Captain Tyrone. Are you staying long this time?"

"I haven't decided, ma'am," he said, although it was a barefaced lie; caution was the watchword around this woman.

"I'm having a small dinner party tomorrow night. If you're free, perhaps—?"

"Unfortunately," he said, "I don't believe I will be. But thank you."

She eyed his noncommittal expression and was undaunted. "Well, come if you can."

"Yes, ma'am."

She glanced past him at the disappearing buggy and, her grievances recalled, said again, "That woman!"

Tyrone had been waiting for it. Mrs. Lettia Symington had a daughter of marriagable age, and had a habit of sweetly—and quite slanderously, he thought—discussing other young women with any unattached man. She also despised Catherine Waltrip because she had never succeeded in cutting her down to the proper size.

"Has Miss Waltrip upset you, ma'am?" he asked, wondering if anything unusual had happened in the month since his last visit to the island.

Mrs. Symington swelled perceptibly with righteous indignation. "She insulted me! She insulted my hat!"

Tyrone eyed the confection of lace, plumes, and what appeared to be at least three birds, and hid his laughter behind a grave expression. "Terribly rude of her," he offered, biting the inside of his cheek to keep himself from asking what, exactly, Miss Waltrip had said about the hat.

"She's a horrid woman," Mrs. Symington said roundly, with none of her usual hinting. "It's a disgrace, the way she treats that delightful father of hers. Why, I wouldn't be a bit surprised if she'd done something just *terrible* back in England, and that was why she dragged him here. Poor man, he's always longing to go back and visit, but, of course, she won't hear of it!"

Tyrone, who thought privately that Lucas Waltrip complained a good deal too much about a great many things, had no comment to make.

And Mrs. Symington, her spleen partially vented, adjusted her hat, smiled brilliantly, and, with a maternal pat on his arm, invited him to "just drop in anytime," before going on her way to spread more joy.

He reflected cynically that she'd be appalled if he *did* visit her opulent home unexpectedly because her daughter wouldn't have time to get herself up properly for the occasion. Tyrone went inside to ask the shopkeeper, Mr. Abernathy, to increase the regular weekly shipment of groceries to his house since he was back on the island. He also ordered a dozen shirts, disregarding the fact that his own ship had likely brought them in, and talked casually for a few moments; aside from Mrs. Symington, Mr. Abernathy was the best source of gossip in town.

"Has anything interesting happened lately?" Tyrone asked.

Mr. Abernathy, a heavily built man who would have looked more at home tending bar or shoeing horses, pursed his lips in thought as he stood negligently behind the long counter.

"We had the magistrate in last week," he offered. "Mrs. Symington accused Miss Waltrip of drowning that little dog of hers in the stream. Said it was sheer spite and nothing more. Got properly tearful about it. Half the town turned up in court."

"And believed Mrs. Symington, no doubt," Tyrone murmured.

"Oh, well, as to that, there was no proof, you know. And a bit hard to picture Miss Waltrip tossing the little dog to its death. Wouldn't want to dirty her hands, I'd guess."

Tyrone looked at him for a moment, reflecting that the townspeople had most certainly believed Mrs.

Symington. They always did. He changed the subject, talked casually for a few more minutes, then lazily took his leave. He unhitched his horse and climbed into the buggy. He drove back the way he'd come, passing the small bank, the equally small hotel, a restaurant, a barbershop, two dressmakers' shops, and the livery stable.

Leaving the town behind, he drew the whip across the chestnut's rump and they moved on briskly. He passed the Waltrip house without a glance. Just around the bend, with the house hidden by tall trees, he drew up and sat listening for a moment. No sound. He glanced around to make certain, then turned his horse off the main road and onto a rutted track that seemed to disappear into the cool depths of the island's inland forest. Within moments the buggy was surrounded by shade and cool.

Sometime later a small cottage appeared suddenly, as if it had grown from the forest. It had a thatched roof, two windows in front, a solid wooden door, and looked to contain perhaps two rooms. Tyrone halted the horse and climbed out of the buggy. The chestnut, having been there before, rested a hind leg and swished his tail lazily, preparing to doze. Tyrone walked to the front door, absently noticing that bright blue curtains hung gaily in the window. They were new. He opened the door without knocking and went in.

"You're late," she said, turning to greet him.

"You're a shrew," he retorted, and pulled her into his arms.

Catherine Waltrip instantly melted against him, her arms sliding up around his neck, her lips warmly responsive. He held her tightly against him. His hands roamed up her slender back until they reached her

hair. Pins scattered about them, and her waist-length
dark hair fell like silk through his fingers.

"You always do that," she murmured, smiling.

"Do what?" He was exploring her throat. It was
soft, fragrant, immensely tempting. He felt the laugh
in her throat as well as heard it, and thought vaguely
that Mrs. Symington would have been amazed. The
whole town would have been amazed.

She was pushing his coat off his shoulders, coping
familiarly with his tie, with buttons. He was aware
of their urgency, hers as well as his; it was always
like this when he first came back to the island. Clothing lay where it fell, discarded carelessly. She would
shake her head about that later.

He held her slender, naked body against his briefly,
but was hardly able to contain his desire when her
full breasts pressed against his chest, when the softness at the base of her belly enticed his swollen loins.
His heart was hammering, his breath coming roughly.
Impatient, he swept her up into his arms and carried
her through the bare central room and to the tiny
bedroom that held only a sturdy brass bed. The covers had already been folded back to the foot of the
bed.

The window in this room, uncurtained, spilled weak
light onto the bed.

She pulled him down half on top of her, refusing to
let him ease himself down as he would have. Her
hands moved over him, long fingers clever and sure.
She raised her head from the pillow and gently bit
his shoulder. The frosty blue eyes were darkened and
gleaming now, veiled by long lashes and deliberation. Her lips were curved in a half smile, and she
was beautiful.

Tyrone held a tight rein on his urgency and allowed himself to become reacquainted with her body. Her slenderness clothed was deceptive; naked, she was sinuous elegance and lusty curves. Her breasts were full and firm, tipped with pink nipples that were hard now under his lips. Her stomach was flat and firm; her hips curved gently; her legs were long and strong.

Her cool, poised exterior disappeared in passion. Her flesh heated as if a fire raged inside her, almost burning him, and there was something essentially greedy in her instant readiness for him. He had, once, aroused her from across a room at a boring party with no more than a veiled look; he had seen her immediate response in darkened eyes and unconsciously parted lips, had smiled secretly at it. Later, she had called him a bastard.

He slid one hand slowly down over her stomach, feeling the deep muscles contract and quiver, hearing her gasp. He rasped his tongue roughly over her breasts, taking his time, rubbing her belly slowly, lightly, until her nails bit into his back and she moaned. He moved his hand quickly then, his palm covering the soft curls of her nest as her legs parted jerkily for him. He explored the slick, swollen flesh, probing her readiness, caressing her with sure knowledge.

She cried out, her hips lifting, arms straining to draw him closer. Tyrone gave in to her need and his own, moving over her, settling between her thighs. He entered her slowly, luxuriating in her tight heat as her body sheathed his. The pleasure was so intense that he gritted his teeth, though not in time to stop the groan from escaping. Her legs closed about him tightly, holding him deep inside her for a moment. Then, when he began thrusting, she answered his rhythm instantly, wildly, taking him as completely as he took her.

This was the Catherine the people of Port Elizabeth would never know, and Tyrone delighted in his own secret knowledge of her. He delighted in her uninhibited passion, her unashamed need. He exulted in the fire he had discovered in her, the laughter, the sharp tongue. He had found, underneath the cool, poised surface of her, a storm raging. She fascinated him endlessly.

Their urgency now caught them, drove them, until movements were quick and sharp with need, until their bodies strove together like two halves of one, with primitive grace. Until the quiet of the tiny bedroom splintered with sounds of release that were barely human.

She stretched languidly beside him, boneless as a cat. Tyrone raised himself on an elbow and looked down at her. He put a gentle hand on her flat stomach, and she made a soft, almost unconscious sound of pleasure, eyes closed, lips smiling.

"I hope," he said, "that you don't have to go home soon."

Catherine opened her eyes and looked at him sleepily. "It isn't even noon," she murmured. "Disgraceful, meeting a lover before lunchtime."

"That wasn't an answer," he told her.

"Ummm. Father's got a game on."

That, he knew, was an answer. Her father occasionally hosted poker games with cronies, and Catherine's absence during those games would never be noticed.

"Good," he said. "Then we have the afternoon."

She wouldn't stay longer, and refused to spend the

night with him. She also refused to visit his house, or to allow him in her own except on extremely rare social occasions. This cottage only.

Tyrone studied her slender, creamy body, aware of familiar stirrings but also aware that this time passion would build slowly and last a very long time. He could wait. Once with her, he could wait easily.

They had been lovers for nearly two years. On his last visit to the island, he had asked her to marry him. With composure, and without explanation, she had refused. It had changed nothing.

From another woman, Tyrone might well have demanded an explanation. But not from Catherine. He had gradually come to realize that there were things she would never share with him, parts of herself that were locked securely away from him. It had begun to trouble him only recently.

He knew well her pride, her cool ability to hide whatever wounds were inflicted by the hostility of the townspeople. She never complained, never defended herself, never explained. She had a wickedly sharp tongue in pointing out pretension, identifying hypocrisy. She didn't hesitate to show him the quickness of her perception and her way with words, but in public her manners, almost without exception, were rigidly polite.

Tyrone had no idea at all of what she really thought of him. He had realized only as he was returning to New York after his last visit that her refusal to marry him had been a blow. To his pride, perhaps. The proposal itself had been made on impulse, and he had shrugged off the rejection as best he could. She had not rejected him as a lover, and if his ability to arouse her so swiftly and completely was one she viewed with rueful acceptance, at least she accepted it.

"You're a bastard, Tyrone," she said, still sleepily.

He was watching her breasts rise and fall as she breathed, and responded absently. "Oh? What have I done now?" He had long ago decided that if she ever called him Marc, it would be because he had finally gotten close to her; she used his surname deliberately to hold him away, and he knew it.

"You know what you've done. If I hadn't seen *The Raven* in the harbor this morning, it would have been a total shock. Appearing out of nowhere in town, no warning. And Lettia Symington not two feet away!"

He chuckled. "What did you say to her about that damned hat? She was livid."

Catherine smiled her secret, private smile, and he watched it in fascination. "I just asked her when those birds were going to hatch their eggs and fly away, since they'd been roosting on that hat since last spring."

Tyrone laughed again. "You definitely touched a nerve. She couldn't wait to tear you to shreds."

"I don't doubt it. Never misses an opportunity, our Lettia."

"Abernathy said she'd had you up before the magistrate. Something about that yapping cur of hers?"

Catherine's smile died. "Yes. Somebody drowned the poor brute, and she naturally settled on me. The magistrate told her not to be foolish and dismissed the case."

"Ummm. And Lettia's supporters?"

Very dryly Catherine said, "Disappointed. They would dearly love to hang me from the nearest tree. But that would be uncivilized, you understand. Hardly the done thing."

Tyrone studied her face thoughtfully. She was too intelligent not to feel the pinpricks, too proud not to be aware of every slighting glance and remark. He wondered suddenly why she stood it, why she didn't just leave the island.

Her lashes flickered up, blue eyes regarding him. "Why are you looking so grave?"

"No reason. You haven't asked how long I'm staying this trip."

She looked faintly surprised. "It's usually a week or so."

"Longer this time. A few months, perhaps." He was watching her intently, and her reaction disturbed him. Alarm stirred in her clear eyes, then wariness; both emotions were fleeting, very quickly gone or hidden.

Calmly she said, "That will be nice. Unless you tire of me, of course."

After a moment he said, "No, there's no chance of that." Abruptly, driven by a need he didn't question, he added, "You've been the only woman in my bed since that first afternoon by the stream."

She was clearly surprised, and looked at him rather searchingly. Slightly hesitant, she said, "I assumed there was a woman in New York."

"No. You're all the woman I can handle." He made it light, mocking.

She laughed, seeming almost relieved by his mockery. "You're a liar, Tyrone. And you know exactly how to appeal to a woman's vanity. Experience, no doubt."

"No doubt," he agreed dryly, knowing she wouldn't take him seriously. Knowing she didn't want to. What he didn't know was *why*. From the beginning of their relationship she had quite coolly and calmly set the boundaries; she would be his lover in secret but not his mistress in public. Her reputation would remain uncompromised, and there would be no tears when it was over. A sensible, adult agreement, unmarred by sentiment.

He had been her first and, as far as he knew, only lover.

Smiling, he bent his head to place a warm kiss on her firm stomach. But when he raised back up, he surprised an expression in her eyes that went through him like a knife. It was quickly gone, replaced by the glow of building passion, and the moment to ask about it vanished.

But he didn't forget it. He didn't think he would ever forget that brief, stark look of sheer agony in her beautiful eyes.

He thought it would haunt him as long as he lived.

Passion did grow slowly this time, almost lazily, as he'd thought it would and he was going to make it last even longer. He teased her, his mouth and hands moving over her heating body with a feather-light touch. His own body was hard, the blood pounding through his veins, but he ignored his own need. She responded, as always, with throaty sounds, her body trembling, breath coming quickly, shallowly. For the first time it wasn't enough for him. He wanted—

"Say my name, Catherine," he commanded, his hands full of her swollen breasts, lips just grazing the tight nipples.

Gleaming sapphire eyes focused on his face, and she bit her lip and tugged at his shoulders mutely.

"Say it." He drew a nipple into his mouth, sucking harshly, one hand sliding down her body suddenly, his fingers raking through dark curls but avoiding the wet, throbbing flesh.

"Tyrone!" she gasped.

"No. My *name*. Say my name, Catherine." He covered her flushed breasts with hot kisses, tiny bites, then captured her lips. He kissed her deeply, lips hard and hot, his tongue delving, exploring, sinuously demanding her instant response. He settled over her, between her thighs, but refused to take her. He let her feel him against her yearning flesh but refused to move, holding himself away from her on rigid arms, muscles bunched and trembling. "Say it!"

There was a sudden flash of pure fury in her darkened eyes, and she made a choked sound of torment. She raked her nails down his back, caught him with her long, strong legs, with silent, desperate insistence.

"Goddammit," he said thickly, and, defeated, sank his hard, throbbing flesh into hers. His hands slid beneath her firm buttocks, lifting her to meet each powerful thrust, trying to bury himself in her. The scalding heat of her held him, captured him. He watched her through angry, slitted eyes, and when her throat suddenly convulsed, he covered her lips with his, catching the cry of release, taking it whether she would give it to him or not, stealing it.

He felt her body contract around his, and that inner caress spurred his own violent, headlong plunge toward satisfaction. He drove into her again and again, into tight heat and wet yearning. And he felt her stiffen even as he lunged a final time, catching her second wild cry with his mouth, mingling it with his own guttural groan of terrible pleasure. . . .

Neither mentioned his failure to force his name from her. They were more quiet than usual, saying little, resting side by side on the wide bed without touching. When the shadows in the room grew longer, the light fainter, he made love to her again. And, again, it was wild, almost a battle, two strong wills clashing, two passionate bodies merging in heat and silence.

He didn't ask her to say his name.

Tyrone reluctantly pulled himself from the bed and went into the other room to gather their clothing, knowing that as usual he would leave first. She would strip the bed and carry the linens back to her house, and on their next meeting would have the bed remade with fresh sheets. He wondered idly what she would say if someone caught her emerging from the woods with a bundle of sex-scented linen. Something daunting, no doubt. He had never seen her lose composure, except in bed. And even then, some part of her mind was composed.

"Tomorrow," he said standing by the bed and shrugging into his coat.

Catherine, lying naked and lazy on the bed, eyed him thoughtfully. "All right. But not until after three."

He bent, bracing a hand on either side of her, and kissed her thoroughly. "Come to my house," he said against her lips.

"No." Her eyes gleamed at him.

He straightened, smiling down at her. "Here."

"Here," she echoed.

"You're a stubborn woman."

Catherine smiled, agreeing with him. She watched him shake his head and turn away, watched him walk to the door and look back at her over one broad shoulder. Then he was gone.

She lay quietly on the bed, her smile gone with him. She listened to the sounds of the buggy moving away from the cottage. She knew she should get up and get dressed in the clothing he had left on the bed for her. She had to hurry home. She didn't move. Her breasts felt heavy, tender, in the aftermath of passion and his caresses. Her entire body was warm, languid.

In the silence of the room she softly released what he had tried to force from her, giving it to the lonely emptiness.

"Marc. . . ."

At the southwestern end of the island the chestnut turned briskly off the main road and onto a private drive. Tyrone didn't hurry the horse now, but merely held the reins, his mind wandering slightly, always returning to Catherine. What pleasure she gave him! What incredible pleasure!

The drive curved up close to the big three-storied stone house, and the horse stopped automatically. There was another buggy waiting near the front door, and as Tyrone stepped down an elderly man carrying a small black bag came out of the house.

Frowning a little, Tyrone met him halfway to the house. "Dr. Scott," he said, and immediately asked, "Is he—?"

"No, no." Behind rimless spectacles Charles Scott's faded blue eyes were still sharp, still intelligent. "He's much the same. Weakening, of course, but I warned you about that. He tires easily, and he'll sleep a great deal from now on." Dr. Scott's voice was surprisingly deep.

After a moment Tyrone said bleakly, "And the end?"

Dr. Scott looked at him intently. "Not long now. As little as a week—perhaps as long as a month. He won't suffer, lad. Likely as not, he'll go to sleep and simply not wake up. To be perfectly truthful, I'm amazed he lasted this long. You've done a fine job of making his last years happy ones."

Tyrone didn't respond but merely stood and gazed broodingly at his front door.

Dr. Scott, who had retired to Port Elizabeth years before only to find himself still in demand for special cases, studied the younger man thoughtfully. A curious man, Captain Tyrone, he thought, and an interesting one. For the most part, he was cynical and hard, a sardonic observer of those around him. Yet Scott had the odd idea that Tyrone was a man who wanted to believe in something, that he had once found something and was fighting even now to preserve it despite its inexorable ending, that there was, somewhere inside him, a core of idealism.

To Dr. Scott's mind, nothing else could explain what Tyrone had done. Nothing else would explain his commitment and caution, his astonishingly selfless care of a man who had no claim upon him. He had disrupted his own life without comment or complaint and had built a secret and safe haven for the man.

"Should I send for you if he becomes worse?" Tyrone asked abruptly, his voice as always without emotion when discussing Dr. Scott's patient with him.

The doctor shook his head. "No need. We've passed the violent stage long ago. If he should grow agitated, give him laudanum; I've left a new bottle with the nurse." He hesitated, then added impersonally, "I've offered her a position with me once he's gone. The island needs a nurse."

Tyrone looked intently at him. "Fine." His voice was even.

Dr. Scott nodded. He went on to his buggy and climbed in, then drove away. He felt he was leaving an enigma behind.

Tyrone had taken one step toward the house, when another man came around the corner. He was middle-aged, stout, placid, and laconic, with mild brown eyes and graying hair.

"Captain. Will you be needing the buggy again today, sir?"

"No. Have it ready for me tomorrow afternoon, if you will, Reuben."

"Yes, sir." Reuben, half of the couple that took care of Tyrone's house and grounds, touched his forehead in a half-forgotten military salute and went to lead the horse around to the stables.

Reuben's wife, Sarah, was known to be plagued by stiffening in her joints, and was often visited by Dr. Scott. No one in town was surprised or curious about his visits. In fact, many had spoken kindly of Tyrone's having sent for the doctor from time to time. Such a nice man, to care like that. And nice to have allowed Sarah's sister to stay as well; no one in town knew that the "sister" was actually a nurse and no kin to Sarah.

Tyrone went inside. The house had been built on noble lines, with large rooms and high ceilings. The furnishings were sparse but all good pieces, which gave the house a spare, clean look. Tyrone liked space around him, openness. There was evidence that this was more a home to him than the apartment he kept in New York: artwork from Europe and the Far East, rugs and tapestries, books everywhere.

He didn't pause downstairs but went directly up the curving staircase to the second floor, where his bedroom was located, bypassed it, and climbed on up to the third floor. This part of the house was quiet, most of the rooms shut off and furniture under dust covers. At the end of the long hallway, however,

were several rooms that were regularly used. The
doors of two of them were open. A third door was
also open and Tyrone entered.

He saw first the nurse, Mrs. Tully, a widow of
undetermined years with gray hair and a kind face.
She was sitting by the window with her knitting, and
looked up with a smile when he came in. "Captain."

"How is he?" Tyrone asked, keeping his voice low
and glancing toward a room off to the right of this
pleasant sitting room.

"Well enough," she answered placidly. "A bit ex-
cited over your having come home. He's got the gifts
you left for him this morning. I told him you'd be
sure to come and see him."

Nodding his thanks, Tyrone went quietly into the
other room. He saw a clutter of picture books and
toys scattered over the rug. Only toy soldiers were
missing from the myriad collection; the man didn't
like soldiers, they upset him. A fire was burning in
the hearth because the man was always cold now.
There were comfortable overstuffed chairs, a divan, a
scarred old oak desk covered with drawings in charcoal. The man, sitting among the clutter on the floor,
lurched to his feet, a big grin on his face.

"Marc!"

"Good evening," Tyrone said cheerfully.

"Tully said you'd come and see me. And the presents! You always bring good presents."

He was a tall, shambling man, dressed warmly in
a fisherman's sweater and heavy trousers. Thick
lace-up boots were on his exceptionally large feet.
His hands were knobby and awkward, hands now
holding an exquisitely detailed wooden coach-and-
four.

"Will you read to me?" he asked eagerly.

"Of course I will. Pick out a book." Tyrone looked at him with a sadness that was no longer understood or even noticed by the man. He accepted the storybook held out to him and settled into a chair with it, preparing to read aloud an old and much-favored story.

Gravely and patiently he began to read. He spoke in a slow rhythm because the man had difficulty in understanding now. There had come a point in the not too distant past when the man had seen and realized what he was losing, what he would become; it had been mercifully brief.

Unusual, Dr. Scott had said clinically.

Tragic, Tyrone had replied without emotion.

He lifted his gaze from the book now and then, his voice going on steadily because he knew the story word for word. He no longer had to pay attention. So he looked into guileless eyes that had already begun to wander. He wouldn't finish reading the story. He never did now.

But Tyrone read on, patiently, to the great shambling childlike wreck of a man.

3

Catherine Waltrip slipped back into her father's house without incident. She heard male laughter from the closed study but ignored it. There were no servants to see her as she made her way to the washroom— a woman came in daily but left shortly after noon. Catherine kept house for her father, and even her detractors in town·admitted grudgingly that she did it well.

She left the bundled sheets in the washroom and then went into her own room to check her appearance since there was no mirror in the cottage. Perhaps she could . . .

She stopped the thought before it could fully form. No. No mirror for the cottage. She'd been foolish in hanging curtains in the windows, foolish in putting a quilt on the bed. Tyrone hadn't commented on either. She hadn't expected him to.

A glance in her mirror showed her that she was neat, calm. On the surface she was the frosty Miss Waltrip that the members of the community of Port Elizabeth knew well. And if she herself was conscious, between her thighs, of the damp reminder of a lover's visit, then no one else could have guessed.

She saw her eyes go cloudy in the mirror and turned away abruptly.

Enough of this. *Enough.*

She went back downstairs, unexpectedly encountering her father in the hall. Lucas Waltrip was a bluff, genial man of great charm. He was her height, which made him a medium-sized man—or would have been if his frame hadn't been padded comfortably. He had iron-gray hair and brilliant blue eyes, and bore no resemblance whatsoever to his daughter ... his daughter, who now looked pointedly at the bottle in his hand.

"Hello, Father," she said.

He didn't try to hide the bottle; she had sharp eyes. "Just a drop or two, Catherine," he wheedled gaily. "Just to wet our throats—"

She plucked the bottle from his hand. "No, Father. Where did this come from?"

His lips firmed in mulish determination, the gaiety instantly gone. "If I want to bring liquor into this house, I'll do it! And if you weren't so busy poking into my affairs instead of finding yourself a husband like any decent girl, you wouldn't worry about it."

Catherine kept her voice soft and calm. "I'll have dinner ready in an hour, Father, and you can have a glass of that wine you enjoy so much. The game should be over now anyway. It is, isn't it?"

"Yes," he admitted grudgingly, calming somewhat.

"You should tell your guests good-bye, then."

"All right, Catherine." He sighed suddenly and turned away toward his study, shoulders slumping.

The meekness wouldn't last, she knew. Something would set him off again, and he'd rampage and roar, and she'd have her hands full until he settled down. She looked at the bottle in her hand, lips twisting, and went away to pour it down the kitchen drain. She remained there to prepare dinner, working quickly and blanking her mind so that she wouldn't think. It had gotten easier with practice, and she had practiced a great deal.

But something was wrong. Something had changed. Her mind kept returning of its own volition to a secret cottage in the woods, slipping away there before she could stop it. And even the mental visits made her body ache and long, made the breath catch in her throat and her heart pound.

Enough.

She ate at the polished rectangular table with her father, responding to his occasional remarks with little attention. She hardly tasted the food she had prepared.

"*The Raven's* back, I noticed."

"Yes, Father. I saw it too."

"Her, Catherine. You saw her. A ship's always female."

"I'll try to remember."

Tyrone. He was the difference. Something had changed between them. He had changed since his last visit. Even, she realized, before his last visit. He had been a remote man for as long as she'd known him, even to a certain degree in bed. A highly sensual man but able to set aside his own needs instantly if something attracted the interest of his keen mind. Until very recently he hadn't done that. Until recently his mind hadn't concerned itself overmuch with the woman in his secret bed. Theirs had been a purely physical relationship, one of simple convenience for them both. Tyrone had found a woman to lie with him without ties or demands, and she—

"I suppose the captain will be staying his usual week," her father commented casually.

"I suppose."

"You could do worse than Tyrone, Catherine. He's a rich man. A cold bastard, but then—" He broke off, looking guilty.

But then, so are you, she finished in her mind. Not a bastard, of course, but cold. Even her father thought so. "I have no interest in marrying, Father."

"You need a man, Catherine." Lucas spoke quickly, trying to smooth away his cruel words of moments before. "Someone to take care of you when I'm gone." Even he couldn't quite put conviction into the words; he believed too strongly that his daughter needed no one to take care of her.

She glanced up at him, then returned her attention to her plate. "I'll be fine," she said colorlessly.

Lucas grunted and fell silent.

Catherine ate without tasting the food. Tyrone, she thought, had been satisfied with a bed partner, asking nothing more. And she had been satisfied. More than satisfied. It hadn't been easy for her to set aside the morals her mother had long ago instilled in her, but she had recognized that if she had not accepted Tyrone's attentions, she would certainly have never known what it was like to lie in a man's arms and feel his passion. Her own unexpected passion.

Faced with the need he evoked and her own impossible situation, Catherine had chosen, eyes wide open, to make herself a whore.

He didn't treat her that way, of course. He treated her as a man might, she imagined, treat a mistress. Except that she had made it clear she would accept nothing from him, not money or gifts. For the rest, he respected her insistence on secrecy, taking pains never to mar her reputation. He was never cruel to her, never insulting. He made love to her with sensitivity and skill, never putting his own pleasure above hers.

He had for these past two years been a steady part of her life. He would appear in Port Elizabeth, his ship anchored in the harbor and usually loaded with supplies and merchandise for the town. He would remain for a few days or a week, meeting her several times at the cottage, occasionally in public. And then he would be gone again, usually without good-byes.

"Catherine, Lettia has invited me to a dinner party tomorrow night. I accepted."

She looked up slowly as her father made the defiant statement. His face was mulish. "I see. Father, Dr. Scott said that you should rest more—"

"The hell with Scott. Man's a goddamned quack. Lettia sets a fine table, Catherine, and I'm going."

Well, then she would go too, though she hadn't been invited. It was just one of the things she forced herself to do, facing Lettia Symington's stiff scorn, intruding where she wasn't wanted. She didn't look forward to it.

"I'm going," Lucas repeated in a rising voice.

"All right," Catherine said calmly. "That's fine, Father."

He subsided, muttering to himself.

She hoped Tyrone wouldn't be at the dinner party. It was doubtful that he would be. He generally took care to avoid Lettia's matchmaking snares. Still, he occasionally appeared at a reception or dinner party, especially if he knew she would be attending. And that was dangerous.

He was looking at her differently now, she realized. It was obvious that he had for some reason grown discontented with their relationship. He was a highly perceptive man, a man given to observing those around him with unusual clarity; if he had for some reason become interested in the part of herself she withheld from him, then he wouldn't stop until he knew it all.

Catherine felt her throat close up, felt panic stir in her mind.

"You aren't eating, Catherine. Do you feel unwell?"

"I'm fine, Father. Quite all right."

Something flashed across his brilliant blue eyes, something like disappointment. He was half hoping, she knew, that she wouldn't feel well enough to accompany him to Lettia's dinner party. He always hoped he could go alone, and he would be unusually affectionate toward her both to hide his guilt and to convince her that there really was no need for her to accompany him.

They both knew she would go.

"You should have an early night, Catherine," he said now, persuasively.

"Yes. Perhaps I will."

"It will do you good. You're pale."

"Yes. All right."

Satisfied, he returned to the meal, sipping the wine she allowed him. One glass. Only one glass.

Catherine pushed the food around on her own plate, trying to fight the dread she felt, trying not to feel at all. But she couldn't stop feeling now. She had forced herself to be content with her life, to avoid asking for more. But the ache that was longing tormented her more with every day that passed.

Tyrone. *Damn him.*

He was staying longer this time. Looking at her in a new way, with a new intensity. He would see more, see things she didn't want him to see. As an occasional lover he had been kept apart from the rest of her life, kept separate. Kept safe.

"I'll have another glass," her father said suddenly, truculently.

Catherine looked at him for a moment, then murmured, "I'll pour it for you, Father." She rose and went around to get his glass, then stepped to the sideboard, where a bottle of wine stood open; she would, as always, return it to the kitchen after dinner, hide it away where he couldn't easily find it. She glanced back once to see a glimpse of her father's satisfied expression. He thought he had won a point. Fine. She slipped a hand into the pocket of her skirt and smoothly pulled out a small bottle. Quickly, making certain Lucas didn't see, she poured a splash of liquid into the wineglass and then capped the bottle and returned it to her pocket. Within seconds wine had been poured to join the liquid, and she stirred it quickly with one finger.

She took the glass back to her father.

"Thank you, Catherine," he said genially.

"You're welcome, Father." She returned to her chair, wondering tiredly how long she could keep from him the knowledge that she had been systematically drugging him for months.

"Catherine."

She halted on the sidewalk but concentrated on pulling on her gloves, keeping her expression icily aloof. It was early the following afternoon, and she had had a wakeful, restless night. A glance around beneath her lashes had shown her that the street was deserted, but she knew only too well the interest that would be kindled if she were seen talking to Marc Tyrone for no apparent reason.

For the first time, that consideration seemed to have no power to sway him. He stood squarely before her, tall and powerful, innate danger hidden in the depths of his impersonal gray eyes—except that now they weren't impersonal. Now they were intent, almost, she thought dimly, disturbed.

"Not here," she whispered, conscious, as always, of the pulse of awareness he could bring to life with no more than his presence.

He ignored that but kept his voice low. "Catherine, why did you go to see Dr. Scott this morning?"

She felt a jolt, and tried not to let it show. After a moment she said calmly, "Father has a touch of the gout. I wanted to consult with the doctor about the advisibility of his drinking."

"That was all?"

"Of course." She gave him a veiled glance. "I didn't see you."

"I was just riding by. Exercising one of the horses." He sounded as though he might be irritated with her. "If it was such an innocent visit, why did you go to see Scott at his house? He's in his office here in town most days."

Catherine smoothed the fabric over her fingers, fixing all her attention on the task. Just the sound of his voice . . . She could feel her body react to him, feel her heart pound, her breath quicken. She fought the sensations, knowing it wouldn't do any any good. "We live next door. It was easier to walk to his house. I must go now."

"No." He glanced around them. "No one's watching."

"Someone's always watching." She made up her mind suddenly, even though she had a feeling her words would prolong this dangerous meeting, even though she didn't want to say them. "I can't come today. Perhaps tomorrow."

"Why not today?" he asked sharply.

Catherine raised her eyes and let him see anger at being pressed, at being questioned, even though what she felt was desperation. "Not today."

"Catherine—"

"Excuse me," she said abruptly, and stepped past him before he could stop her. She felt his gaze on her all the way down the street but didn't hesitate or stop until she reached her buggy. She climbed in, and, looking neither left nor right, she drove out of town.

She didn't start to shake until she was unhitching the horse at her father's stable behind the house. Her fingers became all thumbs, and she leaned her forehead against the patient horse's neck for a moment. She didn't cry. She thought that she might have forgotten how. After a moment she finished unhitching and caring for the horse. Then she went to the house.

She got through the remainder of the afternoon almost mechanically. Her father remained in his study until late, reading. When he finally emerged, the look he gave her was questioning.

"I don't suppose you'll—"

"I'll be dressed and ready by the time you are, Father," she said calmly.

Lucas made a faint grimace but turned and went upstairs, his back stiff. She watched after him for a moment, then sighed and climbed to her own room.

Lettia Symington's dinner parties were an excuse for guests to wear their best finery, and Catherine kept that in mind as she quickly selected a gown and began getting ready. She usually chose to wear unrevealing garments, and evening social events were a distinct problem for her since ladies' evening gowns were almost always designed to display the charms of shoulders and bosoms. A new seamstress had come recently to Port Elizabeth, so that now there were two dressmakers on the island. Catherine had decided to have the new seamstress make several gowns for her for these occasions. In the meantime, however, she could do only her best.

The gown was one she had not worn since their departure from England. It was pale blue, off the shoulders, and quite revealing. Her bosom was bared almost to the nipples, and the tight bodice and full skirt gave a greater emphasis to her figure than her usual dresses. Catherine looked in the mirror, bit her bottom lip, and got a lace shawl from a drawer. Cast around her shoulders and pinned in place with a cameo brooch, it hid both creamy flesh and the thrust of her breasts.

It would have to do. She checked her hair but didn't bother to change the braided coronet. She picked up a small evening purse and looped it over her wrist. Then, composing her face into a mask of cool tranquility, she went downstairs to wait while her father hitched up the horse and brought the buggy around.

They didn't say much on the journey. Lettia's opulent home was on the northeast portion of the island and just outside town. It was, as usual during Lettia's parties, ringed with buggies and carriages; there were about a dozen "upper-class" families on the island, and it looked as though all were attending.

Including Captain Tyrone.

Catherine felt her throat close up when she saw the

familiar chestnut gelding. Panic stirred within her. Ever since a party some months before, when, by merely looking at her, he had aroused her to a degree that had shocked her, Catherine had been wary of meeting him during social gatherings. Yet she knew there was no avoiding it, that with such a small community social meetings were inevitable.

She accepted her father's brusque help in getting out of the carriage and walked beside him with outward composure to the house. With the same composure she endured Lettia Symington's exaggerated surprise at seeing her, endured the simpering smile at her father. She greeted George Symington calmly, and said hello to their nervous, high-strung seventeen-year-old daughter, Lucy, in the same tone.

None of them could ignore her during this type of social gathering, and Catherine wasn't sure which she preferred: polite scorn or being looked at as though they wished she would become invisible. Neither, really. She never got used to it.

More than a score of people filled the Symingtons' large drawing room, laughing and talking and drinking. Catherine moved among them, keeping an unobtrusive eye on her father. He was being good, she saw, holding a glass but drinking from it only occasionally; he knew she was watching.

Someone else was watching her. She could feel his gaze but refused to look his way. Still, tension grew inside her like a coil tightening. *Don't look at me*, she thought desperately. *Don't let them see what we are! Please don't let them see. . . .*

After an eternity, dinner was announced. In no particular order the guests went into the dining room to sit around its very long and highly polished oak table. Catherine found herself seated with Dr. Scott on her left and Gerald Odell on her right. She recognized and accepted the spite of her hostess, knowing she had been deliberately seated between two bachelors who were each old enough to be her grandfather. It wasn't unexpected.

"You're looking well tonight, Miss Catherine," Gerald Odell said in a slightly wheezy and avuncular voice. He owned the two dressmakers' shops in town and valued her patronage; whatever he thought of her personally he kept to himself. A shrewd businessman.

"Thank you, Mr. Odell," she muttered.

"I've a new selection of fabric and French lace," he said cannily. "Captain Tyrone's ship brought it in. Perhaps you'd care to come and look it over."

"Yes, of course," she responded, hardly paying attention. She had just realized that Tyrone, seated across near the head of the table beside Miss Lucy, was directly in her line of sight. Her father was on her side, also near the head of the table. Vaguely, Catherine recognized yet another intended slight; she had been placed between a doctor and a merchant, both, in Lettia's eyes, at the bottom of the social scale of acceptance. It didn't disturb her, being also expected.

Tyrone was looking at her. Catherine met his gaze only glancingly, and even then felt her breath catch. *Damn him!* She looked fixedly at her plate, aware of composure scattering like leaves in the wind. She felt her nipples prickle instantly, felt the heavy consciousness of a slow pulse inside her. And it came to her then that this was more than passion, that Tyrone had somehow touched something deeper inside her, something infinite.

It was terrifying.

"Miss Catherine?" It was Dr. Scott's voice, low and concerned. "You've gone pale. Are you all right?"

She looked at him blindly, focused on him with an effort. Sharp eyes behind rimless glasses, kind features. She wondered if he knew what she was afraid of. She had, nearly two years ago, gone to him with certain questions; he had gotten what she required without question or comment, had never once said that an unmarried woman shouldn't need what she had needed. She would always be grateful to him for that. "I'm fine, Doctor." Her voice was low, calm.

"Are you sure?"

Catherine wanted to laugh suddenly but not with humor. "I'm quite all right. Thank you."

He seemed unconvinced but accepted her assurances and returned to the meal. Catherine followed suit. She heard, as if from a great distance, sounds of conversation, heard the high, nervous sound of Lucy's voice rising above the rest as she flirted coyly with Tyrone.

She wished the evening were over.

But it wasn't, of course. Lettia wanted her guests to relax after dinner. Drinks were produced again. The French doors opening onto the veranda were flung wide, and an invitation entered from the warm night. Catherine wanted to keep an eye on her father but found she was even more concerned with avoiding Tyrone.

She managed it for more than an hour. She was conscious from time to time of his gaze but refused to meet it. She had taken pains to make certain there was never a chance to speak to him, though she spoke to everyone else at least briefly.

Much later she would realize that she should have

spoken to him casually. It might have changed so much if she had.

The laughter grew louder and more easy as drinks were consumed, though Catherine was relieved to see that her father was still being good, still drinking only moderately. She herself drank hardly at all and even, finally, set her almost untouched glass aside on a convenient table. She felt a little dizzy with tension and worry, with the faint throbbing yearning of her body. It was made worse by the noise of the crowd, the almost sickeningly sweet scent of perfume.

She glanced around swiftly and warily, then retreated smoothly from the room. There was a short hallway with several doors opening off it; she chose a room at random and found herself inside George Symington's study. It was deserted; she closed the door softly behind her and went to stand by the darkened window.

She didn't know how long she stood there gazing blindly out at the night. The sounds of the crowd were distant now, and she hardly heard them. She didn't hear the sound of the door opening and softly closing, or footsteps behind her. But there was, somehow, no surprise at arms slipping around her from behind, pulling her back against a hard male body.

"Damn you," Tyrone said thickly. "Not a glance. Not even one of your cold, haughty stares. What are you trying to do to me, Catherine?"

With his touch her body came alive. She felt her breasts swell in the hands that slid up to hold them, felt her legs go weak, her heart thud rapidly. Between her thighs was a sudden heavy fullness, a pulsing ache. And she felt the swelling response of his body as he pressed himself against her. Her head fell helplessly back onto his shoulder, and she bit her lip to hold back a moan that half escaped before she could stop it.

"Don't," she whispered. "Not here. Not now."

"Here," he said. "Now. It's your fault for ignoring me all evening." He was exploring the soft flesh of her neck, his lips hot and hard. His hands impatiently brushed aside the lacy shawl, then expertly unfastened the brooch and pulled the shawl free of her, dropping both to the floor.

"Stop—"

"I made you angry today, didn't I? Because I pressed you, because I questioned. But you made me angry as well, Catherine. So I came to this damned party, just to see you again. And then you wouldn't even look at me. I won't allow you to be cold with me. With them . . . but not with me."

"No." Catherine was trying to think, to remain calm. "Someone could come in. Tyrone—"

"I locked the door." His hands closed over her breasts, squeezing gently. "I want you, Catherine. Now. With half the town in the next room smiling their empty smiles and looking at one another with treacherous eyes." His voice was unusually rough, urgent, almost violent. "I want you."

"No." But he knew too well how to arouse her, how to make her forget everything but him and need. The fever rose in her body, hot and dizzying. She could hardly stand, hardly breathe. One of his hands slipped down over her stomach, lower, pressing hard through the layers of clothing, and she gasped as the stark caress triggered a rush of flaming need.

"Now," he said roughly.

Catherine half sobbed. "Yes. Damn you, yes!"

Without another word he moved back and pulled her several steps to one side, to George Symington's desk. There was an armless chair behind it, and Tyrone pulled it away from the desk. Quickly he freed himself and sat down, drawing her forward to straddle his legs as he pulled up her rustling skirts.

She caught at his shoulders, biting back a moan when his knowing fingers slid up her trembling thighs and found the wet, hot flesh that was pulsing for him. Except for petticoats and a thin linen shift, she wore nothing beneath the gown, and she could see his gleaming gray eyes flicker in satisfaction.

"You're ready for me," he murmured, fingers probing surely.

Catherine shuddered when his hands slipped around to cup her buttocks, when he eased her down slowly. She felt the long, throbbing hardness of his manhood enter her yearning body, filling her, and the pleasure was so intense that her eyes closed, breath coming quickly from between parted lips. And she could hardly breathe at all by the time she settled fully against him, clutching his shoulders and swaying slightly.

"Yes," he muttered thickly, staring at her face through slitted eyes. "This is my Catherine, the Catherine only I know." One of his hands lifted to the nape of her neck and he pulled her upper body toward him, kissing her hard, his tongue filling her mouth with sinuous passion. "All woman. Warm and soft with wanting me. Mine."

On some level of her mind Catherine was conscious of the danger of this, the recklessness, but she didn't care. The throbbing inside her was a pleasure so potent she would have risked almost anything for it. A moan broke from her throat as he began lifting and lowering her slowly, and she smothered the sound against his shoulder, biting into fine cloth.

She thought she would burst, that her straining body couldn't possibly hold the feelings inside. The heat was liquid, flowing, rushing. Her body pulsed in a faster and faster rhythm, tension gathering in a bittersweet agony. She heard his harsh breaths, felt his chest laboring, felt the bunching muscles of his shoulders and arms as he controlled her movements.

Catherine had never felt so intensely, and she was only dimly aware of the sounds tangling behind her clenched teeth. The heat was swallowing her, consuming her. And then she felt the tension snap with violence, tossing her wildly to a crest of pleasure she had never known before. She collapsed against him with a whimper, her forehead resting heavily on his shoulder, dimly aware of his shudder and rasping groan.

Limp, boneless, she couldn't move and didn't want to, despite a niggling urgency. No matter what happened, she realized, she would always be grateful that she had known this, felt this. It was the single reason the entire situation was bearable.

She floated for a few precious moments, content, sated. Her breathing gradually returned to normal, and she felt his slow as well. *If only I don't lose this*, she thought. *Lose him* . . . She forced the thoughts away and slowly raised her head.

Tyrone kissed her, his mouth not hard now but warm and gentle. Then he looked at her with eyes that were still intense. "Catherine, are you pregnant?"

The unexpected question jolted her, and her head snapped back almost as if he had slapped her. But after an instant she was able to reply in the same blunt tone. "No. I'm not."

His eyes searched hers, and then he half nodded. "I

wondered. When I saw you at Scott's this morning. That's why I stopped you in town."

"No, I was there for the reason I gave you. Because of Father." Contentment was draining away, and she grieved its passing. With an effort she made her voice dry. "You don't have to worry, Tyrone. There are ways to—to prevent it happening. There won't be a child."

He was silent for a moment, then touched her cheek with gentle fingers and said huskily, "I wouldn't mind."

Another shock. When her voice emerged this time, it was too sharp, too revealing. "I would. There won't be a child."

Tyrone's brows drew together in a swift frown. "Catherine—"

She shook her head to stop the question and then withdrew from him, forcing her weak legs to support her. The trickle of wetness down her thighs was unnervingly sensual, and she gritted her teeth as she moved away from him. She didn't look at him as she bent to gather the shawl and brooch from the floor, replacing them to demurely cover her flushed bosom again.

When she turned around, Tyrone was there before her, his own clothing adjusted and fit for public viewing. He was still frowning. Before she could move, he captured her face in one hand gently, and forced her to stand still.

"Catherine," he said slowly, "I would never abandon you if you were to become pregnant. You know that, don't you?"

The question, she realized, was important to him; her answer was important to him. After a moment she said steadily, "Yes. I know that. But there won't be a child."

He kissed her lightly, briefly. "Just as long as you know."

She moved a little away from him and lifted one hand to touch her hot cheek. The dangers of this suddenly recalled, she wondered hopelessly if she could manage to return to the party without giving away what had happened in this locked room.

"Oh, God," she blurted out.

Tyrone chuckled, realizing what was wrong. "I'm afraid your haughty mask is gone. You look very much a woman who's just met a lover. Our secret is about to become public knowl—" He broke off because she'd turned on him abruptly, and what he saw in her face wiped the amusement from his own. "Catherine," he began in an entirely different tone of voice.

But she had herself under control now. "This must never happen again, Tyrone. I mean that."

He was expressionless. "And if it does?"

She hesitated, knowing the dangers of pushing a man like him. He was a strong man, and strong men disliked ultimatums. But what choice did she have? None. No choice at all. *Damn! Damn!* Carefully she said, "We agreed, long ago, how it was going to be. Nothing has changed. If you aren't . . . satisfied with our agreement, then it's over. I won't be held up in public as a whore."

Some emotion she couldn't identify seemed to pass fleetingly over his face, but his voice remained steady. "I see. That's the one line you won't cross, then."

She was a little puzzled. "What do you mean?"

"The fine citizens of Port Elizabeth, that's what I mean. They treat you like dirt, and we both know it.

They smile their genteel smiles while they cut at you."

After a moment she said, "They're just people, no better or worse than any others. Just people."

"Why won't you defend yourself with them?" he asked, suddenly rough.

Catherine felt a prickle of foreboding. *He's different. He looks at me differently. Oh, God!* She kept her voice calm. "I've done nothing to defend. I can't help their attitudes."

"You could change them. We both know that too. You could drop your haughty mask and show them you're human. Show them you're a woman with a heart that beats, lips that can smile. Show them the warmth beneath that icy surface. But you won't. Why won't you, Catherine?"

What could she say to him? She could say that pride was all she had left, and that with it she had built a cold wall to contain her fear and worry. She could say that scorn was more bearable than pity, and easier to deflect. She could say that her own hurt was nothing compared to the pain of others.

But she didn't say any of that. She couldn't, not to him. So she simply ignored the question.

"I meant what I said. This can't happen again."

His eyes narrowed slightly. "You wanted me just as much, Catherine. Even here and now."

She felt her lips curve in a terrible smile. "Yes."

He made a rough sound. "God, don't look like that! You can't hate it that much, what I make you feel. You can't hate it that much, Catherine!"

She couldn't answer, couldn't tell him he was wrong. Because then the next question would come, and she couldn't answer it either. *Then why did you look like that?* "I want your word this won't happen again," she said softly.

His eyes were restless, and a muscle leapt in his jaw. "You'll meet me tomorrow?"

Catherine felt a quiver deep inside her. Meet him. Like a moth to the flame, bent on destruction. "Yes. I'll meet you. Give me your word this won't happen again, Tyrone."

"All right." He sighed. "You have my word."

A breath she hadn't been conscious of holding escaped in a soft rush. "Thank you," she said. She moved toward the locked door, wondering suddenly how long they had been absent from the party. It felt like hours, but she knew it hadn't been nearly that long. And before she could say anything, Tyrone spoke flatly.

"I know. We leave the room separately. But, Catherine—don't ignore me again. Don't do that to me."

She half nodded, then quickly unlocked the door and slipped out into the hall. Hoping desperately that Tyrone had been wrong in saying her mask was gone, she composed her features into cool remoteness and moved steadily down the hall and back to the drawing room.

No one seemed to notice her reappearance. Or even to have noticed she had been gone. The talk and laughter was still loud and cheerful. Smoothly she merged with the crowd and searched until she found her father. He was talking to George Symington, as cheerful as the rest. His eyes were clear, and there was no flush on his face. Catherine relaxed and moved away. All right, then. Everything was all right.

She found her abandoned drink just where she'd left it, and stood sipping it. She was glancing toward the doorway a few moments later and saw Tyrone stroll in lazily, looking as if he'd just stepped out for a breath of air.

With veiled eyes she studied him. A big man, powerful and graceful. His face was handsome in a somewhat cold manner; a smile made his face warm and charming. There was no sign in him now of urgent passion in a locked room, of questions, of intensity. He moved with deliberation, with muscles under unthinking control. He was, somehow, innately dangerous.

And she loved him.

Catherine felt the shock as the realization dropped gently into her mind. No. Oh, dear God, no. She tore her gaze away to stare down at her glass, breathing fast, shaken to her soul.

The noise of the room faded away, distant and unimportant. She felt cold, hot, terrified. *No!* When had it happened? Ten minutes ago? Yesterday? Or nearly two years ago? When had he gotten inside the walls she had built, and done it so effortlessly that she hadn't even noticed? Her mind flashed back unexpectedly almost two years, to a sudden encounter by the tiny inland stream.

Cool gray eyes abruptly warming, going intent. "You're beautiful, you know," he had said, and she had shaken her head, queerly disturbed. "No. I'm not." He had smiled, nodded with certainty. "You hide it behind a mask. I know all about masks." She had been silent, and melting inside, because it had taken no more than that. He had walked steadily to her as if he saw, as if he knew. He had taken her into his arms and kissed her as a lover would, with hunger. He had removed her clothing and his own because she had been too shaken to help. And beside a stream of quiet water he had become her first lover. With tenderness. With care. With passion.

Catherine half heard a sigh escape her. Then. She had loved him even then. That was why she had risked so much to lie in his arms when she could. Because she loved him, helplessly, against all reason. Because she loved him.

"Catherine?" His voice, low and concerned.

She didn't dare meet his eyes. She had, with determination, convinced him that an affair suited her. No ties, no sentiment. That couldn't be allowed to change.

"I hate these parties," she said, amazed at her own calm tone.

He was reassured by her tone, and his laugh was no more than a breath of sound. "Even this one?" he asked softly.

She never got the chance to respond.

"Kate . . ."

Shock rippled through her, and she jerked around so suddenly that part of her drink spilled over her fingers. Her father stood a couple of feet away from her. He was smiling faintly. His brilliant blue eyes were oddly glazed, and a flush mottled his cheeks.

"Kate, my dear, we must go," he said softly. His gaze flickered from her face to that of the man beside her. He looked back at her again. His smile widened. "We must go."

"Yes." She felt numb. She set her glass aside and stepped away from Tyrone without a glance. "Of course." Mechanically she took the arm her father held for her and walked away with him.

What the hell?

It wasn't the first time Tyrone had asked himself that question. He had been asking himself that since the party. Or, more specifically, since Catherine had been summoned by her father to leave. Even before then, when he had spoken to her in the drawing room, when her face had been so still, her lips trembling with a vulnerability he'd never seen in her before. But her voice, calm and dry, had reassured him.

Then . . . her father had called her. He had called her Kate, something Tyrone had never before heard him do. And she had, in a single instant, gone dead white. The veiling lashes and lifted, revealing eyes darkened with shock, with—fear? And her voice had been oddly hollow when she had spoken to her father.

Frowning as he drove back toward his own house, Tyrone tried to understand what it might mean. It was difficult, almost impossible, because Catherine was a puzzle. He didn't know, not really, the woman she was inside herself—only pieces of her, glimpses he caught from time to time.

Warm and willing. Cold and forbidding. Humorless, frosty blue eyes. Eyes bright with laughter, dark with fire. Stiff, precise posture. Sinuous, elegant grace. Self-mocking coolness. A look of sheer agony in her eyes. Calm. Panic. Fear.

Who was she?

And why, suddenly, did that matter to him? Why did her insistence on secrecy, amusing to him in the past, anger him now? Why had he tried recklessly to catch her eye at the very public party, and then discarded all reason to deliberately arouse her so that they ended up making love on a chair in a locked room in their host's crowded house? Why did he abruptly resent, on her behalf, the treatment she received from the townspeople? And why had the possibility she could have been carrying his child filled him with a riot of emotions he didn't even understand?

Tyrone pushed the baffling questions away. When they would meet the next day he would try again to understand her, try to discover what lay beneath Catherine's various masks.

He knew all about masks.

The buggy passed the harbor just then and he automatically looked to see that his ship was safe. And she was, floating dark and still on the calm water. A symbol, he sometimes fancifully thought, of all he had become. A symbol of struggle and danger, of outrageous risks, of dark nights and peril.

He wondered, suddenly, if one of these perils, a nemesis out of his past, would follow *The Raven* to Port Elizabeth. It was likely. No, he thought, it was certain. Falcon Delaney would follow the trail that would bring him there.

Only death would stop him.

4

Washington

Leon Hamilton had waited until Falcon and his new wife left the party before moving quietly through the crowd and asking several men along his way to meet him in the gentlemen's smoking lounge. He was cheerful, casual, teasing wives who rolled their eyes in resignation at being deserted by husbands. Still, this was the nation's capital, and most of the wives had grown accustomed to the demands of public office.

No one was overly surprised by Leon's summons.

They gathered in the small lounge down the hall from the ballroom. These men knew one another well; they were still casual and smiling. But they didn't smile long when Leon spoke one word flatly.

"Camelot."

There was a moment's suspended silence while four men stared at Leon in varying degrees of shock.

"That was years ago," Senator Ryan Stewart said. He was a nondescript man of middle years, middle height, middle weight, and average coloring; only shrewd gray eyes hinted at the exceptional intelligence beneath that ordinary-looking exterior. "Why are you bringing it up now, Leon?"

"Because it's . . . it's come up again."

"It can't have," Judge Steven Franks said firmly, sitting down in a wing chair in a decisive way as if he could ignore the very notion. Elderly, silver-haired, and nervous, he had grown forgetful in recent years and tended to disregard problems that might threaten his comfort.

"I'm afraid it has."

"Look," Senator James Sheridan said, "we took care of everything, every detail. There's no danger at all now. Everyone's put the war behind him, and no one wants to remember. We're safe."

Slowly the fourth man, Paul Anderson, spoke in his deep, thoughtful voice. He was a cabinet member known for his organizational abilities. Middle-aged, he was slim and handsome and, a bachelor, had a distinct eye for the ladies. "There was one thread left dangling," he reminded the rest. "It didn't seem dangerous—at the time."

Senator Sheridan turned to Leon with a frown. "Tyrone? Is that what you're talking about?"

"Yes. Captain Tyrone."

Sheridan's frown grew. He was a short, thin man with the aggressive charm of a born politician, and also, unfortunately, an impatience that often got away from him. "Tyrone's kept his mouth shut all this time; why would he talk now? He'd have nothing to gain by it. If it comes down to it, he's as much to blame as we are."

"Is he?" Leon asked quietly. "He agreed with us at the time that ours was the only possible solution; he understood there was no choice. Everything was fine up to that point. But then it went wrong."

"That wasn't our fault," Sheridan said instantly. "We couldn't have anticipated such an accident."

Broodingly, Leon asked, "But was it an accident?"

In a sharp tone Senator Stewart asked, "Do you think it wasn't? Christ, Leon, who would have planned such a thing?"

"Any of us," Leon said flatly. "Any of us could have. You remember what Tyrone said when he came back to tell us what had happened? It was a clumsy, brutal attack, and succeeded only by the sheer unexpectedness of it."

"What would any of us have had to gain by planning such a thing?" Sheridan demanded.

"Everything. Remember, we had our own man standing by in the wings and ready to step in. Once that attack succeeded, our man was safe for good. The whole thing was so impossible that no one would ever have suspected the truth."

Uneasily, Judge Franks said, "We hired Tyrone to get him out of the way, that's all. To take him up to New England. The rest was an accident. It had to be!"

"I hope so," Leon added gravely. "I really hope so."

There was a moment of silence, and then Anderson asked, "But you said it had come up again? What did you mean?"

"One of my own men," Leon said in a grim tone, "has stumbled onto it. Falcon Delaney has been looking for that stolen shipment of Union gold, and it looks as if Tyrone is the man who ended up with it somehow."

Impatiently Sheridan said, "If he did, it's got nothing to do with Camelot."

"Falcon thinks it has. And you all have me to thank that he didn't question you about it tonight."

Another shocked pause.

Subdued, Sheridan asked, "Us? But—why?"

"Because Tyrone, damn his black heart, left a few sweet little notes in a ledger before he set off for God only knows where. And Falcon saw them. The word Camelot, underlined, and a list with all our names on it."

"Call your man off," Anderson suggested quietly.

"I can't. Hell, that's one of the reasons I put him onto the gold in the first place. He's one of the Arizona Delaneys, and you don't call those men off. You just *don't*. He's been tracking the gold for eight years, and now he's convinced that Camelot is somehow connected to the gold. Maybe it's because Tyrone's involved in both. God knows. I don't doubt he'll head for New York at dawn to pick up Tyrone's trail."

There was a moment of silence, and then Anderson spoke again. "Would Tyrone tell Delaney?"

Leon bit the inside of his cheek, then shrugged. "I don't know. There's always been a peculiar kind of understanding between those two, or at least it seemed so to me. Not quite enemies; not quite friends. Mutual respect between them, I'd say, and a high degree of wariness. Tyrone might tell him the entire story. He might tell him nothing at all. I just don't know. But I do know one thing." He looked at the other men steadily. "If Falcon Delaney finds out about Camelot, he could jump either way. He could keep it to himself and take it to his grave; or he could take it public."

"We'd be crucified politically," Anderson murmured.

"Crucified?" Sheridan exclaimed, and then hastily lowered his voice. "Jesus Christ, Paul, we'd be lucky

to escape being hung! There's only our word for it, the way things were then; his doctor's been dead and buried for five years. Tyrone could call us all liars, say that *accident* was meant from the start, all our idea. Our word against his, or course, but we're not exactly on the side of the angels in this case."

In a quavering voice Judge Franks said, "Surely your man could see the necessity of what we did, Leon? And why would he stir it all up now? There's no reason!"

Leon sighed. "I just don't know, I tell you. But Falcon's got a strong sense of right and wrong. He's not puritanical, but if he decides the public should know what we did, he'll damn well tell them."

"You have to stop him," Sheridan said numbly. "We have too much to lose and—God, you have to stop him!"

"I can't."

"Then what do we do?"

"Wait." Leon shrugged. "Hope that Tyrone keeps his mouth shut about Camelot. Or, at least, that if he talks, he makes Falcon understand how it was then. That we had no choice. What else can we do?"

There was no answer.

New York

It was actually three days later that Falcon and Victoria arrived in New York and made their way to the waterfront. Falcon had felt no particular urgency and, truth to tell, was reluctant to ask his new brother-in-law questions that would be rightly viewed as an intrusion and possibly as a personal insult. Still, he had no choice.

They entered Marc Tyrone's waterfront office early that morning to find Jesse Beaumont at the desk and coping with paperwork, his shirt sleeves rolled up, his fair hair mussed as if he had been clutching it in despair, and his green eyes a little wild.

He looked up as they came in, and instantly groaned. "No. Tory, it's always nice to see you, but take that husband of yours away. He's got a determined look on his face, and I don't want to hear whatever he's going to say."

"Hello, Jesse," Victoria said, smiling.

"Hello. You look beautiful today," Jesse told her in a polite tone, while keeping a wary eye on Falcon.

"Thank you. You look upset."

"Upset?" He gave the word an incredulous emphasis. "Why would I be upset? Marc dumps his business in my lap and sails off into the wild blue, leaving me to cope with paperwork when I haven't even gotten over being saddlesore yet— Stop laughing!" he ordered Falcon in a fierce tone.

"Sorry." Falcon cleared his throat and made his face grave. "About Tyrone—"

"No," Jesse interrupted, a certain mulishness settling into his handsome, sunburned features. "I've told you before, brother-in-law or not, there's no way I'm going to help you put Marc's head in a noose!"

"You won't. I just need to talk to him."

"Then wait until he's back in New York."

"How long will he be away?"

"I don't know," Jesse said flatly.

"Jesse, it's important."

"If it's your damned gold you're talking about— and I know it is!—you've been after it for eight years. A few more months won't make that much difference."

"Months!" Falcon exclaimed.

Jesse gritted his teeth and fought back a sheepish expression. "Damn you, I wasn't going to say that. Tory, if you love your brother, take your husband *away*."

Quietly Victoria said, "I can't, Jesse. I'm sorry, we're both sorry, but Falcon needs to talk to Captain Tyrone. He'll find out where the captain's gone eventually, you know. He's very good at things like that. Why not tell us?"

Jesse sat back in the chair and raked long brown fingers through his hair. "Damn," he said miserably. "Damn you, Marc. Why you had to go away when everyone wants you—"

"Everyone?" Falcon's voice was sharp. "What do you mean by that?"

Jesse looked at him and shrugged. "Only that one of Marc's business friends had to get in touch with him. He came rushing in here a couple of days ago, wild to find Marc. Something about papers that had to be signed right away. I couldn't help him; I've got Marc's power of attorney, but only for current business."

"What was his name?" Falcon asked slowly.

"Well, he was a senator, actually. Senator Sheridan."

Victoria gasped softly. "Isn't that—"

"One of the names on the list. Yes." Falcon looked at her, frowning, his green eyes remote. "Now, I find that to be just too damned coincidental."

Blankly Jesse said, "What are you talking about? What list?"

Falcon looked back at him, still frowning. "Jesse, you said the senator was wild to find Tyrone. Wild in what way?"

"Nervous, jumpy. Very intense and insistent." Jesse began to look worried. "What the hell's going on?"

Victoria spoke first, perhaps answering her brother's question but looking at her husband. "Leon was . . . afraid, you said. He didn't want you looking into this Camelot. The other men on that list might be just as afraid. Maybe even more so. Afraid of what you might be able to uncover. Afraid of what Captain Tyrone might tell you."

"And if they are," Falcon said, picking up her train of thought, "one of them might well attempt to get to Tyrone before I do. But for what? To try and bribe him to keep quiet? Or to shut him up permanently?"

"God," Jesse whispered, staring at them. He might not have understood fully what they were talking about, but it was clear there was danger to Marc Tyrone. Jesse went white. "I told him. It seemed more than reasonable. Important, really. So of course I told him where Marc was."

"We have to warn him," Victoria said.

Falcon looked at Jesse. "A telegram?"

"No. No, there's no— It's an island, and there's no way to reach it except by ship!"

"What about Sheridan? Has he gone yet?"

Jesse sucked in breath. "Christ, I helped him. I booked passage for him that day, even persuaded the captain to detour by Port Elizabeth and drop him off. He's had two days; he must be halfway there by now."

Falcon swore bitterly. Then, grim, he said, "We'll just have to take the fastest ship we can find. Jesse, where, exactly, is this Port Elizabeth?"

There was a moment's silence while Jesse stared at him. And then the younger man said slowly, "I'm going with you."

"Jesse—"

"Look," Jesse said flatly, "nothing out there in the

harbor is heading south until tomorrow afternoon, and there's no way you could catch Sheridan if you waited that long. But there is a ship out there with a chance of catching him—the second fastest ship in Tyrone's fleet. *My* ship. *The Robyn*. We can leave today, on the afternoon tide. And even if we can't catch Sheridan, we'll damned well be running up his stern by the time he gets to Port Elizabeth."

The Robyn, like her sister ship *The Raven*, was a clipper built for speed. She was two hundred feet long, and her three tall masts held numerous sails. She could, Jesse told them proudly, do twenty knots when she was pushed; he intended to push her.

Falcon and Victoria stayed out of his way. Within the few hours before they could sail it became obvious that however distressed or uncertain he was on land, Jesse was utterly and completely comfortable with a deck beneath his feet. And he handled the many details of an unexpected departure briskly and without hesitation, recalling a crew on liberty, stocking the ship for a journey, and coolly summoning one of Tyrone's attorneys to handle the necessary business matters until either Jesse or Tyrone returned to New York.

"Will he like that?" Falcon asked curiously when the lawyer had received his orders and gone.

"Marc?" Jesse grinned. "No. He doesn't trust lawyers. Even his own. *Especially* his own."

"Then aren't you taking a bit of a risk by, ah, dumping his business matters into the lawyer's lap?"

Jesse's grin turned savage. "Serves him right, dammit. Next time, maybe he won't be so quick to saddle me with a mess."

Falcon watched the younger man step aside to deal

with a minor crisis among the crew, reflecting that
Jesse was badly worried. But then, so was he. In his
life at various times, Falcon had been both hunter
and hunted; he knew what it was like to have enemies stalking him the way Tyrone's were stalking. . . .
He wondered suddenly if Tyrone thought of him like
that, as an enemy, and found the thought disturbing.

Victoria came to his side then, slipping a hand into
his and looking at him gravely. "What will you do if
Captain Tyrone has the gold?" she asked him.

Falcon wasn't surprised by the question. The longer
he and Victoria were together, the closer they seemed
to grow; she had read his face if not his thoughts
themselves. "I don't know, sweet," he said finally,
troubled by his own uncertainty. "I really don't know."

"Is this Camelot more important?"

"It may be. It may well be. Somehow, they're connected, I know that. I *feel* it. And I think . . ."

"What?"

Slowly he said, "I think the gold may turn out to
be the least important part of the story, because I
believe there was, originally, no connection. I think
Tyrone himself became the connection."

"Deliberately?" she asked.

He frowned. "I—there's a sense of irony." He looked
at Victoria almost blindly, as if his gaze were turned
inward, searching feelings, instincts.

She tried to help him focus. "In what way?"

"Illusion," he said, and his eyes narrowed. "Yes,
that's it. Illusion. What you think you see is wrong;
it's what you're led to see."

"What *we* see? You mean someone has led us to
look at the entire thing wrongly?"

"Yes, I think so. Parts of it anyway. But which

parts? There are two separate threads, the gold and this Camelot. Tyrone, somehow, for some reason, is holding them both."

Victoria waited, watching him intently. After a moment his eyes cleared and he looked at her wryly. "Damn. It's gone. I thought I had something, but it's gone."

"You don't have all the pieces yet," she reminded him. "There are some only Captain Tyrone can provide."

"Yes. But will he?"

The Robyn sailed out of New York Harbor in mid-afternoon, heading south. She was slightly more than two days behind a slower packet on the same course. There wasn't a great deal of wind, but *The Robyn*'s many sails unfurled and snatched all she could get. Her heading was directly east for a time, then southeast, and finally due south. Her narrow, streamlined keel cut through the water neatly, her crew was experienced, and her captain canny. She began to make up lost ground, as though someone had whispered to her of the importance of this race.

Or perhaps she heard whispers of another kind; perhaps she heard the call of her sister ship.

If so, she responded. Against all reason, *The Robyn* was breaking her own speed records.

5

Port Elizabeth

The scream woke him from a deep sleep. It was a shriek of terror, of agony, and even as Tyrone sat up and threw back the covers, he realized that it wasn't a human cry. He dressed quickly in trousers and a shirt left unbuttoned, thrusting his feet into boots, then headed downstairs. The house was silent, unaware, and he knew that only he had been awakened.

He paused in his study long enough to get his pistol out of the desk drawer where he kept it, then slipped out of the house. The night was queerly silent. He stood for a moment listening, then went around to the stables in back of the house. His stables were completely enclosed, rather like an old-fashioned barn, and were built sturdily of stone to withstand the often violent storms off the Atlantic.

The main door to the stables was flung open.

Tyrone cocked the pistol and held it ready as he moved silently closer. He kept half a dozen horses here, and he could hear the soft stamping and blowing of nervous animals. But nothing else. Carefully, he edged through the doorway, flattening himself against an inner wall. And he listened.

His eyes quickly grew accustomed to the darkness, and he found he could see quite well. Ten stalls, the last four at the other end empty, their doors latched open. He moved slowly down the wide hallway, stopping finally before the only other opened stall. The chestnut gelding, his favorite carriage horse, was gone.

Tyrone stood frowning. Not the most valuable of his horses, and not the most beautiful. Hardly a target for theft, he would have thought. And it had to be that, because the stable doors held bolts made of iron, sturdy things the horses couldn't even reach, let alone unfasten. But it didn't make sense. The scream he had heard, shrill with terror, wasn't a sound that a horse would make while being led quietly from a barn.

He suddenly felt cold. He turned and left the stables, securely fastening the big door. Then, without pausing, his pistol still held ready, he walked southwest, away from the house. This was the end of the island that was built up from the sea, a jagged forty-foot cliff rising from a narrow ribbon of sand. Tyrone had built his house here partly for that reason, because his land was inaccessible from the sea.

About thirty feet from the cliff's edge he had put up a barbed wire fence to safeguard his stock; all the horses had been loose in this small pasture from time to time, and none had ever even ventured close to the fence, perhaps sensing the sheer drop. Tyrone stood at the fence and studied it for a moment, seeing even in the faint light that the three strands of wicked wire had been neatly cut.

He walked on to the cliff's edge. The sandy ground here had been churned violently. He bent to pick up a heavy stick and felt sick when he realized that one end of it was wet with blood. He no longer had to

look, but did anyway. He stepped closer to the edge
and gazed down. The big, dark hump was clearly
visible against the pale sand, and very still.

The chestnut hadn't had a chance.

It wasn't Tyrone's way to turn to others with his
problems, and he didn't now. In the morning he told
Reuben about the horse, making it sound like an
accident. He himself had smoothed the telltale evidence of an animal beaten into leaping to its death,
had taken away the bloodstained stick. If Reuben
thought it unlikely that a horse raised on the island
would have been so incautious, he didn't comment,
but merely obeyed Tyrone's orders and repaired the
fence.

The tide had come in by morning, and the chestnut's carcass was carried out to sea.

Tyrone brooded over the matter all morning. It
wasn't only losing a favorite horse that disturbed
him, but how that horse had been taken from him.
The violence of the act, the sheer cruelty of beating
an animal bloody, of killing it in that manner, sickened him.

Reluctantly he had asked Tully about her patient,
but she had been certain. The man slept deeply now,
and she would have heard if he'd gotten up during
the night. And the violent stage was past, she reminded him; they hadn't had trouble like that for
more than two years.

Relieved, Tyrone accepted the assurances. But relief was short-lived. If not the sick man in his own
house, then who? Who on the island could commit
such an act? Aside from everything else, his property
was isolated, miles from anyone else. Who had come
there in the night, by stealth, intending to kill a poor
beast after putting it through agony?

He remembered, suddenly, Lettia Symington's little dog. Drowned? It seemed odd now that he thought about it for a dog to have accidentally drowned in the narrow, shallow stream that ran a couple of miles through the center of the island. Killed deliberately like his horse?

After lunch he hitched a muscled bay mare to the buggy and drove her into town. He stopped first at the harbor and went out to *The Raven*, questioning the mate, Lyle, about the other men. All had been on board during the night, Lyle reported, mystified.

Deep in thought, Tyrone drove on into town. He stopped at the mercantile and went in.

"Good afternoon, Captain," Mr. Abernathy said cheerfully. Except for Tyrone, the store was empty of customers.

"Abernathy."

"How can I help you?"

Tyrone leaned against the counter and drew out a long, thin cigar, lighting it slowly. After a moment he said, "You mentioned the other day about Mrs. Symington's dog being killed. Have there been any other animals killed recently?"

Abernathy looked puzzled but frowned in thought. "How recent might you mean, Captain?"

"In the last few months, say."

"Well, aside from the little dog, I can't think—No, wait. About six months ago Dr. Scott lost that old hack of his. The animal must have stepped in a hole in its pasture; broke a leg and had to be put down. Is that what you mean?"

"Yes," Tyrone said slowly. "That's what I mean. Do you recall anything else?"

The storekeeper leaned on the counter, his eyes distant and thoughtful. "Last summer," he said, "Mrs.

Jessop's hound turned up missing. Everybody figured it went off and died; it was old. And just before that Miss Lander's yellow tomcat was found dead."

Tyrone hesitated, then asked, "Did any of those people, aside from Mrs. Symington, claim their animals had been killed deliberately?"

Abernathy's eyes widened, then narrowed. "No. No, I can't remember that they did."

Two dogs, a cat, and now two horses killed within the past six or eight months. Tyrone wondered if it meant anything at all. "All right. Thanks, Abernathy." He was halfway to the door when the storekeeper's quiet voice stopped him.

"Captain?"

"Yes?"

"Captain, your questions are a bit ... suggestive. Would I be wrong in thinking you'd rather I kept them under my hat?"

Tyrone smiled a little, knowing that Mr. Abernathy could be trusted to keep secrets, as long as he knew they were secrets. "I would appreciate that," he said.

Abernathy nodded. "I'll let you know if I hear anything else."

"Thanks." Tyrone left the store. He stood on the sidewalk for a moment, thinking, then tossed his cigar into the street and drew out his watch. Almost two o'clock. Catherine might be waiting for him ... or she might not. He was beginning to feel frustrated by the uncertainty of their meetings, by her inaccessibility.

He climbed into his buggy and slapped the reins against the mare's rump, guiding her down the main street. Bothered by what he increasingly felt to be the presence of an elusive enemy—and a coldly ruthless one—he badly needed Catherine. It surprised him, this need for her that was more than sexual, and he pondered it as he drove from town.

Desire for her was something he had felt from the first; that hadn't changed. Or had it? Slowly he realized that he wanted her more often now, that he thought of her more often. When he was with her, he felt . . . greedy, as if he couldn't get enough of her. Her public coldness was beginning to anger him just as her private elusiveness angered him.

Tyrone took the usual precautions before turning off the main road and onto the track into the woods, but he was frowning as he stopped the buggy before the cottage. He pulled a tether block from the back of the buggy and tied the mare, who hadn't been there before and couldn't be counted on to stand and wait patiently for hours as the chestnut had learned to do.

He patted the mare's glossy neck, reminding himself to double-check the stables each night before he turned in. But, somehow, he didn't think one of his horses would be targeted again. It was a feeling, an instinct. He hoped he was right.

Tyrone went into the cottage. It was empty. He paced slowly around the main room, looking without really seeing at the bare, almost rotting wood floor, at walls damp with mildew. He walked to the door of the tiny bedroom and gazed at the brass bed that had, now, only a colorful quilt to hide the mattress. He had brought that bed himself.

Catherine had suggested the cottage as a meeting place. It wasn't much, she had said dryly, but there was a roof and walls. And, of course, privacy. The first few times, they had made love on a thick pallet of blankets on the floor. On his next visit to the island, Tyrone had brought the bed and set it up before she saw it. She had, typically, said nothing

about it, but at their next meeting had provided
linens.

The cottage had been built, Tyrone knew, when the
land had first been settled, around twenty years before. It had been abandoned and vitually forgotten
when larger and more permanent homes had been
built closer to the coast. For Catherine and him it
had been a haven for almost two years. A place of
quiet and passion, a place free of strain.

The door opened suddenly. "You're driving the little mare," Catherine said, clearly surprised. "I thought
she was in foal."

"She is," he said, turning to face her. "But she
won't foal until spring. The work will do her good."
He realized only then that he wasn't going to tell her
about the chestnut. He didn't know why.

Catherine started toward him and the bedroom,
her arms full of folded linen. Briskly she said, "Let
me put these on the bed. You're early."

"Last time I was late." He watched her as she
moved past him toward the bed, catching a fleeting
scent of cinnamon. Desire washed over him so abruptly
and strongly that he caught his breath, feeling his
belly knot hard, his loins swell achingly. "Never mind
the sheets," he said thickly.

She turned to face him, surprised. But her eyes
darkened almost instantly, her lips parting. "For heav-
en's sake, Tyrone—" It was a breathless protest without strength.

He stepped to her, taking the sheets from her and
dropping them onto the floor. His hands went to her
hair, and he pulled the pins away and cast them
aside until her hair fell about her shoulders in a
shining dark brown mass. She stood without moving, staring up at him with veiled eyes. The calico

material over her breasts, demurely buttoned to her throat, rose and fell quickly, and the heat of an inner fire was rising in her creamy cheeks.

Tyrone thought she was beautiful. He always had, even before he had seen this hidden part of her.

He reached for buttons and began unfastening them slowly, one by one, from her throat down. It took a tremendous effort to keep from crushing her in his arms, but he held on to control with all his will. Their time together was so brief, and he was conscious of the desire to make it last.

When the dress was unbuttoned to below her waist, he lifted his hands and very slowly pulled the edges apart. The thin linen of her shift was straining over her full breasts, and as he lingeringly pushed the dress off her shoulders, the hardened tips of her nipples thrust against the cloth.

Catherine caught her breath but didn't move.

Tyrone guided the dress down her arms, pushed it over her hips, until she stood before him wearing only the shift, her stockings, and shoes. She made a slight movement toward him, as if she would have begun undressing him, but he caught her wrists firmly. He guided her a step backward, then gently pushed her down until she was sitting on the bed.

He knelt before her, lifted one foot, and removed the shoe. His hands slid caressingly up her leg until he found the top of her stocking just above the knee. Taking his time, he rolled the stocking down her leg, then pulled it off and set it aside. The other shoe followed, the other stocking. Catherine was gazing down at him with eyes that were wide and dark, veiled now only with desire. Her body was trembling, her breath quick and shallow. Her hands were small fists clutching the quilt.

Tyrone rose to his feet and slowly pulled her up. For a moment he just stood looking at her. She was primitive like this. Her glorious dark hair spilled around her shoulders, gleaming softly in the dim light. Through the almost transparent linen of her shift he could see the dark smudges of her areolas and, at the base of her belly, a shadow so enticing that his loins throbbed with a sudden, almost unbearable ache.

"Oh, Christ," he muttered in a hoarse, guttural voice. He reached quickly for the hem of her shift and, with one smooth motion, skinned it up over her head.

Catherine had lifted her arms automatically, lowering them slowly as the shift was tossed aside. His eyes moved over her with exquisite slowness, lingering on her breasts, on the soft nest of dark curls at the base of her belly. He reached one hand out and touched her breast with just the tips of this fingers, circling the tight, hard center very lightly.

Her eyes closed and she swayed toward him, a moan breaking from her lips. His hand closed around her breast, squeezing.

"I wanted you like this last night," he said roughly. "Naked like this, wanting me until nothing else mattered." He yanked her against him suddenly, his arms almost crushing her. One hand tangled in her hair to pull her head back, and he kissed her with a driving, almost punishing hunger, his tongue plunging deeply to twine with hers. For the first time, he possessed her mouth, taking, demanding everything.

And Catherine, her mind and senses whirling, refused nothing. The roughness of his clothing against her soft skin was a sweet torment. She couldn't breathe, was barely aware of the sounds that escaped her. Her heart was pounding throughout her body and she was burning . . . burning for him.

He lifted her into his arms and bent to place her on the bed, straightening to swiftly discard his clothing. His eyes never left her, and they were molten silver, glittering with passion and promise. She reached up for him as he joined her on top of the colorful quilt, her arms wreathing around his neck.

Tyrone captured her mouth, still demanding, still insistent. His hands moved over her body with hard, urgent need, caressing until she was writhing against him. And she almost sobbed when he parted her thighs and moved between them, when the heavy bluntness of his manhood probed her wet, pulsing flesh.

She looked up at his face, stark and hard, into the feverish eyes that were like none she had ever seen before. Her hands lifted, fingers thrusting into the thick silk of his hair, her legs closing about his muscled body. A whimper broke from her as she felt his rigid flesh sink slowly into her, filling her with its throbbing hunger.

And she moved with him, answering his thrusts as her lithe body accepted and returned his passion. She held him with her arms, her legs, as wild and unrestrained as he was. The rhythm quickened and they rushed with it, caught up in something beyond their control, helpless to slow the primitive race toward satisfaction. Until, finally, pleasure washed over them both in a torrent of heat that threatened to burn them alive.

"Jesus." Tyrone's breath came raspingly, and muscles quivered as he eased himself up on his elbows. He looked down at her flushed face, the closed eyes and half smile. Reluctant, but concerned that his

weight was uncomfortable for her, he began to with-
draw from her.

"No." Her legs tightened around his hips. She didn't
open her eyes.

"I'm too heavy," he said huskily, kissing her softly.

"Don't leave me." Her voice was low, almost slurred.
"Don't leave me yet."

Tyrone relaxed but kept his upper body propped
on his elbows. He felt her fingers moving almost
convulsively in his hair and turned his head to kiss
the inside of her forearm, where the skin was soft and
warm. That was when he saw the bruise.

He pulled her arm down gently and stared at the
purplish mottling that went almost completely around
her arm between her wrist and forearm. It had taken,
he knew, a powerful grip to mark her like that. And
he couldn't remember . . .

"Catherine, did I do this?"

Her eyes fluttered open, looked at the arm he held.
Something stirred in the darkened blue depths, but
it was gone before he could identify it. She shrugged
faintly. "If you did, I don't remember it."

"If I did, I'm sorry. So very sorry." He was appalled to think he could have hurt her like that.

She shook her head a little, as if it were unimportant. Then the faint smile returned, and her eyes grew
sleepy. "Mmmm."

He felt her inner muscles tighten slowly around
him, caressing him, and his breath caught. Heat
rushed through him, and he knew she could feel the
slow, swelling renewal of need.

"Catherine," he muttered somewhat thickly. "Where
the hell did you learn to do that?"

"Do what?" she asked, and the lips he kissed were
smiling with an ancient female wisdom.

*   *   *

"I must go."

Tyrone didn't want to move, but he shifted slightly and raised up on one elbow to look down at her. She was lying on her back beside him, and the serenity of only moments before had left her. Her face was still, eyes caught somewhere between light frost and dark fire fixed on the ceiling.

He reached out a hand to lie just beneath her breasts. "Not yet. It's still early."

Her hands lifted to catch his, holding it against her. The gesture was oddly jerky, almost as if it were made against her will, and her lips twisted a little as if she realized it.

He was trying to understand her, and meant to no matter how long it took. And, more than anything, he wanted to understand why she had refused to marry him. He could understand her desire to keep their illicit relationship secret; what he couldn't understand was her unwillingness to marry him, especially when what they had together was so damned *good*.

"Catherine, was there a man in your life before me? Back in England?" He could feel her tense, but her face remained calm.

"You know there wasn't."

"Not a lover, I know, of course. But was there a man?"

She was silent for a moment, and then said without looking at him, "I was engaged. Briefly."

"What happened?"

Her lips firmed. She still didn't look at him, but her fingers toyed with his. "Things changed. My mother died. Father and I decided to come here. It ended."

"Did you love him?" He felt, suddenly, a hard tension, a tightness in his chest. Had she loved before and, losing that love, made up her mind not to risk her heart again? Could it be that simple? And, if it was, could he bear it? "Catherine, did you love him?"

She sent him a startled glance. "You sound—"

He knew how he sounded. Harsh, demanding. With an effort he spoke in an even tone. "Did you love him?"

She hesitated, then half shrugged. "I thought I did. But it was . . . it was a tame thing. I'd known him most of my life. And I knew him very well. There weren't any secrets between us." *Except one*, she thought.

"And there are between us," he said a bit grimly.

She felt panic stir, and spoke quickly and dryly so that he wouldn't see. "And why not? This is what we are, Tyrone." She lifted a hand to gesture at them, naked together in a small room of an abandoned cottage. "*This*. Our lives touch only here."

"Not by my choice," he said in a flat tone.

"It was your choice in the beginning, just as it was—is—mine," she reminded him, wishing the contentment would return, wishing she didn't have to cope with this conversation. "And if you don't like it now, then—" She broke off, unable to end it, desperate to have what time she could steal with him.

"Then what?" His voice was quiet, dangerous.

Her control snapped suddenly, frayed by fear and worry. "Oh, don't do this," she whispered. "Please, don't." Her hands held his tightly against her, and she thought she was weeping somewhere inside herself. She closed her eyes, wishing the tears could escape because trapped within they hurt so.

"Catherine . . ."

She felt his lips brush her cheek, her mouth, gently, heard surprise and something else in his voice. She kept her eyes closed tightly, afraid of what he might have seen in them.

Tyrone began talking quietly. He told her about his background, orphaned young and forced to earn his living by signing on a ship when no more than a boy. He told her about a man named Morgan Fontaine, a man who had once been a kind of gentleman pirate, and who had seen something he liked in a much younger Tyrone. About the encouragement of that man and, later, solid help in the shape of the loan that had purchased *The Raven*. He talked about the war and his part in it as a blockade runner. About danger and struggle.

And Catherine, listening with a hunger she hoped didn't show on her face, realized that for the first time he was giving of himself. Not passion or desire or gentleness, but himself. He was allowing her to see and understand the life that had shaped the man he had become. She almost held her breath for fear that he would realize what he was doing, and stop.

But then it hit her with the force of a blow. He knew. He was sharing himself quite deliberately.

When his voice died finally into silence, she opened her eyes slowly and looked up at him. His face was grave, eyes direct and steady. He had opened himself up for her, and it hurt her unbearably that she couldn't do the same. Huskily she said, "I have to leave now."

Tyrone's face tightened, and his eyes went bleak. "You're a stubborn woman, Catherine."

"I have to leave," she repeated.

He rolled away from her abruptly, and she felt cold. Alone. She watched him dress, wondering in pain if she would ever see him like this again. Won-

dering if he would end it now after the slap she had
dealt him. Her hands were folded tightly over her
stomach, pressing hard as if to hold in feelings that
were wild to escape.

Then he stepped to the side of the bed and bent to
kiss her with a possession she could feel branding
her. Hands braced on either side of her, he said, "My
name, Catherine."

Through a tight, aching throat, she murmured,
"Tyrone."

He half nodded, expecting it. His face was expressionless. "One of these days you're going to call me
Marc. And then I'm going to ask you to marry
me—again."

She felt a jolt that was pleasure and pain com-
bined, hot and sweet and tormenting. He wasn't going
to end it; he wasn't going to leave her.

"One of these days. And soon, Catherine," he said
flatly, then straightened, turned, and left the cottage.

Long minutes passed before Catherine could force
herself to leave the bed. She picked up the sheets
from the floor but left them on the bed, ready for
next time. Slowly she began dressing. The shift first,
and the memory of how he had gazed at her. The
dress, remembering how he had slowly unbuttoned
it. Stockings and shoes, and the ghostly touch of his
hands on her legs.

She collected the pins from the floor, then got the
hairbrush and sat on the bed restoring order to her
hair. She braided it, pinned it in place. She just sat
there for a while, one hand gripping the brass footrail,
staring at the bed they shared.

How much longer could she risk this? It had seemed
so simple at first. He was seldom on the island and

willing to be careful, to keep these meetings secret. But now ... Her common sense told her to end it quickly, to regain control of her life, but she needed him so badly, needed *this* so much.

If only he would keep to his usual habit and leave in a few days! Everything would be all right. She would be alone again, and able to cope. But he wouldn't. He would stay this time, and every day he remained would be an added strain, a wearing combination of worry, pleasure, and fear.

Catherine could feel the tension inside herself and knew it had never been so great. Between his changed attitude and her own realization of being in love with him, she had seen how desperately important her time with him was. And how agonized she was at the threat of losing it.

But it's no threat. It will happen. The only question is ... when.

She got to her feet slowly and paused in the room long enough to straighten the quilt on the bed. She would be willing to make a bed for Tyrone anywhere, she realized. On his ship, in New York, at the big, silent house here on the island that the townspeople had been politely but firmly discouraged from visiting. And she wouldn't have asked for marriage even if she could have. Just him. Just him, for as long as possible.

Not long.

Catherine left the cottage, conscious suddenly of a great weariness. It was the tension, she knew. She had held herself guardedly for so long now, fought her own nature to project a cold, forbidding surface, and she was very tired.

She walked through the woods, emerging at the road around the bend from her father's house. She paused there, looking and listening, then slipped quickly across the road. She angled across Dr. Scott's drive and onto her father's property, approaching the house through the overgrown garden. Flowers were scarce this time of year, but Catherine picked a few, breaking the stems because she didn't have her shears.

She gathered the threads of her emotional control carefully and held them tight, composed her features, willed the weariness away. Then, carrying the flowers, she strolled around toward the front of the house. Her father was standing near the door, frowning down the walkway at the opened gate of their white picket fence.

"Hello, Father."

He turned and stared at her. "That Tommy Jenkins has been swinging on the gate," he said irritably, "and now he's bent the hinge."

Concentrating, trying to keep her mind calm and to avoid painful thoughts, Catherine only half heard him. "Boys are like that," she said.

"Where have you been?" Lucas asked, still irritable.

"Just walking."

"You're doing a lot of that these days."

Catherine looked at him. "Did you want me for something?" she asked calmly.

He shrugged. "No, no. But you might take better care of me, you know. I've caught a chill somewhere."

As far as she could see, he looked fine. But she said, "Then you should be in bed, Father. Why don't you go now, and—"

"I want my dinner," he said petulantly.

"All right. I'll bring it to you in bed." She took his arm gently and turned him toward the house.

"You'll put the bell by my bed? In case I need you?"

"Yes, Father."

"And hot bricks for my feet? I'm getting dreadfully cold, Catherine."

"I'll see to it, Father. You'll be fine."

But he wasn't. By midnight he was feverish, restless, complaining of being too hot, too cold, or being thirsty. His pulse was rapid, and he was querulous. The little crystal bell on his nightstand rang often as he summoned her to replace the warmed bricks, straighten his bedclothes, fetch him more cool water, bathe his hot brow.

In the lonely hours of darkness, Catherine went up and down the stairs, fetching and carrying patiently. She remained calm when he swore at her in irritation, when he threw the water glass across the room, when he wept at his own weakness.

Just after dawn, strained and exhausted, she slipped from the house and made her way through the garden to Dr. Scott's front door.

Sometime later, as he walked beside her downstairs after leaving her father's room, the doctor said reassuringly, "It's a bad cold, Miss Catherine. Has he been out in the night air? You know how it affects him."

"I don't think so. The other night after Mrs. Symington's party, of course, but it was a warm, dry night.

"Mmm. Well, he caught a chill somewhere. At any rate, his fever's down a bit now; the worst should be over." He eyed her in concern. "He isn't a good patient. You must have had a bad night with him."

"Bad enough," she said briefly.

"You're worn out. I can ask one of the women in town—"

"No." She managed a smile. "No, thank you. I'll take care of him."

"See that you get some rest," he told her sternly. "Don't run up and down these stairs just because he wants his pillow turned. I don't want you as my next patient. Understood?"

"Yes. All right."

"And eat something," Dr. Scott ordered.

She smiled again. "I will. Thank you for coming."

"I'll stop by later in the day."

When he had gone, Catherine closed the door and leaned back against it. God, she was tired. She pushed herself away from the door and went slowly upstairs, holding on the railing with one hand. At her father's bedroom door she stood and listened for a moment, watching the solid shape under the covers that was blessedly still, hearing a faint snore.

With luck he would sleep a few hours. Catherine knew from experience that her father was indeed a bad patient, concerned only with his own discomforts and swelling those all out of proportion. She would get very little rest until he was back on his feet.

She hesitated, feeling her stomach complain of hunger, then went along to her own bedroom. Food could wait; she didn't know when she would get another chance to sleep. She loosened her dress and pulled off her shoes, then lay down on her bed. Muscles that had been taut with strain eased; her aching head was soothed by the softness of the pillow. She felt herself grow limp, felt everything slip away from her.

The bell woke her an hour later.

That day and the next became a test of Catherine's endurance. She fetched and carried, sat with her father when he demanded it, prepared soup and hot tea, carried trays up and down the stairs. She read to him, listened to him talk ramblingly about years gone by.

She slept when she could, an hour here, an hour there snatched when her father was napping. She tried not to let herself think of Tyrone, but was conscious of a desire to be held in strong arms, to go limp and content—even if the contentment was brief. She couldn't help but wonder if he had gone to the cottage and waited for her, if he knew that her father was ill, knew that she wouldn't be able to meet him. She didn't dare try to send him a message.

She needed him, and it frightened her.

"Catherine . . ."

"Yes, Father?" She was sitting by his bed on the second day, watching his hands pull fretfully at the covers.

"I love your mother."

"I know."

"But did she know?"

"I'm sure she did."

His eyes filled with tears and his voice dropped to a low, pathetic mutter. "I loved her. I did, really. But I was a fool. There was a time, when you were just a child . . . She'd gotten angry at me, and she took you and went back to her family."

"Yes. You told me, Father." And he had, months ago, when a similar illness had made him feel guilty and maudlin. He had confessed his unfaithfulness to her mother with a whore he had picked up on the street, had punished both himself and her with the sordid details. Sickened, she had listened with outward composure, then tried to forget what he had told her, although his confession had finally explained the violent arguments she remembered overhearing when she was no more than ten.

"Did I?" he asked vaguely, then sniffed miserably. "I told her too. Begged her forgiveness. Then I got sick and she seemed to forgive me."

"She did, Father," Catherine said in a quiet voice.

"She was going to have another baby after that, but it died before it could be born. And then there was another, dead even before she knew it was inside her."

Catherine half closed her eyes. "Father—"

"We just stopped trying then."

Catherine remembered. She remembered her mother's weakness after the miscarriage. Remembered her mother's tears. Remembered her parents occupying separate bedrooms after that.

"I killed her," Lucas said starkly.

"She got sick, Father. You couldn't have stopped it."

He laughed, a curious sound that held a thread of horror. "No, no, you don't understand. *I killed her.* She knew. She knew I killed her. She haunts me, Catherine."

"Father, please. You have to rest. Close your eyes and try to sleep."

"She haunts me," he whispered, but obediently closed his eyes.

Catherine watched him silently. It was a good hour before she was certain he was asleep. When she was sure, she silently left his bedside and went away to snatch sleep for herself, too tired even to think.

Dr. Scott came to visit the following day, and Catherine left him upstairs alone with her father. He had told her that he'd earlier spread the word in town that Lucas was mildly infectious, discouraging visitors; she was grateful for that. She stood downstairs now, looking around, thinking vaguely of furniture that needed dusting, or other things needing to be done.

When someone knocked at the front door, she went to answer the summons without thought. But she went first hot and then cold when she saw who was standing on the doorstep.

Tyrone.

His eyes narrowed quickly, but his voice was calm and polite when he spoke. "Mr. Abernathy had some groceries ready to send you, so I offered to deliver them." He held a large box, and lifted it slightly to emphasize this sensible reason for his forbidden visit. "Just tell me where to put them."

Catherine hesitated, then stepped back to allow him inside. "Kind of you to trouble yourself," she said in a voice she tried hard to keep steady and without emotion. "If you'd take them into the kitchen, please?"

"Certainly." He had been there before, and knew the way.

She followed, stopping to wait for him outside her father's study door. Her throat felt tight, her body stiff and sore. She had left the front door partly open.

He returned to stand before her. And he reached out suddenly to touch her cheek, his voice dropping to a low, husky note.

"You look so tired, Catherine."

6

Catherine felt herself quiver, and tried to keep the reaction from showing on her face. "Father's better. He should be up and about by tomorrow." She could see the stairs from here, and kept a wary eye out for Dr. Scott's return.

"You've been waiting on him hand and foot, haven't you?" Tyrone's tone was impatient.

She didn't answer. Even in weariness her body had begun pulsing slowly, awakening to his presence. It was hard to breathe, hard to think. But she tried. "Thank you for bringing the groceries. It was kind of you."

Tyrone knew a dismissal when he heard one; he decided to ignore it. He grasped one of her hands firmly and pulled her through the doorway into her father's study. "Stop watching the damned stairs," he said roughly. "And talk to me, Catherine!"

With an effort that felt unbearably great, she managed a faintly mocking smile. "Missing your bedmate, Tyrone?"

His free hand encircled her neck abruptly and he kissed her with the starkly branding possession that was so new in him, uncaring that they could be observed at any moment. "What do you think?" he asked.

She caught at stolen breath. "I think you are."

"Damned right." A grin slashed across his dark face, and he glanced around the study. "However . . ."

"However," she agreed through dry lips. No love-making here. Never here.

His glance had settled on a large oil painting behind her father's desk, and his eyes narrowed. "Your mother?"

"Yes."

"You're the living image of her."

"So I've been told."

Tyrone looked back at her face, his gaze intense. "God, I've missed you," he said softly.

"You said that," she managed to say.

"Not just a bedmate. You. I've missed you."

Catherine was very conscious of his hand still holding her own firmly, of the other hand at the nape of her neck, fingers moving caressingly. "If Father's better, perhaps tomorrow."

"I want to be with you." He seemed to be trying to explain something to her. Or to himself. "I want to look at you, talk to you. Touch you. I want to be with you, Catherine."

I want to be with you! She wanted to repeat his incredible words, savor them aloud, return them and their sentiment to him. But she didn't, or course. "Yes. But, you have to go now. Dr. Scott is upstairs—my father. You have to go."

Gray eyes probed hers in an intent search. Very quietly he said, "I wish you'd tell me what you're afraid of. Tell me what's hurting you."

She stiffened, then backed up a step so that he was forced to release her. "I told you."

"That you're afraid of being a whore in the eyes of the town?" he said bluntly. "That isn't it. You're like me, Catherine; you don't give a tinker's damn what other people think of you. So it has to be something else. What is it?"

"Tyrone—"

"Whatever it is, let me help."

You can't help me. No one can. Steadily she said, "I'll come tomorrow if I can. If Father's better."

Tyrone sighed heavily. "All right, dammit." His mouth was tight, hard, his eyes glittering. "But I'll find out. I will, Catherine. You can't keep it from me forever."

That was part of what she was afraid of. She turned away and preceded him out into the hall, then to the front door. Without a word she opened the door wider and waited for him to go, to leave her.

He paused a moment in the doorway, saying in a different voice, "You should let someone take care of you." Without waiting for a response, he left the house.

Catherine closed the door and leaned back against it. She watched her hands shake, felt the tremors inside. She knew she should end it. Knew she wouldn't. Knew she would go to him tomorrow if it was at all possible.

Like a moth to the flame. Bent on destruction.

Tyrone felt tense, angry. He thought of Catherine's pale, strained face, and anger tangled with a surge of concern, of tenderness. He had wanted to hold her, simply hold her, had wanted to wipe the weariness and tension from her face.

He felt so damned helpless. It wasn't a feeling he

was familiar with. And the mystery that was Catherine grew more bewildering by the hour.

She wanted him, and yet her own desire seemed to cause her pain. She zealously guarded their secret, even though he was certain the opinion's of the townfolk meant next to nothing to her. She gave of her passion, her body, without reservation, yet refused to share any more than that with him. And she was *afraid*.

He drove the bay at a brisk trot all the way back to his house, frowning in thought. I was as if ... He remembered a jigsaw puzzle he had brought for the sick man in his house, remembered the man's bafflement when a piece proved to be missing, leaving the picture incomplete.

That was Catherine. He had all the pieces but one, and that one was needed to show him what she was. A single piece of her that she protected fiercely, and he hadn't a clue as to what it might be.

He was no closer to the answer when the bay turned in his drive and trotted briskly to the house. He put the horse away himself, checking the other horses before he closed up the barn. There had been no further attempts against his stock, and he was no closer to an answer there either.

He went inside. Much later, reading a story to the man, Tyrone was conscious of a leaden sadness and discouragement within himself. It happened more and more, he knew, because this childlike man with the gaunt face and innocent eyes was slipping away. In a very real sense he had gone already, but Tyrone had kept a memory alive, and that had been enough. For a while.

But now, with the man fading, there seemed nothing to hold on to. It was such a waste, such a terrible, tragic waste. And Tyrone hated waste.

He wished suddenly that he could tell Catherine about the man, share the memory with someone else he cared about—

He realized the truth only then. Leaving the man to be helped into bed by Tully, Tyrone went downstairs and sat alone in his study, gazing at nothing.

Fool, he thought, fool not to have seen it sooner. He was in love with Catherine.

She came quickly into the cottage the next afternoon, a little breathlessly, not ten minutes after he'd arrived himself.

"Mr. Odell came to see Father and they're playing cards," she said immediately. "I can't stay away for long."

Tyrone stopped her breathless rush by pulling her into his arms, kissing her. "Let me hold you," he said huskily, and did, keeping her slender body pressed tightly to his own. She was still for a moment, pliant, but then she pushed back away from him.

"There's no time," she said.

He was struck by her urgency, by the almost wild look in her darkening eyes. Concerned because of her exhaustion and strain, he had meant this interlude between them to be quiet and peaceful. He had wanted, somehow, to comfort her. But she refused that, and he could feel a storm loose in the tiny room.

"Catherine—"

"There's no time." Swiftly she reached to free her hair, scattering pins carelessly over the floor. Her eyes fixed on his face, she began unbuttoning her dress. "This is what we *are*, Tyrone. Just this."

"No. More." He could feel the rising heat, feel his body and senses responding to her strange, desperate urgency. He watched the dress fall away from her.

"There can't be more." Her voice was low, shaking. "You knew that from the beginning. There can't be more, not between us." She kicked her shoes off and stepped toward him wearing the thin linen shift and stockings. Her hands reached for his tie, his coat, dropping them heedlessly to the floor. Unbuttoning his shirt, tugging it from his trousers.

"Catherine . . ." His voice had thickened, gone hoarse.

"I want you. Now, right now. I don't want to talk. I don't want to think."

She took his hand and led him into the tiny bedroom, and they made love on top of the colorful quilt, as they had before. But it had never been so wild between them, so hungry. Catherine was almost ravenous, and yet her urgency held a thread of despair that moved Tyrone unbearably. She seemed determined to take all she could of him, fixedly intent, as if she knew there would never be another opportunity to lie in his arms.

There were no half smiles from her this time, no contentment or ease. She didn't ask him not to leave her. And Tyrone, burned by her fire, seduced by her need, tried to give her the assurances she was so desperate for. He tried—and was unhappily conscious of failure. He could give her passion because she would accept it from him, match it, return it. But she refused his tenderness, rejected comfort.

And if she wouldn't accept those simple, undemanding emotions, he realized in pain, then how would she ever accept his love?

It almost broke his heart.

*   *   *

When it was over, when the tiny room was quiet and still again, Catherine slid from the bed. She retrieved her shift and stockings from the floor, put them on in silence. She got her hairbrush and pins, sitting on the edge of the bed with her back to him, and restored her hair to order.

Tyrone, lying on his side watching her, thought that she had never before left the cottage first. He wondered what it meant, and was afraid he knew. Quietly he said, "What in God's name are you afraid of, Catherine?"

Her back still to him, she continued to braid her hair. After a moment she said, "I have to get back home. I told you."

When she would have risen, he reached over and grasped her wrist gently. "Look at me," he ordered.

She turned her head slowly, looked at him with a still face and eyes that were guarded.

"Let me help you," he said.

"There's nothing to help." Her voice was calm. "Nothing wrong, nothing different. Nothing has changed, Tyrone."

"You don't lie very well, Catherine."

She pulled her wrist free and got to her feet, stood looking down at him for a moment. "I'll be busy for a few days," she said. "I won't be able to come here. Perhaps on Friday."

Friday was three days away. Tyrone looked at her, feeling frustrated, angry, worried. "All right," he said finally. "Friday, then."

She nodded, a flash of relief in her eyes, then turned away and went into the other room. He heard the rustle of her clothing as she finished dressing. The next moment he heard the door open and quietly close.

He didn't leave for a long time.

Catherine slipped back into her father's house in silence and, listening, was relieved to hear Lucas's laugh from the study. Good. Odell was still here, then.

She busied herself in the house, cleaning and dusting, making a start on the work that had piled up while her father had been ill. She had sent word to the woman who came in daily not to return until her father was better, and made a mental note to pass along the news that he was recovering now.

She didn't think about Tyrone. She blanked her mind and worked, concentrating on what she was doing. It was the hardest thing she had ever had to do, but she did it. The only alternative was pain and worry.

The following day her father was better. It was always like that with him; once back on his feet, it was as if he had never been ill. She was relieved, knowing that she could relax a bit now and recover her energy. She badly needed to do that.

"I believe I'll go for a ride, Catherine," he said cheerfully.

"Don't overtire yourself, Father."

"No, no, I won't. The hack needs exercise; so do I. Just down to the harbor and back, perhaps. I'll be all right. Stop fussing, Catherine."

She didn't bother to point out that for the past days he had wanted her to fuss over him. He'd be indignant if she reminded him, would bluster and deny and work himself up to anger. She had learned to avoid that.

Instead, she said, "I'll go into town then. Mr. Abernathy sent groceries, but there are a few things I should get."

"Fine. Get another bottle of wine, will you?"

"Father—"

"Another bottle, Catherine." Lucas was very annoyed.

"Very well." She realized, suddenly, that during his illness she hadn't bothered to drug his nightly glass of wine. But it couldn't matter, she assured herself. It couldn't possibly matter. He was fine now.

He hitched up the buggy for her in a rare burst of helpfulness, then saddled his elderly gray hack and set off toward the harbor at a comfortable pace. Catherine drove herself into town, unable to help herself wishing that she would see Tyrone, even while knowing that such an encounter would be tense and cold and painfully unsatisfying as always.

Not long now, she thought bitterly, *until that's all I'll have.*

She pushed the thought away. Halting the buggy before the mercantile, she was dismayed to find the town busy and filled with people. It was relatively unusual, particularly on a weekday, but half the women and a number of the men of Port Elizabeth seemed to have found some reason for being in town.

There were few young children on the island, since the wealthy families chose to send their youngsters away to boarding school in Europe; only the merchants kept their children with them, and there was a one-room schoolhouse at the northern end of town, where a brisk, middle-aged spinster, enticed to the island from Philadelphia, taught. School was over for the day, however, so the street rang with children's shouts and laughter.

Catherine, wearing composure like an iron mask, hitched her horse to the rail and stepped up onto the sidewalk. There was a clatter of small feet rushing by, almost running into her, and one young boy, sniggering, jerked at her skirt as he passed.

The boy's mother was no more than ten feet away, and Catherine watched her turn away indifferently. Unsurprised, Catherine wondered wryly how she could hope for respect from the children, when their elders were so studiously lacking it.

It hurt though.

She stiffened her spine and went into the store. There were several women and a few men talking and laughing in the big, cluttered store. Catherine quailed, but kept her head high.

Tyrone, standing in a dim corner by the pickle barrel, smoking a cigar and talking to Dr. Scott, saw her come in. He had been asking Scott about the loss of his old hack, still trying as casually as possible to discover if the other animals that had died under mysterious circumstances could have been killed deliberately, if not quite so brutally, as his own horse. But when Catherine entered the store, Tyrone found his mind wandering away from the doctor and dead animals, and fixing on her.

And, instantly, he saw her isolation, her aloneness, more clearly than he had ever seen it before. The people in the store didn't, being "civilized," offer her cold stares or insulting remarks; they simply behaved as if she weren't there. Gazes passed over her and were averted; shoulders were casually turned away; voices were raised slightly higher in volume. And through it all, Catherine, expressionless, silently gathered the items she had come for.

"Poor girl."

Tyrone looked sharply at Dr. Scott, who was gazing meditatively at Catherine. "What do you mean?" he asked, wondering if the doctor saw what he himself saw.

Dr. Scott pursed his lips slightly, still looking at Catherine. "She has a great deal to bear."

"These people hate her," Tyrone said slowly. "I find that hard to understand. She's done nothing to them." He watched the doctor intently, looking for some clue to the answers he sought.

Then Dr. Scott said, "Perhaps they offer the only thing she can accept from them. Have you ever considered that hate might be the lesser of two evils?"

Tyrone frowned. "Why would it be? And what other evil are you talking about?"

Dr. Scott gave him an odd, intense look, then shrugged and began to turn away. Softly he said, "We all have our demons, lad. She has hers."

Tyrone returned his gaze to Catherine, watching her move among people who deliberately didn't see her. He was baffled.

Tommy Jenkins was seven. He was, his ma said, incorrigible. Tommy didn't know what that meant, but it sounded like something Dr. Scott would give medicine for. However, since the doctor had offered no medicine, Tommy concluded that being incorrigible wasn't *that* bad.

Tommy had left his playmates in town the instant they were released from the bondage of Miss Peabody's lessons. He usually did that when there was a ship anchored in the harbor, being more fascinated with ships than with anything else in his disappointingly placid life.

The Raven. Tommy loved *The Raven.* She was an

absolutely perfect ship, and her exciting life practically screamed from every sleek line. Sometimes one or more of her crew could be wheedled into telling stories about *The Raven* and about Captain Tyrone. About blockade running, which sounded to Tommy dreadfully dangerous and wonderful.

Tommy sat on the extreme edge of the dock and dangled his feet above the water, gazing wistfully across the calm harbor at his goddess. Even still and trapped by her anchor, he thought, she was a dainty lady. Tommy wasn't entirely sure what "dainty" meant; his ma had used that word once, and he had liked the sound of it. Dainty. *The Raven* was a dainty lady. He liked that.

He wished passionately that he had the courage to ask Captain Tyrone to let him actually go aboard the ship. He wasn't exactly afraid of the captain, but the tall man was something of a vaguely frightening mystery to his childish mind. Tommy had the feeling that Captain Tyrone could get angry awfully fast, even worse than his pa. Still, he had thought once or twice there might have been a laugh in those queer gray eyes.

I'll ask him, Tommy thought suddenly, screwing up his courage. *I'll be very polite, and—and I'll just ask him!*

Bent on this gathering of his nerve, Tommy didn't hear soft footsteps behind him. He had no sense of danger, and there was no warning. One moment he was sitting securely on the dock, and in the next terrifying, confusing moment he was thrashing about in water far, far over his head.

And Tommy couldn't swim.

"Catherine?"

She concentrated on putting her parcels into the rear of the buggy, and she didn't look at him. "If this town boasted a pillory," she said in a soft, grim tone, "you'd be hell-bent to see me in it, wouldn't you?"

"Not at all." His voice was low but amused. "But, in fact, I have just proved myself to be a heartless man of few scruples and no conscience."

She shot him a glance. "Why?"

"Because," he said, eyes dancing, "I just made a bet with Abernathy. Within earshot of as many people as possible, I bet that I could get a smile out of Miss Waltrip. I now have a dandy excuse to stand here talking to you, and in due course I'll retreat back to the mercantile, crushed, and pay my debt."

She almost smiled.

"Don't, dammit," he said in a near growl. "I have to *lose* the bet."

Catherine noticed that he had planned well. He was standing in such a way as to prevent her getting into the buggy, and to watching eyes it would clearly look as if she were haughtily waiting for him to move. She kept her face cold, her posture stiff. "You *don't* have any scruples," she told him.

"Of course not." He lifted one foot and rested it negligently on the buggy's step. "Not when it comes to getting what I want. Haven't you figured that out yet?"

"I'm beginning to."

"Then why are you still fighting me?" he asked smoothly.

"I don't know what you're talking about."

"Don't lie, Catherine. As I've said, you're not very good at it. You know exactly what I'm talking about. You've held me at arm's length from the beginning, and now you're pushing me even farther away."

"How you can say that after yesterday—" She broke off, trying to still her panic, to keep her face cold.

"Yes, why don't we talk about yesterday?" His deep voice dropped to a lower, more intense note.

"Not here," she said swiftly.

"There's no other place, Catherine. No place you'll allow us. In the cottage you want only passion; you won't come to my house or allow me in yours, and in the streets you offer coldness. Where can I talk to you and have a reasonable hope of being answered?"

She stared into his flickering eyes, vaguely conscious that he wore a half smile that was purely for the benefit of onlookers; there was no smile in those intense gray depths. And she knew her own face was cold, still. Softly, wondering on some dim level if their observers could possibly know her world was falling apart, she said, "You have no right to ask questions."

"Even if you won't share anything else, you share my bed. That gives me the right."

"No." Her lips felt stiff. "Not your bed. A secret bed in an abandoned cottage."

"A lover's bed," he said swiftly. "Where doesn't matter. A lover's bed, Catherine. *Our* bed. The one thing you can't deny is that we *are* lovers. And that gives me the right to question."

"Let me go," she murmured, and she might have been asking him to move away from the buggy. Or she might have been asking him something else. She wasn't sure.

His gaze revealed just how angry he was. "Do you know what this is doing to me?" he asked with the meaningless smile still curving his lips. "You won't tell me anything, won't answer my questions, won't trust me enough to—"

There was a sudden commotion at the harbor end
of the street, a number of people hurrying in that
direction.

"What the hell?" Tyrone muttered. "Wait here for
me, Catherine."

She nodded, welcoming the distraction and aware
that the attention of the town had shifted. She turned
to watch Tyrone stride down the street, absently
admiring his broad shoulders and graceful carriage.
Then her eyes wandered past him, and she felt herself go cold.

A man she recognized as being one of Tyrone's
crew was walking toward the townspeople, carrying
a soaked, sobbing Tommy Jenkins in his arms.

An accident, she thought wildly. Of course, an accident. Little boys were constantly getting into things
they shouldn't, and Tommy was forever at the harbor looking wistfully at whatever ship was anchored
there. An accident . . .

She watched as the boy was handed to his grateful
mother, saw several people shake the embarrassed
rescuer by the hand. Gradually, though, the crowd
dispersed, and Tyrone was left talking alone with his
crewman. He was frowning; the man was talking
earnestly, gesturing. After a few minutes Tyrone nodded, said something that elicited a big grin from the
man, and then they parted.

The rescuer headed happily for the hotel and, Catherine knew, the well-stocked bar. Tyrone returned to
her.

"What happened?" she asked.

Tyrone looked at her, then shook his head. "Lyle,
my ships's mate, saw the little boy struggling in the
water just off the end of the dock. Luckily, *The Raven*'s
anchored close in; Lyle managed to get the longboat

to him in time and fish him out. The child will be all right, I think. He's just wet and miserable and frightened. Dr. Scott will look him over."

Catherine studied his face, feeling herself grow colder. "There's something else, isn't there?"

Tyrone sighed explosively. "I'm damned if I know. Lyle wasn't sure enough to mention it to anyone else, but he told me he thinks the boy was pushed into the water."

She heard her voice emerge calmly. "What did he see?"

"Not much. The sun was reflecting off the water, and there was a glare. He just glanced toward the dock, expecting to see Tommy there because the boy apparently spends hours looking at the ship. Then he believes he saw a flicker of movement. More of an impression than anything else. Lyle's a good man. He doesn't see things that aren't there. If he believes the boy was pushed, then there's a good chance he was."

"Did Tommy say—?"

"He's too scared to say anything right now. Maybe later, when he's calmed down. But if it happened fast enough, he may not remember being pushed."

Catherine felt numb. "Perhaps another boy meant to have some fun? A joke gone badly wrong?"

Tyrone's frown eased. "Yes, that's likely enough. And the other boy panicked, probably, when he realized Tommy couldn't swim. Nothing else makes sense."

Taking advantage of his distraction, Catherine quickly climbed into the buggy before he could stop her.

"Catherine—"

"Go and pay your debt," she told him calmly. "I have to head home now."

"Damn you," he answered. "Always running from me."

Without responding, she slapped the reins against her horse's rump and moved off down the street. She didn't look left or right. She didn't look back. Head high, face cold and remote, she drove from the town.

The fear inside her was a living thing, clawing bloody wounds in its efforts to escape. And she could hear the dry sobs that began forcing themselves through her tight throat, terrible rasping sobs without the wetness of tears to ease their passing. She was shuddering and gasping by the time she had stabled the horse, and paused for a few moments before leaving the barn in an effort to control herself.

But control wouldn't come this time. She could no longer ignore the danger, could no longer convince herself that seeing Tyrone was worth the risk. She was willing to risk almost anything to be with him, to lie in his arms, but there was one thing she wouldn't risk, couldn't risk. And she couldn't explain it to him.

Oh, God.

She could feel something dying inside her, bleeding its life away in agony. She loved Marc Tyrone, and because she hadn't meant to, that love was all the stronger. She loved him, and needed him desperately, and the fates had conspired to hold him tauntingly, forever out of her reach.

You always knew it wasn't forever. Always knew it couldn't be.

But . . . for a while . . . she had let herself dream. The passionate interludes with him and the memories of them had allowed her to pretend that everything was all right. Passion was safe, unthreatening, as long as it was secret. The little cottage was safe, what happened in it was a series of memories she would cherish always to sustain her through the rest of her life.

"Fool," she whispered. Fool to have allowed herself even that. She wouldn't have missed what she had never had. She wouldn't have fallen in love. She wouldn't have let anyone inside her careful walls.

Catherine straightened slowly, unaware until then that she had been bent over like an old woman. But it didn't surprise her. She felt old. Immeasurably old. Her parcels were at her feet; she made herself pick them up. She forced herself to walk to the house, wondering if the expression on her face reflected how empty she felt inside.

You'll get through this, she told herself forcefully. Then she snorted. Of course she would; she had no choice.

"Catherine, where have you been?" Lucas asked irritably the moment he saw her.

"In town, Father. I told you I was going."

"Oh." He frowned at her. "You're pale." It was almost an accusation.

She put her parcels down on the sideboard and slowly drew off her gloves. "There was an accident today," she said calmly. "Tommy Jenkins nearly drowned."

Her father grunted. "Down at the harbor, I suppose, watching that ship. Boys are always fascinated by ships."

"Didn't you see him there?" she asked.

"What? Oh, no, I didn't go to the harbor. I just rode along the road for half a mile or so. Then I got tired, so I came back home. Did you get my wine?"

"Yes, Father. You can have a glass with dinner."

"Stop trying to manage me!" he suddenly roared.

Catherine didn't flinch. "We're having roast chicken for dinner," she said. "And baby peas. You like that."

He glared at her. But slowly the glare died and his brilliant eyes softened. "I like that. You're a good cook, Kate. A very good cook. I've always said so."

"Thank you," she whispered.

He smiled happily.

It was late afternoon when Tyrone, conscious of feeling quite frustrated, finally left town. He had spoken casually to the four people who had lost animals during the past months, having managed to introduce the subject in an offhand way to each of them. Only Lettia Symington thought her dog had been deliberately killed, and she stubbornly believed that Catherine had done it.

She hadn't been able to give him a reason other than "sheer spite."

Tyrone, who knew that Catherine wasn't spiteful or cruel, had no difficulty in dismissing Lettia's groundless accusation. Having done that without hesitation, he was left with his original question and no answers. No answers at all. But he trusted his instincts, and his instincts told him that the animals had been deliberately killed.

Why? As a sick sort of revenge? It made sense in a twisted way, but Tyrone couldn't remember having angered or hurt anyone on the island so much that his horse would become a target. Still, the violent cruelty in killing his horse told him that, indeed, he had made an enemy—a bad one.

Tyrone didn't like it. It was bad enough when you knew your enemy, when you could assign him a face and a name. Then, at least, it was possible to be on guard. But with a ghostly enemy wearing God knew what face, it was nothing short of impossible to be more than careful.

Both before and during the war Tyrone had developed a keen sense of danger; it had served him well in his blockade-running years, and had never since deserted him. That sense was tingling now, leaving him with an itch between his shoulder blades that warned of an unfriendly hand with a naked blade at his back. And it was all the worse because he hadn't the faintest idea who was holding the knife.

Tyrone drove slowly out of town, frowning. Passing the Jenkins house, he saw little Tommy sitting disconsolately on the front steps and staring at the ground. Tyrone hesitated, then drew his horse to a halt at the end of the walkway. "Tommy, come here for a moment, please."

The boy looked up, fright passing swiftly over his small face. He rose and came down the walk with lagging steps, stopping a couple of feet from the buggy. He looked at Tyrone with huge eyes, and spoke quickly and breathlessly. "I didn't mean to cause trouble, Captain, I swear I didn't!"

Tyrone smiled, trying to put the boy at ease. "Of course not, Tommy. It was an accident, wasn't it?"

"I was just looking at the ship," Tommy mumbled, hanging his head and scuffing one foot. "I know Ma told me not to go near the water, but I wanted to get near the ship. She's such a pretty ship and I . . . and I wanted to see her!"

Tyrone listened, still smiling. When the boy's breathless explanation was over, he asked softly, "Tommy, do you think someone might have pushed you off the dock?"

Tommy's mouth made a perfectly round O, and his

eyes grew larger. "Why would anybody go and do that, Captain?" he asked in total astonishment.

"As a joke perhaps? Not knowing you couldn't swim? Did you hear someone come up behind you?"

Tommy scuffed his foot harder and frowned. "I didn't hear anybody. But maybe somebody pushed me, Captain. I wouldn't never go and fall off the dock by my own self. I'm real careful." He said the last with a strong trace of defiance, and Tyrone knew that had probably been the boy's repeated defense to an angry, worried mother.

Still, it was clear that if someone had pushed Tommy, he couldn't remember it. Not unnatural, but certainly frustrating to Tyrone. "All right, Tommy. Thank you." He fished into a pocket and found a coin, tossing it to the boy. "Buy yourself some sweets."

"Oh, thank you, Captain!" Tommy said, catching the coin neatly.

Tyrone remembered his own fascination with ships at that age, and made an offer on impulse. "Tell you what. You get your pa to take you down to the harbor tomorrow afternoon, and I'll see to it that you're taken out to visit the ship." He was rewarded instantly by the expression of blissful happiness that spread across the boy's small face.

Tommy stuttered his thanks, and Tyrone lifted his reins and drove on, reflecting wryly that it didn't take much to make a boy of that age happy. It became more difficult, as one grew older, to find contentment. To cope with problems. At Tommy's age, Tyrone thought, an enemy could be faced and thrashed and anger forgotten, likely with a return to friendship in the next hour. Boys were like that.

But men, Tyrone knew, couldn't settle their hostilities quite so easily. Men carried knives and guns . . . and hated for a very long time indeed.

Tyrone had a sense of time and events rushing beyond his control, and it disturbed him. An enemy here on the island, faceless and more dangerous because of it; an enemy—or at least a determined man— very likely on his way here for a long-avoided confrontation. Then there were his growing feelings for Catherine, and her hidden worry and fear.

Secrets. Too many secrets all suddenly too close to the surface and exposure. An enemy's secret hate; Tyrone's secret deeds, his secret commitment; Catherine's secret fears.

He felt an elusive sense of understanding, as though the answers to everything lay buried in his own mind, but he couldn't seem to grasp them.

Frowning, he drove on, absently remembering to stop by the harbor and arrange Tommy's visit to *The Raven*.

Boys were easily made happy. He wondered if men ever could be.

7

On Friday Catherine made up her mind to end her relationship with Tyrone. It was the only rational thing to do. She couldn't go on living with her nerves stretched to the breaking point, terrified someone would find out about them. So there was really no choice. It had to be over, finished. Then she would get on with her life.

It sounded so simple. Reasonable. She was a reasonable, intelligent woman, after all. She wasn't a schoolgirl languishing in heartbreak for what she couldn't have. She was a mature woman of twenty-eight who had lived long enough to know that hearts didn't break, that they only ached as if they could and would, and that there were certain things she would never be able to call her own.

Captain Marc Tyrone was one of them.

And Catherine's reasonable, rational, intelligent decision to end things between them cost her more pain than she would have believed possible. She had caught herself looking at her reflection in a mirror on Thursday afternoon, wondering why the pain didn't show. It should show plainly, she thought; nothing that hurt so badly could avoid leaving marks—claw marks—in the flesh.

But she looked the same as always—calm, remote, cold. It was with a different kind of pain that she wondered then if this "public" mask, discarded in relief in Tyrone's presence, would gradually become her real self. With no Tyrone to evoke passion and laughter, how could she avoid it? Would she wake one morning and feel no conscious forming of the mask because the mask had become a normal part of her? Would the violence of her secret feelings simply churn wildly for a while before slowing, and finally dying, smothered to death inside her?

Oh, dear God . . .

"Did you say something, Catherine?"

She looked at her father across the table as they ate lunch on Friday. "No. No, Father, I didn't say anything."

"I thought you did."

"No."

Catherine glanced back down at her plate, wondering if the anguish inside her had escaped in some thread of sound. Dangerous. Her loss of control was dangerous. And it was so important, especially now, to maintain control. No one could be allowed to guess what she felt, not the town, not her father—and not Tyrone, especially not Tyrone.

He wouldn't want it to end. She knew that, without vanity. She had, somehow, made an impression on Marc Tyrone's life—or perhaps she had simply become a habit with him. In any case, he saw her as being a part of his life, so much so that he had flatly told her he would propose marriage a second time. When he heard her say his name.

Marc. It was in her head, always, a whisper away

from her lips. She had managed, somehow, not to give in when he had tried, in passion, to force it from her. He knew then, had guessed, that she withheld that because it was her single defense against a total and complete intimacy. By using his surname, whether briskly or in passion, she held him firmly at a distance. With her mask and her morals stripped away by him, it was all she had left.

"I'm riding over to Gerald's after lunch, Catherine," her father said absently. "There's a book he's promised to lend me."

"All right, Father."

"What have you planned for this afternoon?"

She wondered briefly what his reaction would be if she told him the truth. *I'm going to cut my heart out, Father.* But she didn't, of course. She said, "A walk perhaps."

"It would do you good, no doubt. You're looking quite peaked, Catherine."

If her father saw that, what would Tyrone's sharper gaze see? She couldn't allow herself to appear at all uncertain or distressed by what she was about to do; if Tyrone found the chinks in her armor, she would never be able to hide the truth from him. She would have to appear calm and certain, and she couldn't be pale or shaky.

I won't shake. I won't. And I'll rouge my cheeks so that he won't notice a pallor. That's it. I'll paint my face like a whore when I go to him this last time.

The decision made, Catherine resolutely began wrapping layers of cold calm about herself. As she had never been forced to before, she called on all her willpower to hold her features expressionless, her eyes steady and cool, her body stiff. It was so vital now. She reminded herself over and over that it was desperately important not to betray her feelings—and not to allow her body to respond to his.

That would be hardest. The mask she could cling to, even with him, but her body . . .

Catherine felt heat, felt a slow throbbing begin deep inside her, and bent her head over her plate so that her father wouldn't see. *It's worse!* she thought wildly. Worse, this longing of her body for his, worse because she knew she would never have him again. And her body refused to be willed into submission by her despairing mind, refused to feel cold and uncaring. Refused to stop wanting him.

From the first he had been able to instantly arouse her with no more than his presence, a veiled look, a slow smile; how in God's name could she convince him that response no longer existed?

She had to. Somehow, she had to.

"Is there anything you need from town, Catherine?" her father asked casually a short time later.

"No, Father. Will you be long?"

"Two or three hours, I suppose. You should take that walk, you know. Get some color in your cheeks."

"Yes, I will."

"All right, then." He left, whistling cheerfully. A few minutes later she heard his old hack trotting from the stables and past the house. She waited a few more minutes, then went slowly up to her bedroom.

The pot of rouge, caked and dry, was in the drawer of her bureau; she had used it only rarely in England for masquerades and the like, but never here on the island. There had never been a reason to use it. Now there was. With a steady hand Catherine very lightly and carefully colored her pale cheeks. She studied her reflection, half nodded to herself. She looked, she decided, normal enough.

The dress she was wearing was dark blue and without frills; it could have been a gown of mourning. *Was* a gown of mourning.

Catherine went downstairs and then slipped from the house. She made her way through the garden and out to the road. She was careful to wait, to look and listen. When she was sure there was no one about to see her, she crossed the road and allowed the forest swallow her. Dim, cool. She walked steadily, reminding herself with every step that this was her only choice.

Only choice . . . only choice . . . It echoed in her mind, a litany. Only choice. Only. Choice.

Who would she have to talk to after this?

Only choice. Only choice.

Never again to feel his passion . . .

Only choice. Only choice.

Never again to feel her own . . .

Only choice.

Never to say his name out loud . . .

She walked steadily to the cottage, went inside. She took down the blue curtains, folded them neatly, and put them on the floor in the main room. The fresh sheets they had not yet used were removed from the bed, folded, and placed on top of the curtains. The colorful quilt was added to the pile. Her hairbrush was placed on top.

She stood looking at the pathetic little stack. Not much, she thought wearily, to mark the end of passion, the end of joy. The end of happiness. She went into the bedroom and sat down on the edge of the bare mattress. She folded her hands in her lap and stared at the wall.

Gazing at a patch of mildew, she realized how odd it was that she had never felt sordid in this decaying, abandoned little cottage. Never. Though knowing the town would have branded her a whore for what went on here, she had never known the least bit of shame in this place. Suddenly it occurred to her why that was so: because she had loved him from the first. Anyplace with him would have been a place of joy and passion, a place where laughter would have come easily. Anyplace.

She heard hoofbeats, vaguely wondered why he was riding today instead of driving the buggy. She looked down at her hands and laced her fingers together. She heard the door open, a pause, heard it close. He had seen the curtains, the quilt, the sheets, her hairbrush. He would know what it meant.

Footsteps came slowly across the main room, stopped in the doorway. She braced herself inwardly and turned her head to look at him.

Tyrone leaned against the doorjamb, hands in his pockets. His face was set, grim. His eyes reminded Catherine of a stormy gray sky just before the Atlantic loosed one of its violent tempests. He didn't move, didn't say a word. He simply stared at her and waited.

"It's over," she said.

The room was very silent for a few moments. Tyrone never changed expression; his voice was level, steady. "I see. And I have nothing to say about the matter, Catherine?"

Suddenly she couldn't look at him. She couldn't continue to meet those oddly flat, violent eyes. And even now, even sensing his anger, she also felt the painful longing of her body for him. The slow, steady, pulsing awareness of him so near. Every beat of her heart hurt. She looked down at her hands, fought to keep her voice even. "There's nothing to say, Tyrone. We both knew it was a temporary arrangement."

"It may have begun that way," he said. "But two years isn't temporary."

"It's over," she repeated.

"Why?" The single word, abruptly harsh.

Catherine was silent.

"Is it because you've grown to hate the way I can make you feel? Is that it, Catherine? Because you want to be with me, because I've disrupted your neat, *unfeeling* existence?"

She endured that jab, but felt a rush of bitterness, and wished with a sudden wildness that it were true. She could barely breathe past the tightness of her throat, could hardly speak for the anguish of her own emotions. If only she didn't feel, *couldn't* feel! Tonelessly she said, "There's no reason to do this. It's over, Tyrone. Just let it end."

He didn't. In the same harsh voice he said, "It's the one thing you can't control, isn't it, Catherine? I can make you want me with half the town watching, and you can't stand that. So I'm to be put out of your life like a stray cat, like something too bothersome to be tolerated."

"Please," she murmured, feeling buffeted, caught in the storm of his eyes. How could he do that, she wondered. How could he, without moving, lash her with the violence of his voice and his eyes? She wanted to avoid meeting that turbulent gaze, afraid of giving herself away, yet she found herself casting stolen glances at him without meaning to, again and again.

"Please, what, Catherine? Please take my dismissal like a gent, tip my hat and say thank you, ma'am?

Well, I can't do that. I'm a gentleman the way you're a lady—all and only on the surface."

She winced, half closed her eyes. Why not, she asked herself tiredly. Why shouldn't he think that? It was the truth, wasn't it?

"I'm sorry," he said roughly. "I didn't mean that."

"Yes, you did," she said. "And it's true enough. Why should I cavil at it?"

"Catherine—"

"Why can't you let it end? Just . . . let it end." She felt beaten, physically battered.

"No. I want the truth from you now. Why?"

Torn between lies and the truth, she fumbled for a reason he could accept. "It's too much. I'm tired of the tension, tired of secrecy."

"It doesn't have to be secret," he bit out tautly. "I asked you to marry me, Catherine."

"I don't want marriage," she said. *I can't have it.*

"Is it marriage you don't want? Or is it me?"

"Don't ask me that," she whispered, holding on desperately to the last fragile tendrils of control. They were slipping from her grasp; she could feel herself breaking.

Tyrone laughed, a terrible sound. "So that's part of it as well. I'm good enough for a lover, but I don't have the blue blood for a husband. Well, as you said, it's true enough, and why should I cavil at it? I'm the mongrel offspring of an Irish parlormaid and a Greek sailor, and all that I have now I have fought for all my life."

"Don't." She was aching inside, unbearably hurt that he could believe her so shallow. And she was surprised by the touch of bitter defiance in his voice, surprised that it mattered to him, that he was sensitive about his beginnings. How little she really knew about him. But it was better to hurt only his pride, she thought dimly. He would have a reason to hate her, and that would end this between them.

She didn't want him to hate her.

"I never suspected you were like the other fine citizens of Port Elizabeth," he went on inexorably in the same bitterly caustic voice. "But you are, aren't you, Catherine? *Civilized* behavior is everything, ruling here like a god. Never mind the rot underneath. You'll happily take a lowly ship's captain for a secret lover, and then coolly throw him out when you're done with him, like garbage."

"Stop." She heard the thin note in her voice, the quiver of strain. "Don't do this." She felt sick, dizzy, cold.

"Oh, pardon me. Pardon me for feeling, Miss Waltrip. It seems I'm lacking all the way around, doesn't it?"

Catherine realized she was standing, knew she had to get out of there, get away from him before the cry of anguished protest in her throat could escape. But something did escape, a thread of sound like a lost thing, soft and dazed. She went blindly toward the door, intent on pushing past him.

"Catherine!" He caught her shoulders hard, held her with fingers that bit into her.

"Let me go," she whispered, staring fixedly at his tie.

There was a moment of thick silence, and then he grasped her chin in one hand and roughly turned her face up. "Look at me," he ordered.

Unable to resist, she did, trying to keep her eyes blank, her face still. He was pale, a muscle jerking erratically beside his hard mouth. And his eyes were a stormy gray hell, wildly glittering with savage emotion. She wondered how she had ever thought him a remote man, an unfeeling man. He felt a great deal, it seemed. Catherine tried desperately to hide her own agonized feelings, tried to hide from him the knowledge that her body was his, her heart, her soul.

Tyrone bent his head suddenly and fitted his mouth to hers. Catherine stiffened at the first touch, attempting to keep her body still, frozen. And if he had kissed her with anger, with demand, she might have been able to do it. But Tyrone didn't kiss her that way at all.

His hard mouth was incredibly gentle, asking rather than demanding, seducing with sweetness. Almost pleading for her response. It wasn't passion, it was caring, and it broke more than her will. She felt her body sway toward his, felt her mouth open to the tender, seeking warmth of his. She was drowning, and he was a lifeline; she was dying, and he was life. Dying—

"No!" she gasped, jerking back away from him.

"You don't hate me," he said thickly.

"Let me—"

Tyrone was staring into her eyes, his own suddenly darkening with realization and remorse, with the certain knowledge that he had hurt her unforgivably. His hand reached up to touch her cheek, his thumb rubbing briefly; they both looked at the smudge of red that had been transferred from her flesh to his. "Dutch courage," he murmured.

"No."

"I was wrong," he said in a slow, husky voice. "Everything I said was wrong. Catherine—"

She ran. Blindly, forgetting the things left forlornly in the middle of the floor, she fled the cottage . . . and him. She was vaguely aware of his horse shying nervously as she burst through the door; she heard a violent oath from Tyrone, but she didn't stop. She ran through the woods and scarcely paused at the road before hurrying across and into her father's garden.

"Catherine!" He caught her wrist, there in the overgrown garden, swung her around to face him.

She felt sheer panic sweep over her, and a cry of alarm escaped wildly. "No!"

He didn't try to draw her into his arms, but refused to release her wrist. "Catherine, please, you have to let me apologize! The things I said were cruel. Wrong. I'm sorry. You hurt me, and I struck out without thinking—"

"You weren't wrong!" *End it, just end it now.* She fought to lower her voice, terrified that someone might be coming along the road and hear them. "You were right, Tyrone, right about everything. I don't want you anymore." She made her voice hard and cold. "You were just . . . just a convenience, something I wanted and took. But no longer. I'm through with you, do you understand? Finished, as you said, like garbage." The last came out in a whisper, and she braced herself instinctively against a rage she had earned.

But, incredibly, Tyrone wasn't angry. He didn't flinch from what she said to him, didn't lash out at her because of the pain she had tried to inflict. Instead, he looked at her steadily with eyes that were clear now, a tiny frown forming between his brows. "You've been frightened all along," he said slowly. "And now you're half out of your mind with fear. For God's sake, Catherine, tell me what you're afraid of!"

She searched despairingly for something to tell him, anything but the truth. "I'm afraid everyone will find out about us," she got out finally in a choked voice.

He impatiently dismissed her words. "That isn't it."

"Yes, it is." She tried to shore up the truth with lies. "I'm treated badly enough now; if they found out— Go away, Tyrone! Let me go, and leave me alone."

"I can't. You're a large part of my life, Catherine, and I can't simply walk away."

"You have to. I won't see you again. It's over." She jerked her wrist free and turned away from him. His quiet voice stopped her two steps later.

"Catherine?"

She paused, looking back at him over her shoulder.

"It's an island," he said. "How far can you run?"

She felt a wave of cold fear, hoped it didn't show on her face. Turning away again, she went on toward the house with a steady stride. *He'll be gone soon. Even if he stays longer this time, he'll be gone.* He'd go back to that larger part of his life, that part of business and work. And if there hadn't been a woman there for him before, there soon would be.

She wanted to be glad for his sake, but all she could feel was tearing pain.

"Kate . . ."

With one foot on the bottom step of the veranda at the side of the house, she froze. Her father was standing there, and she knew without a doubt that he had seen too much. She tried to swallow the lump in her throat.

"I—"

"You met Tyrone." His voice was low, harsh. "You met Tyrone on your walk, didn't you?"

Catherine hurried past him into the house, trying

to think quickly, to find some excuse. She stopped a
few steps through the door, in his study, staring at
the half-empty wine bottle on his desk. "You've been
drinking," she said. "You said you were going to Mr.
Odell's for a book—"

"And *you* said you were going for a walk!" Lucas
came into the room, looked at her with glittering
eyes.

"Father—"

He laughed curtly. "*That* won't help you. I want to
know why Tyrone was with you, Kate."

She forced her voice to be calm. "A chance encounter. He just spoke to me."

"What was he doing in my garden?"

"He saw me go into the garden from the road."

Lucas's voice dropped to a gentle note. "You were
both upset. You'd been arguing, hadn't you, Kate?
About what, I wonder?"

"Nothing." Catherine swallowed hard. "He's ...
he's a cold man, as you said. A difficult man."

Slowly Lucas reached out and touched her cheek
with one finger. "You painted your face. For him,
Kate?"

"No," she whispered. "You said I was pale."

"I don't like paint. Go and wash if off."

"Yes, of course."

"Right now!"

She went, quickly, hoping it would calm him down.
Her heart was hammering, and she felt cold and sick.
She went to the kitchen because it was closest, and
dampened a towel to wipe the rouge from her cheeks.
When it was gone, she went reluctantly back to her
father's study, speaking quickly before he could and
trying to gain the upper hand.

"You shouldn't drink, Father. You know you shouldn't. Dr. Scott told you it worsens your gout."

"Blast Scott," Lucas said. He was standing by the veranda door staring out, and his voice was absent. "A glass of wine never hurt anyone."

Catherine glided silently to the desk, corked the bottle, and quickly held it behind her back. Perhaps the worst was over, she thought hopefully. Perhaps he'd settle down now. She began to edge toward the hall door, holding her breath.

"Have you disgraced your good name?" he asked suddenly without turning around.

Catherine froze. "Of course not."

"Have you dishonored me, Kate?"

"No."

"I hope not."

She waited, stiff and silent, staring at his back. Several very long minutes passed, until Lucas turned from the veranda door and said petulantly, "I want my wine."

"With dinner, Father," she said in a careful calm.

He looked annoyed. "Isn't it dinnertime?"

"Not yet. A couple of hours."

"I'm hungry now," he said.

"All right, Father. I'll get started on it."

She slipped from the room and went to the kitchen, carrying the wine bottle. It was put away in a different cabinet this time, on a shelf behind stacks of canned goods. Then she began preparing an early dinner, thoughts chasing themselves violently around and around in her mind.

Why *now*? Just when she was trying to end it with Tyrone. It would have been over, safely over, if only her father hadn't seen enough to be suspicious. And now . . . she didn't know. But she felt so alone, and so frightened. She didn't know how much longer she could stand it.

Marc.

Tyrone went to his ship. He tied his horse at the harbor and rowed himself out to *The Raven* in the longboat. Lyle and the other men on board were unsurprised by his arrival, since he often checked the ship while in harbor. They greeted him casually, waited to see if he had any orders. He hadn't.

He went to his cabin, shut himself inside. There was a logbook on his small desk, and he made a brief entry. Today's date. *The Raven* was still tied at anchor in Port Elizabeth. He stared at the entry for a long moment, then closed the log and sat back in his chair.

The captain's cabin was large for a ship of *The Raven*'s size, almost luxurious. It was actually two rooms, this study area and a second room partitioned from the first and holding a full-sized bed. In the study were the desk and a couple of chairs, a number of books, maps, charts; in the bedroom were more books as well as the satin draperies and ornate furnishings that had amused him when he had had them installed years before.

Like a Turk's harem, he had thought ruefully. More than one woman had been impressed by the luxury, and more than woman had happily shared the draped and ornate bed.

Tyrone sat at his desk and stared blindly across the room. She didn't hate him. She didn't, really, want to end it between them because she still felt something for him. He knew that.

It had been slow in coming to him, that knowledge. He had stepped into the cottage, had seen that small bundle on the floor, and it was a knife in his heart. It had taken all his will to face her there in the bedroom doorway, all his control to hold in his pain and bitterness.

And, in the end, he hadn't done a very good job of it. He had lashed out at her, and knew that forever he would regret the things he had said. Those dim, long-ago feelings of inferiority—laid to rest, he had thought, fifteen years before—had gripped him like vicious furies, blinding him to what had lain beneath her iron calm.

God, he hadn't meant to hurt her! But he had. Every word he had said had cut her ruthlessly. He had all but called her a heartless whore, and that was something no woman should ever have to hear from a man.

She had been in so much pain and so afraid, beneath the calm, so terribly afraid. He hadn't seen that, ruthless bastard that he was. Until he had cut at her, had hurt her even more. Then he had seen it, in her eyes, had heard it in the strange wrenching sound that had softly escaped her lips.

"Captain?"

Tyrone focused on the door of his cabin, realizing that he hadn't heard the knock. "Yes, Lyle?"

His first mate stepped into the cabin, a bit hesitant. "Sorry, to disturb you, sir, but some of the men were wondering if you're planning to go back soon."

For a brief instant Tyrone was tempted. Tempted to sail away from there and to keep sailing until the sea and the winds cleansed all the darkness and pain from his soul. He had before. Especially during the war years, when the insanity of that time and his own bitterly divided loyalties had tormented him. But he couldn't do it this time, he knew. This time, if he sailed away, he'd be leaving more than his heart behind.

"No," he said then, flatly. "No, my plans haven't changed. We'll be here for weeks, perhaps months."

Lyle nodded, then grinned suddenly. "That Mick, I think he's got a sweetheart in town. Worried about having to leave her, I gather."

"If he causes trouble in town," Tyrone said mildly, "I'll have him keelhauled."

"He knows that, Captain." Lyle sobered. "She's a decent girl, a shopkeeper's daughter. Mick's minding his manners."

"All right." Tyrone thought of the young Mick, who was a hard worker and was considerably brighter than the average sailor. Much as Marc Tyrone had once been ... "Tell Mick he can spend time in town if he wants, Lyle. As long as he's back on the ship each night. And tell him that if he trifles with a decent girl, I'll personally beat the hell out of him."

Lyle blinked. "Yes, sir, I'll tell him."

"Fine, then."

Lyle retreated, closing the door softly behind him.

Tyrone stared at the door, his lips twisting slightly. Trifling with a decent girl ... And wasn't that what he himself had done at least in the beginning? An older woman, yes, but innocent—and a lady through to her bones. He had become her secret lover without an ounce of compunction, concerned by nothing except his own pleasure and her willingness. She had certainly been willing, though that hardly excused him.

He had unlocked an inner part of Catherine, had taught her to want him. And now, for whatever reason, she was being terribly hurt by it. He had been deceived just as the town had been, he realized now.

Deceived in Catherine. The passion and the laughter had been real, but he knew no more of the true Catherine than anyone else on Port Elizabeth.

But he was in love with her. In love with a woman who was frightened and in pain, and who refused to tell him what was wrong. In love with a woman who had today told him she wanted nothing more to do with him, who had, with surface remoteness, ordered him out of her life. In love with a woman who would coldly ignore him in public and who would no longer permit even the briefest of private meetings.

And he had to respect her wishes, if only because she was so afraid. Until he discovered *why* she was afraid, he dared not make things more difficult for her by calling attention to them in any way. Yet there was no one else he could go to for answers.

He could only wait.

All his life Tyrone had been good at waiting. The sea had taught him that. It was always there, was steady, constant, enduring. Tyrone had watched the sea as a boy, and the rhythm of the tides had taught him patience.

But he didn't know, now, if he could wait for Catherine to give him the answers he needed. He didn't know if he would ever be patient enough for that. Because he loved her, and she was in pain—and he couldn't bear that.

"Good morning, Captain."

"Mrs. Symington." Tyrone inclined his head politely.

"You look sinfully lazy," she said, regarding his relaxed form as he leaned against the front of the mercantile.

He smiled faintly. "It's a lazy Saturday."

"Are you waiting for someone?" she asked archly.

Tyrone cursed inwardly but held on to his bland smile. "No, ma'am. Why do you ask?"

"Oh, no reason." She hesitated, then said, "I hear you lost a bet the other day." Her birdlike eyes were very bright and watchful on his face.

Tyrone created a puzzled frown, then allowed it to melt away. "Ah. You mean my failure to drag a smile from Miss Waltrip?"

"People talk so," she said sweetly, entirely unconscious of irony.

"My vanity suffered a blow," he said ruefully.

"But your heart remains untouched?" Her voice was light now, but the sharp gaze never left his face.

Tyrone thanked the fates for poker games over the years. He even managed a laugh that sounded, to his ears at least, natural. "You obviously haven't heard about ships' captains, Mrs. Symington. We give our hearts to the sea."

Mrs. Symington looked faintly dissatisfied, but clearly realized she couldn't probe further without being considered unforgivably rude. "A sad waste," she said dryly.

"Thank you," he said in a polite tone.

She sniffed, then inclined her head regally and moved on down the sidewalk.

Tyrone stared after her, feeling grim. Lettia had been somehow alerted, he thought, and the lost wager was only a part of it. She was suspicious, and if she found out even a part of the truth, she wouldn't be kind to Catherine.

Kind! he thought savagely. If Catherine had been isolated before, she'd be a pariah, a leper, when Lettia got through with her. And he wasn't helping matters, lingering here in town for no obvious reason except to watch the streets; it wasn't a habit with him, and Lettia knew it.

Damn . . . damn . . . damn!

"Are you planning to murder someone, lad?"

Tyrone started and turned his head to find Dr. Scott watching him intently. Consciously, he relaxed taut muscles and forced a smile. "Of course not."

"You looked it."

So much for the benefits of poker games. Tyrone shook his head a little. "No. Mrs. Symington rather annoyed me, I'm afraid."

"She matchmaking again?"

Tyrone controlled a start. Damn! If he kept jumping like a cat on hot bricks, the whole bloody town would get the wind up there was something going on. "Just being her usual self," he replied with all the calm he could muster.

"Umm." Dr. Scott continued to look at the younger man for a long moment, then turned his gaze abstractedly down the street. "You know," he said in a slow, thoughtful tone, "things aren't always what they seem, lad."

"What things?"

Dr. Scott smiled a little. "Most things," he said, still slow and thoughtful. "Most people. Lettia, for instance. She's not a bad woman. Inquisitive, and convinced her own opinion is the right one, but she'll admit she's wrong—if she's forced to. It's just that she hates secrets."

Tyrone could feel himself stiffen. He knew without doubt that Dr. Scott wasn't referring to the sick man in his house but to something else. And that could only be— "Doctor, are you trying to warn me about something?" he asked pleasantly.

There was a moment of silence while Dr. Scott met

his gaze, then the doctor said calmly, "You're giving yourself away, lad."

"Am I? In what way?"

"You're looking at her differently. I noticed that night at Lettia's party."

Tyrone knew all too well that Dr. Scott's discretion could be counted on. With a mental apology to Catherine he said flatly, "You've known longer than that, though, haven't you?"

Very softly, in a voice that couldn't have been heard from a foot away, Dr. Scott said, "I was the only one she could turn to, you see. I was the only one who could get her what she needed to prevent a pregnancy. Good morning, Captain." He turned quickly and strolled briskly away.

Tyrone stared after him.

8

On Sunday morning Captain Tyrone walked into Port Elizabeth's only church, causing a considerable stir among the congregation. He had never been known to attend services—though many of his ship's crew often slid in to occupy the back pews in respectful silence—and more than one of the town's citizens wondered why he was there.

Tyrone didn't enlighten them. He made certain his gaze was casual as he took a seat near the back, but it took only one glance to find Catherine. She was sitting in the third pew beside her father, a small, neat hat atop the braided coronet of her dark hair. With an effort he kept his eyes away from her.

Stupid to come here, he knew. Dr. Scott had been right; he was going to give himself away. But he was worried about her, and had to see that she was all right. He told himself that was all he meant to do, but he knew only too well that given half a chance, he would try to talk to her.

There was no chance, of course, during the service, or immediately afterward. As was true in most small communities, people stood around outside the church, chatting, laughing, and making plans for the day.

Tyrone found himself talking to the shop owner Mr.
Odell about the shockingly high cost of French lace
and fabrics, and it was sheer luck that he managed
to overhear a conversation going on a couple of feet
behind him.

"Just a few people, casually, of course, for Sunday
dinner. And perhaps a quiet game of bridge afterward," Mrs. Symington was saying brightly. "The
Lydgates are coming, and the Ralstons. The dear
vicar, of course. And you'll come, won't you, Lucas?"

"Delighted, Lettia," Lucas Waltrip responded with
heavy cheerfulness. "You won't mind, Catherine?"
he went on, more a statement than a question.

"Of course not, Father," Catherine responded in a
colorless voice.

"Fine. You take the buggy then, and I'll go along
with the others."

Tyrone couldn't remember ever feeling such rage.
Her own father! Her own damned father treating her
as if she had no feelings, no sensitivity, as if she were
nothing. It took all his will to hold the anger in, all
his control to continue his conversation with Odell
as if nothing were wrong. He forced himself to wait
until he heard several buggies leaving the church-
yard, then bid a polite good-bye to Odell and headed
for his own.

A glance showed him that Catherine was only then
moving toward town, her horse trotting briskly. He
climbed into his buggy without haste and turned in
the same direction; both had to drive through town
in order to reach their homes, and no one would
think twice about it.

The shops in town were closed up, the street quiet
since most of the populace was still leaving church.
Tyrone, about fifty yards behind Catherine, had his

gaze fixed so intently on her stiff, slender back that a sudden movement off to her right caught him by surprise. He saw no more than a flash of motion, but the ringing, childish voice was all too clear.

"Dog killers are bitches!"

Three small boys had leapt from the alleyway between two buildings, and before Catherine could do more than turn her face toward them in surprise, they had flung handfuls of mud at her with the practiced accuracy of small boys, and had darted back into the alley and vanished.

Only Tyrone saw what happened. And, even as some part of him knew that the boys had aped their elders in attitude if not in action, his earlier rage swelled inside him and escaped in a vicious curse. He snapped the reins against his surprised horse's rump and the buggy leapt forward.

But so had Catherine's. He couldn't tell if it was because the horse had been startled by the shout and sudden splatter of mud, some of which had landed on its hindquarters, or if she had urged the animal forward; in any case, her horse sprang into a reckless gallop that made the buggy sway.

Tyrone's worry grew when the horse showed no signs of slowing at the Waltrip drive but sped past it, and his heart lurched when the racing animal took the harbor fork far too fast, the buggy skidding sideways. She wasn't driving, he realized, the horse was running away and Catherine didn't care.

Maybe Catherine was running away as well.

The road ended literally at the dock. And the horse would never have halted its mad, blind rush in time if it hadn't been for Lyle. The ship's mate, assiduous in his concern over the ship, had returned to the harbor immediately after church to wait for the remainder of the crew. He was quick when he saw and heard the runaway, rushing directly toward the animal's head.

Blocked, the horse slid on his haunches, almost flipping backward in its efforts to stop and crying out in fear. But it stopped—with both forehooves resting solidly on the first plank of the dock.

Tyrone saw it all as he slowed, and stopped his own horse, then leapt from his buggy as Lyle was turning Catherine's horse slowly away from the dock. Tyrone hesitated, looking at Catherine's still, stiff body; she hadn't moved or made a sound.

"Lyle," he called quietly.

The other man patted the trembling horse and, satisfied it wouldn't bolt again, walked back to where Tyrone stood by his buggy. "Captain," he said, his thin face anxious, "I spoke to the lady, and she wouldn't say a word. And there's mud on her! Who'd throw mud on a lady like her?"

Grim, Tyrone said, "Several nameless whelps who'd better thank God I didn't get a good look at them." He hesitated, glanced toward Catherine, and then at the anchored ship. "Lyle, is there anyone on board?"

"No, sir. Everybody went to church this morning."

"All right. I'm going to take Miss Waltrip out to the ship for a while. When I get her into the longboat, I want you to take her buggy over there into the grove and tie up the horse, give him a chance to calm down. Leave my horse tied here. You and the men stay in town until I come and get you."

"Aye, Captain."

"And, Lyle—"

"Sir?"

"Miss Waltrip is a lady. I wouldn't want to hear any gossip about this later."

"Of course not, Captain," the first mate said severely.

Tyrone smiled faintly, then went over to Catherine's buggy. She turned her head away as he approached, and he swallowed a curse as he got a good look at the mud clinging to her velvet dress. There was more on her neck, and he could see a smear along one white cheekbone. She wouldn't look at him.

"Catherine . . ."

"Go away." Her voice was low, shaking. "Go away and leave me alone."

"I'll take you out to the ship, Catherine," he said very softly. "You don't want anyone to see you like this."

"I don't want *you* to see," she whispered.

She was still holding the reins in rigid gloved hands, and he reached out to gently pry them away. "I've already seen," he said with more calm than he felt. "But no one else will. Your father won't be home for hours, and I've made sure my men won't return to the ship until I send for them. Lyle won't say a word. Come with me, Catherine, and let me take care of you."

"No, not the ship—" Her voice was a thin thread of sound.

"There's no other place." He took her hands firmly, relieved when she allowed him to assist her in stepping down from the buggy. But she kept her face turned away, and it wasn't until he helped her into the longboat that he saw why.

The boys had been accurate with their pitches. The mud on the left side of her face, caked and ugly against her pallor, covered her skin from just below her eye all the way down her neck.

Gently he said, "It's all right, my sweet. I won't let them hurt you anymore."

She didn't say a word, didn't look at him. She sat perfectly still in the seat, hands folded tightly together in her lap, and stared down at them blindly. Tyrone could feel her strain, knew she was closer than she had ever been to breaking. He rowed the longboat out to the ship quickly, glancing past her only once to see that Lyle had taken her buggy into the grove, where it would be hidden from anyone passing by.

Reaching *The Raven*, Tyrone tied the longboat to the side and then helped Catherine onto the ship. She looked around with the same blank, still gaze, and made no protest when he took her hand and led her to his cabin.

He pushed her gently down into one of the chairs in front of his desk. "Wait here. I'll be right back." He was worried by her meekness, recognizing by that unusual trait alone just how near the edge she was. He went quickly to fetch water and a cloth, returning within minutes with a large basin, which he placed on the desk beside her. He stripped off his coat and tossed it over the other chair, then knelt beside her chair.

"Don't," she said, almost involuntarily.

"Shhh." He pulled her gloves off smoothly, then removed her hat and placed it on the desk beside the basin.

"I can do this," she whispered.

"Be quiet, Catherine." His voice was very gentle. He turned away for a moment to wring water from the folded cloth, then began to tenderly wipe the mud from her face. Her wide blue eyes flickered to his face for a moment, and then slowly closed. Her lips trembled.

"They were just boys," she said softly.

"Cruel boys." He kept his voice low and even with an effort, feeling a return of rage.

"Just thoughtless children."

Tyrone, very gently wiping the dry mud from her pale face, couldn't find it in himself to excuse them. "You recognized them," he said flatly. "And you won't do a damned thing about it, will you?"

"It doesn't matter." Her voice sounded weary. "Why . . . why did you bring me here? To the ship?"

He accepted the change of subject, answering her question in a wry tone. "Neutral territory."

"Oh." Her bottom lip quivered. "I wouldn't have gone back to the cottage."

"I know. Not after what I said to you there."

Her eyes opened, and she stared at him. "It doesn't matter."

"Stop saying that," he ordered roughly. "Everything that hurts you matters, dammit."

For the first time, a hint of a smile curved her lips, a glint of life shone in her eyes. "You must have a soft spot for lost causes," she murmured.

"You aren't that," he told her firmly.

There was a moment of silence while he finished wiping the last of the mud from her neck, and then she spoke in a newly fierce tone.

"I pushed you away. You wouldn't go."

"No," he agreed calmly, returning the damp, stained cloth to the basin. "I wouldn't go." He rose to his feet and pulled her up. In a matter-of-fact tone, he said, "The mud on your dress will have to dry so it can be brushed out. You won't be comfortable in it. Turn around, Catherine."

She looked up at him for a moment, hesitating, then slowly turned around. He unfastened the long row of tiny hooks and eyes while she unbuttoned the tight cuffs. The dress slipped off, and she stepped out of it. Tyrone gathered up the dress and spread the stained blue velvet over one of the chairs.

He looked at her as she stood before him with downcast eyes. She was wearing only her shift, a thin petticoat, stockings, and small kid boots. He frowned suddenly, reached out to gently brush away a smudge of dried mud at the base of her throat. He could see a pulse beating rapidly beneath her pale flesh, heard her catch her breath.

Unsteadily she said, "I—I'd like to go out on deck for a while. Until the dress is dry."

He drew a deep breath, aware suddenly of how alone they were here, how isolated. After a moment he turned away from her, going into the bedroom briefly and returning with a long black cloak. "Put this on," he said a little roughly.

When she was decently covered again, he followed her out onto the deck. Nothing had changed, he reminded himself bitterly. She would allow the towns-people to hurt her, him to hurt her, and would say it didn't matter. He leaned against the side and watched her broodingly as she wandered around the ship. At least the blank look had left her eyes, but she was still far too pale and guarded . . . too aware that she had said they were finished.

She came back toward him finally, but halted more than an arm's reach away as she gazed out toward the open sea. "Does it call to you?" she asked suddenly. "The sea, I mean."

It was the first time she had ever asked anything

like that, and Tyrone gave her an honest answer. "Sometimes."

Catherine sent him a tentative smile, obviously trying to ease the tension between them. "A siren song?"

He shook his head. "No. The sea whispers."

She tilted her head a bit, and her eyes widened as she heard the hint of a breeze through the rigging of the ship. All soft motions and sounds, she realized, listening to the faint, hollow slap of the ocean against *The Raven*'s wooden sides and the gentle creaking of seams and joints, feeling the slight, steady rise and fall of the ship. A living thing, the ship.

It was curiously lulling, unexpectedly peaceful. The only time Catherine had been aboard a ship was when she and her father had sailed to this island. She didn't remember feeling lulled or peaceful during the voyage of the packet, and she wondered if a large part of her new awareness was because of the quiet man beside her.

"I hear it," she said. "It's very calming."

"I've always thought so." He stirred slightly and joined her in looking out to sea. "Rain on the way," he said absently. "The edge of a storm."

"How do you know?"

"Thirty-five years on and near the ocean." He glanced at her, then said flatly, "I was born in a waterfront shack."

Catherine felt her throat close up. *He's willing to risk himself again*, she realized, willing to open himself up to her, let her see him for what he was. He had done it once before, had told her things about his past. And she had rebuffed him, had turned coldly away. She couldn't this time.

"Your parents?"

An indefinable tension seemed to drain from him, and he shrugged. "They did the best they could, but they were hardly more than children. Orphans, both of them. My mother was barely eighteen when I was born. She bore me alone, with no one to help her. And she kept the rats off me at night."

She half turned toward him, watching his face. He was expressionless, his gaze still fixed on the sea. She wondered, suddenly, how much pain was locked inside this man. "Where was your father?" she asked softly.

"At sea. It was the only thing he knew, the sea and ships. He hadn't much education, but he could read a little, and write his name. My mother couldn't do either. She respected it, though, books and learning. She worked herself to death to see to it that I got schooling."

"You mean she . . ."

"Killed herself to give me a better chance than she'd had?" Tyrone's lips twisted suddenly. "Yes, she did. She was barely thirty when she died—and she looked fifty. My father hadn't been much help, but it was hardly his fault. He drowned somewhere in the Atlantic when I was five. They never found his body. Sailors are often afraid of the sea even while they love it. Not many learned to swim in those days. Some still don't." He hesitated, then added, "I make certain all my men can swim."

"What happened after your mother died?"

"I worked. At the docks mostly. When I was fifteen I signed on a ship. It took me almost ten years to work my way up to captain. It would have taken longer, but Morgan believed in me for some reason."

She remembered. "You said that he made sure you had books to read, that he insisted on it."

"Yes. He said the sea wasn't everything, that one day I'd want more for my life. I'll always be grateful to him for that. And for the loan that helped me buy my first ship." His hand settled gently on the wooden side of *The Raven*. "This ship."

Catherine watched his face for a long moment. "During the war you ran the blockade with this ship. But you aren't a Southerner." And she realized instantly that she had touched a raw spot, because his face tightened and his eyes went bleak.

"No," he said in a voice that held a note of harshness, "I'm not a Southerner. I built my fortune on the broken back of the South."

Catherine heard pain, and spoke gently. "You brought them badly needed goods and supplies."

"And took their gold." He turned toward her suddenly, eyes glittering. "I didn't give a tinker's damn for their precious cause, Catherine. The South's cause was dead before it started, and I knew it. But I didn't let that stop me. Yes, I brought them goods and supplies. I also brought them guns, and with those guns I helped prolong their agony."

"If you hadn't run the blockade—"

"Someone else would have?" He smiled a terrible, twisted smile. "But I did it. And if that wasn't enough, I saw the war from both sides. I knew Lincoln. I called him a friend. I *believed* in him, Catherine, believed in what he stood for. But that didn't stop me either. I ran the Union blockade carrying guns for the South, took their gold and sailed away—and left the mess for someone else to clean up."

A throb near her heart echoed his pain, and Catherine tried to help him. "It's *over*," she said intensely. "You can't go back and change anything. And you

can't let it haunt you. You have to put it behind you
and go on."

"No. It isn't over, not for me." He looked back out
at the sea, his eyes quartering the horizon with
the habitual gaze of a ship's captain. His voice
was heavy, tired. "There's a man out there somewhere, Catherine. A determined man. I've known for
years he wouldn't let the past just die. He has the
questions, and I have the answers. And now he'll come
here."

Catherine felt a chill, and stepped toward him almost unconsciously. "How do you know that?"

"I know. I know him."

"What will he do?"

Tyrone smiled thinly. "Ask his questions."

"And will you answer?"

"Yes." Just that, flat and calm.

It didn't ease Catherine's sudden fear. "Will your
answers hurt you?"

He frowned slightly, still staring out to sea. "I
don't know. Perhaps. It depends on him, I think." He
turned back to her suddenly. "We all have secrets,
Catherine. Dark rooms in our lives. We'd rather not
open the doors, but fate has a way of doing that for
us."

"We can . . . can lock the doors," she said huskily.

Tyrone shook his head. "No, that would be too
easy. If we could lock the doors, the secrets wouldn't
trouble us, because they'd be safe. But secrets are
never safe. And we never forget the doors that don't
have locks."

Catherine thought of her own secrets, and realized
that he was right. All this time she'd been desperately guarding the dark rooms because there were no
locks on the doors. And she knew that one day, one

day soon, the doors would open and all the darkness would come spilling out.

"Sail away," she said suddenly. "Take your ship and sail away before that man comes here, before he opens the door." She heard fear in her voice, fear for him. He could escape, she thought wildly, could keep the door shut tight.

"I can't do that, Catherine." He lifted a hand and touched her cheek, cupped it gently. "This time I have to face the darkness. I've stopped running."

She had known that, had felt certain of it. She stepped away from him and turned to the side, staring off across the ocean. She could smell the rain on the breeze now, and watched the clouds rolling slowly toward the island. She could still feel his hand on her cheek. Her body ached for him incessantly, and he wouldn't be pushed away, wouldn't leave the island. There was a flood of tears inside her, the pressure building, and she was so tired she didn't think she could bear it any longer.

"I love you, Catherine," he said quietly.

Catherine heard a gasp escape her, as if she'd been struck or stabbed, as if all the breath had been driven from her lungs. Joy and agony washed through her, and she caught at the railing on the side of the ship to steady herself when her legs went suddenly weak "Don't," she whispered.

"I love you," he repeated.

She could feel the flood of tears, hot and stinging, pressing harder inside her. "Don't love me," she said starkly. "You can't love me."

"I do. I can't stop it, can't change it . . . can't run away from it. And you realized I was falling in love with you, Catherine, and that's why you tried to end it between us."

On some dim level of her mind she wondered if it was true, wondered if her own instincts had alerted her that the unthinkable was happening. She didn't know . . .

She was afraid to look at him, afraid her own violent emotions would leap at him out of her eyes. "Why did you have to change things?" she murmured helplessly. "I was so happy. Never again will I be that happy—"

His hands caught her shoulders, turning her to face him, and when she would have pulled away, his fingers bit into her. In a hoarse voice he said, "Tell me you hate me, Catherine. Tell me you can't bear my hands on you. Because that's the only way you're going to get me out of your life!"

She looked up at him, and at first she thought the rain had come, because she was blinded by it. But then he pulled her into his arms with a groan, and she realized that she was weeping. Sobs tore out of her like things alive and on the wing, clawing her throat in ragged pain. She couldn't stop them. Once the flood was released, it poured out of her violently.

She thought she was moving, thought he might have been carrying her, but it didn't seem to matter. Nothing mattered except for her wild grief, the awful, unbearable pain of loving and being loved. She heard his voice, rough yet tender, felt his hands trying to soothe her shaking body. She couldn't say anything, could barely breathe through the racking sobs.

She didn't know how long it went on, but she was drained and limp when it was finally over. She was lying on her back on a bed and staring up at what looked like a canopy of scarlet satin. Yards and yards of the stuff, she thought. She felt a cool damp cloth move over her face, knew that Tyrone was doing that for her just the way he had earlier knelt beside her to wash away the mud.

"I must look like hell," she said suddenly.

A shaken laugh escaped Tyrone, and he said tautly, "Dammit, Catherine, don't do that to me again!"

She turned her head to find him lying beside her, raised on an elbow as he stared down at her. There was a silver glitter in his eyes, and his face was pale. She felt an echo of pain, and reached up to touch his cheek. "I'm sorry."

He tossed the damp cloth aside and held her hand against his face, kissing the inside of her wrist. "You should be," he said somewhat thickly. "I've lost ten years of my life during the past half hour."

She felt oddly peaceful. The dark rooms were still there, but she believed she might almost be ready to face them. She was still afraid, and still hurting, but her long-denied tears had let the worst escape. "Thank you," she said to him.

"For what? For making you cry?" He was incredulous.

"Yes. For that."

"Catherine—"

She lifted her head from the pillow and kissed him lightly. "It's raining, isn't it?" she asked. "I can hear it, and feel the ship moving more strongly. It's very peaceful." She raised her other hand and touched his face, looking at him gravely, conscious of a need to settle things between them. "You've made me very happy since that day by the stream," she told him. "I hope you know that."

His mouth tightened. "If you're saying good-bye again—"

She covered his lips with the tips of her fingers.

"Please. Can we forget all that for now? I don't want to think, or hurt, or be afraid. Make love to me?"

"Is that all you're ever going to take from me, Catherine? Is that all you're willing to give me?" His voice was low, bleak.

She stroked his face with gentle fingers. She wanted to ask, *Would that be so bad?* But she didn't. Because she knew it would be. "Don't you want me?"

"That's a stupid question," he muttered.

Catherine almost smiled. "Don't be angry. Just— make love to me in this amazing bed of yours."

He laughed reluctantly, a glint of honest appreciation in his eye. "You never say the expected, do you?"

"You just don't expect the right thing. And it *is* an amazing bed."

"Mmmm. Do you like it?" He was smiling a little, watching her face.

Catherine looked up at yards and yards of scarlet satin, twisted her head to see the ornate headboard. Then she looked back at him and widened her eyes. "Which sultan did you rob? And how many harem girls did you manage to fling across your saddle before the flight through the desert?"

"Damn!" He laughed, but there was a trace of sheepishness in his expression. "It isn't that bad."

"It should be in a cathouse," she said roundly.

"What do you know about cathouses?"

"Only what I've heard." She smiled. "What you told me, in fact. I asked, and you described. A number of them. All over the world."

He winced. "Hell, I did, didn't I?"

"Certainly you did. You told me all sorts of things I'd never known before. Very interesting. I especially recall that memorable visit to the house in Spain—"

He bent his head and kissed her. "Shut up." He was half laughing, his mouth curved and a bitter-sweet enjoyment in his eyes. "Just shut up, dammit, and let me make love to you in my sultan's bed."

"You'll have to get me out of this cloak first," she said in a voice that had grown abruptly breathless with more than humor. "I'm all twisted in it."

Tyrone managed to get her untwisted while she laughed and fumbled at the buttons of his shirt. The storm of tears had changed her somehow, leaving behind it a serenity that reminded him of their first days together. He could only be grateful that her pain and fear had gone, at least for now, and tried not to let her see his own pain.

He had told her he loved her, and she had wept for the first time in his presence, bitter, racking tears that had shaken her body wildly and had nearly killed him.

But he would happily give her what she would take from him while he snatched all he could from her. For now.

"You've lost weight," he said in discovery when their clothing had been flung aside haphazardly and her pale body lay naked beside him.

She stretched pleasurably as his hands stroked over her, smiling a little. "Your imagination."

"No." He bent his head, trailing his lips across her breastbone while his hands slid slowly down her ribs, exploring gently. "I can feel it here." His fingers traced slight indentations between her delicate bones, touched the hollows above each leg. "And here."

"How does it feel?" she asked huskily.

"Like silk." He moved a hand smoothly over her belly, felt the deep muscles tighten and quiver. "Silk

over glass. Soft and fragile." His lips nuzzled a tight
nipple, and his tongue flicked lightly, teasing.

"And that?" she whispered.

"Mmmm. You tell me. How does it feel?" His mouth
captured the hard bud, drew it strongly inward.

Catherine moaned. "Heat." Her voice was throaty,
shaken. "Burning me . . ." Her fingers dug into his
shoulders, compulsively stroked the powerful muscles. She sounded bewildered, passionate. "How can
you make me feel this way? I'm alive only when you
do this."

Tyrone felt a sudden rush of hunger more intense
than he had ever felt before. A craving for her, for
Catherine, that was more than desire, more than
need. His entire throbbing body cried out for hers in
a way that was primitive, almost savage. She would
give him only this, only her body, and if that was
their sole tie, he would bind her with it.

He moved slowly down her body, kissing, his tongue
flicking, teeth nipping her soft flesh. He could feel
her tremble, feel the heat inside her. He felt more
than heard a sound break free of him, a guttural groan
of pleasure and yearning.

"Please," she whispered, her head moving restlessly on the pillow. "Tyrone, please . . ."

She wouldn't even give him his name. And he knew,
suddenly, implacably, that this time she would. If he
had to half kill himself, if he had to drag it out of her,
he was going to hear her say his given name.

He eased her legs apart, slowly trailed his lips over
the sensitive skin inside one thigh, then the other.
His mouth hovered over her lower belly, just grazing
the hot flesh, and she writhed suddenly with a gasp.

"Is this what you want?" He hardly recognized his

own voice, hardly knew the thick, rasping sound of
it.

She moaned. "Yes."

His mouth suddenly found the hot, throbbing wetness between her legs, his tongue stroking with sure
skill, and she cried out brokenly.

"This?"

Catherine's body shuddered, and she tried to catch
her breath, tried to find a voice in the searing heat of
her need. He was torturing her and she couldn't
think, couldn't do anything but feel the exquisite
agony lancing through her.

"Oh, God," she whispered.

"Say my name, Catherine," he murmured softly.

"No!"

"Say it!" He prolonged the torture ruthlessly, taking her again and again almost to the peak, letting
her reach for it but refusing her satisfaction. She
became a wild thing, a thing that was hunger and
nothing more, a thing without will. Until finally she
broke.

"*Marc!*"

He went still for an instant, and then he was moving over her swiftly, settling between her thighs. His
swollen, throbbing manhood sank into her, deeply, a
violent plunge. Her legs locked strongly around his
hips and she arched beneath him, whimpering.

"Again," he ordered thickly, holding himself still,
buried inside her, his glittering eyes fixed on her
face.

"Marc," she whispered, filled by him, claimed and
possessed and vanquished by him. "Marc."

An odd sound escaped him, as if he had broken
instead of she. His powerful thrusts scalded her, ig-
nited flames that burned her alive until she couldn't

bear it any longer, until she was dying from the pleasure of it. Blind and deaf, she felt rather than heard her own wild cry of release, felt the harsh rumble of his groan before his heavy, welcome weight bore her down into the bed.

A long time later she felt movement, felt a shifting of weight. He had rolled over, concerned that she might be uncomfortable. She was suddenly on top of him, boneless, still joined to him, and she rested her head on his chest with a sigh.

"Thief," she said softly.

A chuckle vibrated in his chest. "I got it."

"You stole it." But she couldn't feel any anger. She had known, somehow, that he would win at least that.

His hands were belatedly removing pins, spreading her hair over her back, stroking the silky strands. "I got it," he repeated, something fierce in his low voice. "And I won't let you take it back. Not now."

"No." She rubbed her cheek against the springy hair on his chest, enjoying the rough caress. "There wouldn't be much use in that, would there?"

His arms tightened around her.

9

Catherine sat in her buggy, hidden from the road in the cool little grove. She listened to the sounds of birds, the faint hissing of the sea against the thin ribbon of sand around the southern curve of the harbor that was nearest to her. She felt more alive than ever, sensitive to everything around her, as if she'd never allowed herself to see and feel before.

She looked back over her shoulder at *The Raven* floating serenely in the harbor, and realized suddenly that she had spent these last hours in another world, a world where the sea whispered and a graceful wooden vessel floated, where the breeze through rigging could be a kind of siren song, and an ornate bed draped with satin could be a place of wild passion and fragile peace.

A world she could visit. A world she could never call her own.

Nothing had changed, she thought, feeling tension creep back, dragging fear and pain with it. If anything, it was worse now because she knew she could never have what Marc Tyrone wanted to give her, and yet she couldn't end this between them, couldn't send him away. Couldn't stop loving him, needing him.

"Are you going to be all right?" he asked quietly.

She looked down at him where he stood beside the buggy, and her heart lurched. "I have to think," she murmured, knowing it wouldn't do any good.

"About what? About us?"

"You won't let it end, will you?"

His jaw tightened. "No. I love you, Catherine. And you feel something for me, I know you do."

She looked at her gloved hands holding the reins. "It doesn't matter what I feel."

"It matters to *me!*"

Catherine began to lift the reins, but stilled when his hand reached out to catch hers. "Please, Marc—"

"At least I've won that much," he said huskily. "Maybe I stole it, but it's mine. I can't be just Tyrone, your secret lover. Not anymore. Marry me, Catherine."

"Don't!" Perhaps hearts couldn't break, she thought, but they could hurt as if they'd been shattered into pieces.

"I said I would. Marry me."

"No. I can't."

"Is it because you can't love me?" His voice was very steady, controlled.

She felt the hot pressure of tears, and stared down at the hand covering hers. "I can't marry you. Please don't ask me again, Marc."

"You won't even tell me why?"

She shook her head silently.

He racked his brain to think of some way to reach her. He didn't want to hurt her, and God knew he didn't want to add to the fear he could feel in her like something dark and cold, but he was going mad not knowing what was wrong. And the helplessness of not being able to do anything at all ate at him.

"Will I see you again?" he asked finally, defeated.

She lifted her gaze, staring straight again. A queer little smile that was pleasure and pain curved her lips. "I . . . don't think I can give you up."

"Catherine—"

"Do you have a gun?" she asked abruptly.

"Of course I have a gun." He frowned, conscious of a sudden chill.

"You should keep it with you," she said in a far-away voice.

"Why, Catherine?" He made his voice flat and calm.

She pulled her hands away and took a firm grip on the reins. "I have to go. I—I have to think."

He was forced to step back when the buggy moved forward, and he stood there in the grove staring after her. *I?* he thought, bewildered. *I'm in danger?* He shook his head and muttered, "Goddammit," because he couldn't focus his thoughts.

Finally he went back to his own buggy, where his horse waited patiently. He untied the animal and got into the carriage, and headed into town to tell his men to return to the ship.

She believes I'm in danger.

The men were waiting inside the hotel. He took Lyle and a few others in the buggy with him; the rest cheerfully walked. He drove the buggy back to the harbor, responding absently to Lyle's occasional comments, then watched the men take one of the long-boats and begin rowing out to the ship. He turned the buggy around and set off toward his house at a brisk pace that was the horse's idea rather than his own.

She's afraid I'm in danger.

Had that been it all along, he wondered. He could feel his mind groping, feel scattered thoughts and impressions that refused to complete an image in his mind. Frowning, he drove to his house and stabled the horse.

He had missed his lunch, and so had Catherine. He hoped she ate something; he was worried about her slight loss of weight. More, he wished violently that she'd let him take care of her.

"An early dinner, Captain?" Sarah asked brightly as he came into the house. She was standing in the foyer with a dustcloth in one capable hand; she was a middle-aged woman with quiet eyes and an unobtrusive way of taking care of him when he was on the island and under her gaze.

"Please," he said, distracted.

"I'll have it ready for you in an hour or so."

"All right. Thank you." He went into his study, feeling restless and uneasy. Something Catherine had said . . . or was it something that finally clicked in his mind?

The house was very quiet. He wandered over to the window, looking out at lengthening shadows, at approaching night. When Sarah called him, he went and ate his dinner without tasting it, but not forgetting to compliment her cooking—which, in truth, was excellent.

He returned to his study. Paced. He took his gun from the desk drawer, cleaned and reloaded it, but left it lying on the blotter as he resumed pacing. It was dark, and Sarah came in silently to put on the lamps, then went away again.

He called her Kate, Tyrone thought suddenly, bothered by that. Her father had called her Kate, and she'd gone white. It had to mean something. What did it mean?

I won't be held up by the town as a whore.

But that wasn't it; that had never been it. Catherine, accepting the slights and insults of the town, had cared no more for her reputation than Tyrone cared for his. Yet she had insisted on secrecy, was panicky at the threat of being found out, was cold to him in public, as if there were danger even in being seen talking to him on the street.

Do you have a gun?

He forced himself to think. If she were afraid for *him*, had been afraid all this time not of any danger to herself but of a danger to him ... and if that fear had grown recently because he had changed, had begun to love her, had begun to demand more of her. An end of secrecy ...

She wouldn't marry him. *I can't.*

The threat to him was *because* of their relationship. He was in danger because he was her lover. And it was real danger, deadly danger, because nothing else would frighten her so deeply. She was desperately trying to push him away from her because she felt certain that someone could hurt him, perhaps kill him. Because of her. Because he loved her.

Tyrone stopped pacing, staring blindly at nothing. That had to be it. He didn't understand, not completely, but he thought that he could, now, give his enemy a face.

That was when he heard the frantic knocking at his door.

Catherine put the horse away and went into the house. It was silent; her father was still away. She went upstairs and changed out of her velvet dress, trying not to think despite her words to Tyrone. But she couldn't stop, of course.

Stepping into a dark skirt, buttoning a white blouse,

she thought of scarlet satin, and found herself smiling, feeling a sad, sweet understanding. She wondered how old he had been when the "sultan's bed" had been installed. Still young enough, she thought, to carry the vivid memory of a thin, worn mother and rats in a cold shack at night. So, wanting to surround himself with luxury, with sensuous fabrics and the brightest color he could find, he had bought the ornate bed. And if he was, now, older and wiser and inclined to view his younger self with a kind of wry mockery, then that was natural.

But she hurt for that younger Marc Tyrone. And she hurt for the man who still felt the bitter prick of conscience, even after all these years, for his own part in a senseless war.

Dear God, she loved him.

Feeling tired and terribly alone, she went back downstairs. The house was still silent. She went into the kitchen and began preparing dinner, vaguely aware of lengthening shadows. It was almost dark when the meal was ready, and she felt the first uneasy twinge of worry.

Where was her father? He should have been home by now. Could he have come in quietly while she was busy in the kitchen?

She went back through the house, lighting lamps, and felt a surge of relief when she noticed that his study was bright, a soft glow spilling through the doorway.

"Father?" She went into the room, and got as far as his desk, when she suddenly went cold. She could feel her heart hammering against her ribs, feel hot bile rising bitterly in her throat.

Her mother's portrait had been horribly slashed with a knife, utterly and ruthlessly destroyed.

Catherine heard a faint sound behind her and whirled out of instinct, throwing up one arm to protect her face. But she wasn't quick enough, and the flat-handed blow caught her with the full force of his arm, knocked her over the corner of the desk and onto the floor. She tasted blood, felt the stab of agony just beneath her ribs, where the edge of the desk had gouged into her. Tears of pain blinded her for a moment, and as she blinked them away, her face began to throb angrily from the blow.

"Father . . ."

"*Stop saying that!*" he roared.

"Father, please—it's Catherine." She didn't dare get to her feet, and fought to keep her voice steady.

"Catherine is just a child," he said in a shaking voice. "You stop bringing her into this, Kate!"

"I'm not Kate," she whispered, but he wasn't listening. He no longer had the knife he had used on the painting, but that was a small mercy since a pistol was jammed inside his belt.

It had never been this bad before. He'd never hit her before, never really hurt her. And he was terrifying in looks. His face was heavily flushed, his eyes wild and glazed, and a trickle of drool escaped his lips.

She was terrified. "Please."

"Please, what, Kate? Please let you go to your *lover*?"

Oh, God, she thought numbly. "No, I don't have—"

"You went out to his ship today, didn't you?"

"No!"

"I *saw* you, Kate!" He was standing over her, shaking violently, and one hand kept plucking at the pistol under his belt. "I came home hours ago, and I walked out to the harbor. I saw your buggy, and his, and I waited in the woods."

She wiped the trickle of blood from her mouth, tried to think. "It was just a . . . visit," she said desperately. "I wanted to see the ship, and—"

"With all the crew in town? I saw them too. You were alone with him on the ship, Kate. You let him have you! I know you did, you let him crawl between your legs and—"

"Stop it!" she cried. "I'm not your wife! *I'm not Kate!*"

He was beyond hearing.

"I knew all along," he muttered. "I saw that night at Lettia's party. I saw you look at him. With your eyes wide and your lips parted, looking at your lover as if he could have taken you right there in front of us all. But you told me it wasn't true, goddamn you! You lied to me!"

"No!"

He giggled suddenly, his wet lips twisting obscenely. "I got him though. I got him back for looking at you like he did, like you belonged to him."

Catherine caught her breath on a jolt of fear. "What did you do?" she whispered.

"I killed his horse." Lucas snickered softly, eyes bright and hard with remembered enjoyment. "That pretty chestnut of his. I pushed it over the cliff behind his fancy house. That's where I caught that chill, you know. Beating Tyrone's horse until it went over the cliff."

She almost retched. "Oh, God."

"But it didn't stop him. It didn't stop you from going to him, did it, my sweet Kate?"

"Stop. Please stop." It had never gone this far before, had never lasted this long or been so violent. And he had never before armed himself. Her frightened eyes flickered to the gun he was plucking at, gently toying with. It was loaded, she knew. She swallowed hard. "Please."

"It didn't stop you." He was staring down at her, and his voice was bewildered. "I thought it would, but it didn't. You just kept smiling and lying, and going to him like a bitch in heat!" His voice began rising again, shaking. "How long, Kate? How long has it been going on?"

"Don't."

'Months? *Years?*"

"You have to calm yourself, please!" But she knew it wasn't any use, knew that this time he was beyond her reach.

"Do you know where I went after I left the harbor, my darling Kate? I went looking for your secret meeting place. I knew there had to be one, and nearby. I knew you'd gone to him on those so-innocent little walks of yours."

Catherine flinched from the thick disgust in his voice, and swallowed the wild protests that were trying to choke her.

"I saw it, Kate!" His glazed eyes were hot, feral. "Your pretty little lovers' cottage in the woods. I saw the bed, smelled the lust— Oh, Christ, how could you, Kate? How could you let him have you, let him take you like some street-corner whore?"

"No!"

"Admit it!" His voice shook frenziedly, and his hand suddenly gripped the butt of the pistol. "God-damn you, you lying, cheating, heartless bitch—*admit it!*"

Instinctively, trying to stem the tide of his fury, Catherine accepted the role of erring wife. Anything, she thought desperately, to stop this here and now. Anything to save Marc. "All right," she said unsteadily.

"I admit it. But it won't happen again, I promise you."

He went very still. But he didn't let go of the pistol. "You've promised before, Kate," he said almost sadly.

"I—this time I mean it. I do." She took a deep breath. "We can . . . we can go away. Leave the island. We can go somewhere new. We can start over."

"You'll just do it again. Just find another lover. Another bastard like Tyrone to warm your bed."

"No. I swear I won't."

"You'll leave him? Come away with me?"

"Yes." *Anything to save Marc.*

His bright, hot eyes narrowed, and then he laughed bitterly, a terrible sound. "No, you won't."

"I swear!"

"Lying bitch." He was muttering now, and his eyes had moved restlessly away from her face. "I'll have to get him. I will. I'll get the bastard."

"No!" Catherine pushed herself up from the floor, ignoring the screaming pain in her side, conscious of nothing except the overwhelming need to stop him. She tried to grab his arm, throwing all her weight against him.

But he threw her off as if she weighed nothing, slamming her back against the desk with an ease that was terrifying. He waved the pistol in the air, laughing softly, grinning at her. "I'll get him. I'll get him this time, Kate."

"No!" But it was hardly a sound, and she couldn't catch her breath because the desk had caught her another wicked blow beneath her ribs and it hurt so terribly. "No, Father—" She tried to find him with tear-blurred eyes, and fear shot through her when she realized he was gone.

Gone to get Marc . . .

She pushed herself upright, crying out at the pain of contorting muscles and bruised flesh. Her body fiercely resisted her efforts to stand straight. She leaned on the desk for a moment, telling herself it didn't hurt, that she could stand it. Slowly she forced herself upright. Her legs were shaking and she felt sick, but she managed to stumble through the house, out to the barn. It was still closed up, and she felt a surge of hope that she could get to Marc before her father did.

With trembling fingers she pulled a bridle on her sometime saddlehorse, the gelding that had run away with her only hours before; he was fast and loved to run, and she hoped he still had plenty of speed left in him. He was made nervous by her agitated state, shifting away when she led him beside the mounting block just outside the barn, and Catherine tried to be calm.

"Easy," she whispered, patting his neck with a hand that wouldn't stop shaking. "Easy, boy. Just a minute now. Just a minute." She had no hope of getting on him without the block; she hadn't bothered with a saddle, and her entire stomach felt battered and painfully tender.

Snorting, the gelding finally stood still, and she managed to get her leg over his back. She gathered the reins and pressed her knees to his sides, feeling her stomach muscles protest even that action. Gritting her teeth, she urged him down the drive, then turned him south. She could feel his muscles working between her knees as he leapt into a gallop, felt the wind tearing at her hair until all the pins were gone. The tail of her full skirt, bunched up nearly around her waist, whipped out behind her.

.

She leaned forward, barely feeling the horse's mane stinging her face, conscious only of the need to go faster, faster. It was miles to his house, and she didn't slow the headlong gallop through the darkness until she was forced to turn sharply into the drive. The gelding chose the verge of the drive rather than the hard-packed dirt, cantering with little sound along the grass. He was sweating moderately, obviously still fresh even after the wild race.

She had been here before, when Marc was away in New York. She often rode casually by, and stole glances at his big, quiet house. This was the first time she had turned into the drive, had approached the house itself.

Catherine stopped the horse near the door of the house and managed to swing her leg over his neck and slide to the ground. She nearly fell then, catching herself at the last minute but with a terrible cost to her bruised stomach and side. Holding one hand and arm pressed to that tender area, she stumbled to the front door and pounded her fist against it.

He had to be there. If he wasn't there, if he was somewhere her father could find him . . . if she had wasted precious time—

"Catherine!"

He was there, thank God he was there, and her relief was so great she sobbed aloud, fighting to regain her lost breath. "Marc! Marc!" She heard a violent oath from him, thought vaguely that she must look like hell again—he ought to be getting used to it by now—and then she realized he had swung her up into his arms and was carrying her into the house, past two other startled, exclaiming people.

Sarah, she thought hazily. *And Reuben. Won't the town have something to talk about now . . . but it doesn't matter, not anymore.*

He had placed her gently on a long couch and sat half supporting her head and shoulders. She saw that she was still holding her middle, and wished it would stop hurting. "Marc—"

"Shh. Not just yet." He held out a hand commandingly, and someone put a glass into it. "Drink this, Catherine."

She felt the cool rim against her mouth, thinking it was odd of him to hold it to one side like that, but then she realized that her lip must be split and that he was trying to avoid the wound. She started to tell him it hardly mattered since it was split inside as well, and that the brandy burned like hell, but then the liquid was sliding down her throat, and it felt too blessedly warming in the rest of her body to protest. She hadn't realized until then that she was so dreadfully cold.

Courage flowed into her with the brandy. Dutch courage, to be sure, but she was grateful for it nonetheless. The room stopped whirling, and even the pain in her stomach seemed to lessen to a dull throb, like her face.

"Marc—"

"Just lie quietly for a little while, my sweet."

She wanted to. She wanted to turn and burrow closer to the hard warmth of his body, to lose herself in him. But there was no time, she was terrified her father would come and try to hurt Marc.

"No. I have to—" She struggled to sit up, the breath hissing between her gritted teeth when her bruised stomach protested violently.

"Dammit, Catherine!" But he helped her to sit up, keeping one arm around her.

She saw the pistol lying on a table beside him, and remembered suddenly that he'd been holding it when he opened the front door. Good. Good, then; he was being careful. "Marc, my father—"

"Did he do this to you?" Tyrone's voice was level.

She lifted a shaking hand to brush her hair back away from her face, looking at him. "He . . . ran out of the house. He had a gun and he was going to look for you."

He half nodded, unsurprised. Softly he said, "You can't go on protecting him any longer. You know that, don't you?"

She shook her head a little, trying to think. "How did you know about him?"

"I figured out most of it, I think. When you told me today to keep a gun with me, many things started to make sense. At least, some of it did. Who was Kate? Your mother?"

"Yes." She shivered, oddly unsurprised by his perception. "When he gets like that he thinks I'm she. Thinks she—she's been with another man."

Tyrone's mouth tightened. "I see."

"No, you don't. He'll try to hurt you; he's out there now looking for you. If he comes here—"

"I'm not going to give him the chance." He glanced aside, where Sarah and Reuben stood waiting with shocked expressions. "Reuben, saddle my fastest horse."

"No!" She twisted, ignoring the pain, and grasped his shirt with both hands. "You can't go out there!"

Tyrone set the glass he was still holding aside and then touched her cheek gently, his eyes going cold and hard when they dropped briefly to her cut, swollen lip. "Honey," he said in a quiet tone, "I can't let him hurt someone else. I have to go after him, have to stop him."

After a moment she whispered, "The buggy, then. If you're going, I'm going with you."

"Catherine—"

"I might be able to calm him down. Reach him. I have before. And I have to try!"

"You're in no state to go anywhere!"

There was no way on God's earth, Catherine thought with absolute clarity, that she would allow Marc to go without her. Calmly she said, "I'm going. Unless you mean to tie me up or lock me in a closet, I'm *going*."

His lips twisted suddenly, and a glint of humor flashed in his gray eyes. "You're a damned pig-headed, stubborn woman, Catherine."

"So you've told me. More than once."

He sighed, looked back at the waiting Reuben. "The buggy, then. And stable Miss Waltrip's horse, please."

"Yes, sir," Reuben said, fading back out of the room and drawing his wife with him.

Catherine released Tyrone's shirt with one hand and rubbed her stomach absently. "You'll take your gun?"

"Yes." He swore softly. "Did it ever occur to you that you had only to tell me what was going on? I could have—"

"What?" she interrupted tiredly. "There was nothing you could have done. Except . . . except to stop seeing me. Maybe that's why I couldn't tell you, really. And—he's my father."

Tyrone looked at her pale face, half averted from him, and the tightness in his chest wouldn't ease. He couldn't find any compassion within him for Lucas Waltrip, not while he sat staring at Catherine's bruised face, her cut, swollen lip. And she was hurting in other places, he could see that; she moved stiffly, and both her stomach and side were obviously painful.

He hated to think what bruises must lay beneath her clothing.

She had been very tired, he knew, tired and worried and afraid. Yet she had faced a violent confrontation with her father and then, hurt and frightened, had climbed up on a horse bareback and raced miles to get to him and warn him. He had known all along that she was strong, strong enough to shoulder her burdens alone and refuse help, but he hadn't known just how incredibly strong she really was.

He reached out a hand and put it gently over the one rubbing her stomach. "What did he do to you?" he murmured.

She sent him a quick glance. "I fell against the desk, that's all. Just a bruise."

"Has he ever done this before?"

"No. He's never been this violent before."

Suddenly, flatly, Tyrone said, "No matter what happens, you're not going back to his house."

She seemed to realize she was still clutching his shirt, and hastily released it. "I'm all he's got."

"You're all *I've* got." He bent his head and kissed her lightly when she opened her mouth to respond. His voice had gone a little rough and unsteady. "Just shut up, dammit, and let me take care of you."

She thought wistfully of being cared for by him, of letting herself love and be loved, then painfully forced the thoughts away. Stupid thoughts, useless thoughts. He hadn't realized yet what her other secret was. Secret fear, secret dread. And she didn't have the courage to tell him.

"I just want it to be over," she whispered.

They both heard the jingle of harness and the creak of the buggy's wheels outside at that moment, and Catherine accepted his help in getting to her feet. She didn't think she could have done it on her own.

"Will you be warm enough?" he asked, glancing down at her blouse and skirt.

"I'm fine"

He gave her a wry look, then bent to pick up his pistol and slide it under his belt on his left side.

What if he has to kill Father? The sudden realization hit her, prompted by the gun, and she thought Tyrone must have been thinking the same thing, because he stood looking down at her with grave eyes as if he were waiting for something.

"He's—sick," she said slowly.

"I know."

She stared up at him, seeing a tall, powerful man with raven hair lightly silvered at the temples. A man with a hard, handsome face and level gray eyes. His white shirt was open at the top, revealing the strong column of his throat and the first curls of black hair on his chest. The gun in his belt added to his innate air of danger, and for the first time she could clearly see him as the captain of a ship running a deadly blockade.

It was hard to breathe, and she could feel her heart thudding against her ribs. "If I had to choose—"

"You won't," he promised flatly.

"But if I had to . . ." It was terribly important to her that he should know. "I'd choose you, Marc."

Something flashed across the silver sheen of his eyes, then was gone almost instantly. He carried the hand he held to his lips and kissed it gently. Then he led her out to the buggy.

They were half a mile from the harbor when they saw the eerie glow in the night sky.

"What is—" Catherine caught her breath suddenly, dread filling her. "Oh, no!"

"The Raven." Tyrone swore harshly. "Christ, she's burning!"

Horror numbed Catherine. She hadn't expected this, not this. Hadn't expected her father to hit Tyrone where it would hurt the most, with the loss of his beloved *Raven.* And it had to be that, had to be her father's doing, because the crews of wooden vessels were always so careful of fire.

The buggy leapt forward as Tyrone snapped the reins hard against the horse's rump, and she could feel his tension, feel him straining to get to his ship. As they skidded into the fork leading to the harbor, she was vaguely aware of bobbing dots of light coming from the town, and realized that the fire had been spotted, that everyone was rushing to the harbor.

She had eyes only for what lay ahead of them.

It was a scene out of hell. The ship, anchored close in, was blazing wildly, the fire making an ungodly roar in the quiet of the night. *The Raven* had become a torch, her sails and masts burning, the fire casting a flickering reddish glow over the water, the dock, and the men watching in silent anguish.

Tyrone stopped the buggy and jumped out, turning, even in his own pain, to help her out, holding her hand firmly as they went down to the dock.

He automatically counted his men, felt relief when he saw all were present and safe. "What happened?" he asked thickly as soon as they reached the men.

Lyle turned to stare at him, and his voice was almost a moan. "He made us get off her, Captain. He had a gun, and—and he was wild, crazy! He kept saying he'd burn the bastard, he'd burn the bastard. And then he smashed the lamp against the side and said he'd shoot us if we didn't get off her."

"Oh, God," Catherine said numbly.

Tyrone heard the thudding of feet behind them, heard gasps and murmurs from the gathering crowd, but ignored them. Sharply he said, "What about Waltrip? Did he come off her?"

Lyle shook his head slowly. "He wouldn't."

Swearing, Tyrone took a quick step toward the longboats—and halted when Lyle grabbed his arm.

"It's no use, Captain," he said miserably. "Her sides are burning now. You'd never even get close to her."

They all saw him then. Catherine, Tyrone, and his men, the people from the town. They all saw Lucas Waltrip dancing about amidships surrounded by fire, waving a gun in one hand and the smashed remains of a lantern in the other. They all heard his maniacal shrieks of laughter even over the harsh crackle and roar of the fire, heard his deranged chant.

"Burn the bastard, burn the bastard, burn the bastard!"

Tyrone saw the man's sleeve catch fire, and he turned quickly and gathered Catherine into his arms, pressing her face against him, covering her ears. He felt her shudder against him, felt her arms go blindly around his waist. And he held her tightly and did his best to close out the terrible sound of an agonized scream, the awful sight of her mad father burning alive in the fire he had loosed on himself.

The Raven burned brightly, a comet in its final, plunging flight to earth. The flames swallowed her tall masts, engulfed her sides, spread with dreadful speed from bow to stern. She was a blazing pyre embracing the charred remains of her assassin, and there was a kind of stoic glory in her death.

No one who saw her die would ever forget the sight.

* * *

"He . . . he was obviously drunk," Lettia Symington said blankly. "Drunk and crazy."

"No," Dr. Scott said quietly. "Not drunk. He's slowly been going mad for fifteen years."

Mrs. Symington, her wide eyes fixed on the woman still shuddering silently in Tyrone's protective embrace, worked her mouth for a moment before her voice would emerge. "There was never any sign—"

"Of course there wasn't." Dr. Scott never raised his voice or changed the tone of it. "His daughter saw to that. She didn't want anyone to pity him; she wanted him to live as normally as possible. So she took care of him. She bore the rages of his sickness in private. She watched him constantly in public to make certain he didn't betray himself—or hurt anyone. When he got worse these last months, she followed my instructions and drugged his wine each night."

"Don't," Catherine whispered, but only Tyrone heard her. He held her tightly, watching his ship die, listening to the doctor's quiet, implacable voice.

"She even stood up before the magistrate, Lettia, and allowed you to accuse her of killing your dog, even though she knew her father had done it."

"What?" Mrs. Symington's voice was beyond shock.

"Oh, yes. He struck out blindly when someone annoyed him. I don't know what you did or said; probably nothing you'll ever remember. It didn't have to be much. Tommy Jenkins just swung on his gate and bent the hinge."

There was a gasp from the crowd, and Mrs. Symington sucked in her breath with a stark sound. "He pushed that little boy into the water?"

"Yes, I believe he did."

"Then"—her gaze slid past Catherine and focused on the burning *Raven*—"when he set fire to the ship? It was deliberate?"

"It was. As well as any mad act can be deliberate."

"Why? What had Captain Tyrone done to him?"

Tyrone turned his head suddenly toward her, and his voice was harsh when he answered the question. "I fell in love with his daughter."

Mrs. Symington looked at him in bewilderment. "But why would that—"

"Lettia," Dr. Scott said quietly, "Catherine is the image of her mother. Whenever Lucas had one of his spells, that's who he saw. The wife he was obsessively jealous of. Any man's notice of her was a threat, one that enraged him. And Catherine knew that. She knew that all too well. She couldn't look at a man, couldn't draw her father's attention to one. She could only act cold and forbidding, and abandon any hope of love.

"Can you imagine what that must have been like, Lettia?" Dr. Scott's voice roughened suddenly. "Living under that kind of strain? Holding herself aloof no matter how much she wanted some hint of warmth in her life? She never complained, never even allowed herself to share the burdens with the one man who had seen beneath the coldness—and loved her. She couldn't even walk with him in public, Lettia."

Catherine lifted her head from Tyrone's shoulder. Her face was as white as her blouse, the bruise and cut standing out sharply against her pallor, and her eyes were dark blue pools that seemed stark and blind. She didn't look at anyone, and her voice was a strained thread of sound. "Please. Don't say any more."

Gently Dr. Scott said, "Child, they have to know. There's no reason for you to keep it inside any longer."

"I can't—"

"He's dead. You have your own life now."

There was a moment of silence while the townspeople, numbed by tragedy until then, shifted uncomfortably as they were forced to recognize their own roles in Catherine's hell.

Catherine lifted her hands to touch Tyrone's face, her own pale features anguished. "Marc, your beautiful ship ... I'm so sorry. I thought I could control him. I've always been able to before."

"It's all right, Catherine. It wasn't your fault."

"It was! I should have been strong enough to send you away—"

"I wouldn't have gone. You know that." He bent his head and kissed her gently, ignoring the crowd who watched.

Lettia Symington reached out suddenly, her face twisted in guilt and shame and compassion. "You poor child—"

Tyrone drew Catherine hard against him and turned a look on the older woman more savage than anything she had ever seen. "Keep your hands off her," he said with deadly quiet.

10

"Easy lad," Dr. Scott said gently.

The flickering light of the fire lit Tyrone's hard face with a hellish glow, and his eyes glittered silver. "Easy? How easy has Catherine had it, Doctor?"

Lettia Symington almost shrank away from him, knuckles pressed to her lips. "We didn't know," she said. "We couldn't have kno—"

"You could have looked!" He swallowed hard. "I could have looked."

"Don't, Marc." Catherine's voice was little more than a whisper.

Tyrone gazed down at her white face for a moment, then swung her up into his arms. He felt her head fall wearily onto his shoulder, her arms go around his neck, and looked at the silent townspeople with eyes that wouldn't easily forgive. "I'm taking her home," he said, and turned away toward the buggy.

Silent, the crowd parted to let him pass through. He put Catherine gently into the buggy and climbed in beside her. He turned the horse south, slipped an arm around Catherine, and drove away, not looking back to watch the sea claim his ship.

He'd seen her die, and that was enough.

He held Catherine close to his side all the way back to his house. When they arrived, Reuben came out to take the horse, his face questioning. Lifting Catherine from the buggy despite her murmured protest, Tyrone said briefly, "The ship burned. Waltrip's dead."

"I'm sorry, Captain," Reuben said soberly. "Miss."

Tyrone nodded, and carried Catherine into the house. He started toward the stairs, knowing she badly needed rest, sleep, but she stopped him.

"Marc, I want to tell you about it."

"There'll be time for that tomorrow, my love. You're exhausted; you need to sleep."

"No, please. I—I want to tell you now."

He hesitated, met her haunted gaze, and then carried her into his study without argument. The lights still burned, and the room was warm and quiet. Tyrone put Catherine gently into a wing chair and drew a footstool forward for himself. He absently removed the pistol from his belt and set it aside, then sat down on the stool and took her hands in his. They were cold, and he gently rubbed them.

"Have you eaten since this morning?" he asked abruptly.

"No. But I couldn't. Really," she added when he gave her a sharp glance.

"Catherine, you don't have to do this."

"Yes. I do." Her head rested against the high back of the chair, and she watched him steadily. She was aware on some level that it was still early, hours before midnight; it had been the longest day of her life. But she owed this man so much—and he had a right to know it all.

"You're hurting," he said, gazing at her face. "The bruises?"

It had been another kind of pain, but she didn't tell him that. "Just a little sore. Marc, he was a good father."

Tyrone realized that she had to tell him, and squeezed her hands gently. "Was he?"

"When I was a child, he was. Always laughing, and kind. But he had a temper, and I realized later, after I got older, that he sometimes struck out at people if they hurt him, or made him angry. Just in little ways. Then."

Tyrone watched her pale face, listened to her soft, weary voice. The mask was gone, wrenched away from her, and he thought it was gone for good. She was achingly vulnerable now.

"I don't really know when he started to—to change. I was about five or six, I think, when he and my mother began having terrible arguments. I was too young to understand then, but he told me months ago what it had been about."

"What was it?"

"He had done something, out of anger he said. Anger at Mother for some argument they'd had. He'd struck out blindly, without thinking, trying to hurt her. And he had. He had gone to a prostitute."

"He told you that?"

Catherine's lips twisted slightly. "He caught a cold a few months ago, and being ill always made him maudlin. He still felt guilty about it, and he wanted to talk." She shrugged. "He talked to me."

Tyrone nodded silently, not trusting himself to speak.

"I don't know how Mother found out," Catherine went on. "He may have told her himself. Anyway, she knew. She was bitter and hurt; he was eager to be forgiven. I suppose she did forgive him. But things began changing in the next few years. Mother became pregnant and lost the baby. A few months later she had another miscarriage. I remember she was weak and ill for a long time, and that Father was very upset.

"I heard them sometimes at night, fighting. I didn't know what it was about. And then the fighting stopped, and I realized they weren't sleeping in the same bedroom any longer."

"How old were you?" Tyrone asked gently.

"Oh, ten or twelve, I suppose. Old enough to know without really understanding. I could feel the tension between them. And then, it must have been years later, the fighting started again, worse than before."

"What was it about then?"

"Father was convinced that Mother was betraying him. That she had lovers. He was constantly suspicious, questioning anyone she met, everywhere she went, what she did. I didn't understand it then, but since I've been able to piece together what was happening between them."

"Were there lovers?"

Catherine shook her head. "No. I was with Mother every day; I would have known. She denied it over and over, but he never really believed her. By the time I was sixteen I was understanding more of what I overheard between them. And I knew Mother was frightened sometimes. Frightened of him. I think I sensed, even then, that there was something horribly unnatural in his jealousy, something unreasonable and violent. I could see he was getting worse, and I didn't understand what was happening to him."

After a moment of silence Tyrone said, "Catherine, you're too tired for this. Tomorrow—"

She had closed her eyes but opened them now. "No. I want to go on. I want you to understand."

He was worried about her but nodded silently and waited. If she had to talk, he had to listen.

"When I was eighteen," she said slowly, "Mother became ill. Terribly ill. Doctors came and went, and no one would tell me what was wrong with her. Father just looked frightened and horrified when I asked. She died ..." Catherine drew a deep breath and went on in a steady voice.

"Father was very quiet for a long time. But, after a while, he seemed to be better. He began going out again to his club, to parties. Everything seemed fine. It was almost as if those years hadn't been real, that they'd been a nightmare."

Tyrone was frowning a little. "You told me you'd been engaged. When was that?"

Catherine smiled wryly. "I know I gave you the impression it was when my mother was sick. I'm sorry. It was years after she died, a bit over two years ago. I'd known Jeremy all my life, as I told you. He had asked me to marry him several times, but I'd been worried about Father, uncertain about leaving him. Then Father began pressing me to marry Jeremy, and I—"

"You loved him?" Tyrone asked, looking down at her hands.

"I thought I did."

Tyrone nodded, his face expressionless. "And then?"

"There was a formal party to announce the engagement. I danced with Jeremy, and I could see Father watching us, but I didn't think there was anything wrong. It wasn't until later that I realized I had been wearing a gown very like the one Mother wore for her portrait."

"What did he do?"

"That night, when the guests had gone ..." She

steadied her voice with an effort. "He started saying things to me. Terrible things. I didn't understand at first . . . not until he called me Kate. He saw Mother when he looked at me, and he was accusing her of having a lover. It didn't last very long; I managed to calm him down. Then he seemed to forget it, as if it had never happened. I was Catherine again, his daughter, and he talked very cheerfully about the wedding."

She shook her head, looking at Tyrone almost pleadingly. "I didn't think it would happen again. He'd been drinking; that could have confused him. There was no way I could have known."

Tyrone realized then that something bad had happened, something that had ended her engagement. And that Catherine blamed herself for it. He rubbed her cold hands more briskly, trying to warm them. "No, you couldn't have known," he murmured. "Did he strike out at Jeremy?"

"It was a few weeks later. Jeremy came to visit, and we walked in the garden. He left after a little while, and I went into the house. Father was there, and he seemed quiet." Catherine fell silent for a moment, then said very softly, "The message arrived hours later. There had been an accident in the streets. Jeremy's carriage had lost a wheel, tipped over. There was a great deal of traffic in London and he was thrown into the path of an oncoming stage. He was killed."

Tyrone's hands tightened on hers. "It could have been an accident," he said quietly.

"No. That's what I thought at first. Then I looked at Father. And he was smiling."

"Catherine, it wasn't your fault."

"I should have broken the engagement after that first night, when I realized Father was . . . was sick."

She sounded very tired, haunted. "But I didn't. And Jeremy died."

She would, Tyrone knew, carry that feeling of guilt to her grave. God, no wonder she'd been so terrified here on the island, so desperate to keep their relationship secret. The miracle was that she had allowed it to happen at all.

"Catherine—"

"I didn't know what to do." Her voice remained soft and weary, and her eyes rested on his face. "He was my father, all I had left. And I was all he had."

"Did you take him to a doctor?" Tyrone asked finally.

"He wouldn't go, he got so angry and so upset whenever I mentioned it. So I went myself and told the doctor all about it. He—he said the best place was an asylum, that Father would probably get worse. But I couldn't do that to him, Marc. I couldn't lock him away somewhere and forget him."

"No, of course not."

She drew a deep breath, steadied her voice. "I told the doctor that, asked what I could do to help Father. He said that there was another doctor, a specialist in brain disorders. This doctor, he told me, lived on a little island off the coast of America, to which he'd retired. No one knew as much as this specialist, the London doctor said."

"So you brought your father here," Tyrone said, understanding very well since he, too, had come to Port Elizabeth because of Dr. Scott. "It couldn't have been easy to persuade your father to leave England."

"I made it sound like—like an adventure. And I talked about needing to get away from memories. It took several months to get his agreement and to arrange things. When we arrived here and were building the house, I talked to Dr. Scott. He agreed to do what he could. It wasn't easy, because Father refused to see him except socially, and wouldn't be examined. So I talked to the doctor instead, describing things that had happened over the years. He said it was like a puzzle he was trying to put together, and that every memory I could recall would be another piece."

"Does he know why your father was sick?"

Catherine frowned faintly. "He told me months ago that he had a suspicion. He said he was going to write to some of his colleagues in London with questions for them. He was especially interested in questioning my mother's doctors. I don't think he's gotten any answers yet. He hasn't said."

After a moment Tyrone said roughly, "No wonder you were so afraid. And so determined to keep our secret."

With her dark head resting against the back of the chair, Catherine looked at him gravely. "You were . . . unexpected. I knew, when we'd been here a few weeks, that there was a Captain Tyrone who lived sometimes at the other end of the island. People talked about you. I knew you came here every month or so, and stayed a few days. I'd even ridden by your house one day. But when we met . . ."

Remembering that first meeting on the street nearly two years before, Tyrone smiled faintly. "You were so stiff, and carefully polite. So daunting."

"You weren't daunted," she said. "You were the only one who wasn't."

"No. I was intrigued." His smile died, and he gazed at her seriously. "Perhaps Dr. Scott was right, and I immediately saw beneath the icy surface. I remember being struck by your beauty. As I watched you walk away from me, I wondered what you were thinking."

Catherine's eyes gleamed suddenly with wetness, and her lips trembled. "I think I was a little afraid of you; I sensed you saw too much. But I didn't know it would matter. Not until that day by the stream."

He shook his head, and his face was suddenly grim. "I was a selfish bastard, Catherine. I knew you were innocent, and I didn't care—"

"You cared," she interrupted quietly. "You were very gentle with me, Marc. I've always been grateful to you for that."

"Grateful?" His voice was a little harsh, strained. "Catherine, I can see now what you went through. It must have been hell for you, taking a lover after what you'd heard all those years, listening to your father's suspicions, your mother's denials. And for me to be the way I was then, not giving a damn for anything except my own pleasure—"

Her hands tightened in his. "Marc . . . if you'd been any *other* way, I couldn't have borne it, not then. What you wanted from me was the only thing I was free to give you. You wanted a woman in your bed, and the secrecy suited you. You weren't here very often, or for very long. I thought I could keep it hidden from Father, that there was no danger. That's what I told myself. I believed I would never have another chance to . . . to be a woman and lie in a man's arms. To feel wanted."

"Catherine." He felt his heart lurch, felt a terrible need to hold her tightly, to mend the broken note in her voice. But she was going on softly, her eyes blind.

"I thought it would be over soon, you see. I thought you'd weary of me, and I'd have all those memories. But it didn't end. You kept coming to the cottage, and I kept meeting you there, and I told myself it was all right, it was still all right. The secrets were safe, all the secrets. But then you asked me to marry you. And I knew you were changing."

"I was falling in love with you," he said huskily.

"I didn't know that, not then." Her gaze remained blind, fixed on something only she could see. "I knew only that you were changing, you were looking at me differently. And I was afraid you'd see too much. Father was getting worse; he'd started killing animals when he was annoyed at someone. I was putting laudanum in his wine every night so he wouldn't slip out without my knowing, and I was watching so closely to make sure he didn't drink too much because it affected him so.

"I should have stopped seeing you then. I knew the danger, knew what could happen. I'd been so lucky he hadn't found out during all those months, but luck couldn't last forever. It was getting harder for me to slip away, and you were staying longer this time, asking me to meet you more often. Looking at me differently, acting as if you . . . as if you cared about me in a new way. And even though I knew I should have ended it, I didn't have the strength."

While Tyrone watched in helpless pain, two glittering tears welled up in her blind eyes and rolled slowly down her pale cheeks. And when she spoke again, her voice was hardly more than an aching whisper.

"I needed you so desperately."

With a soft groan Tyrone stood and gathered her into his arms, then sat in the big chair with her in his lap, holding her close to him. She was crying quietly, almost silently, and he didn't try to stop her, knowing that these were tears that should have been shed long before now.

"I'm sorry," she uttered finally, sniffing.

"God, don't be sorry." He rubbed his cheek gently against her soft hair, met her gaze steadily when she lifted her head and looked at him. "I don't know how you've kept all this inside for so long, my sweet."

She waved that away with a tired hand. "I'm sorry about your horse, Marc. I—you should have said something to me about it. I didn't know until Father told me tonight."

Slowly Tyrone said, "He called you Kate at the party that night. Had he seen me looking at you? Was that what set him off then?"

She nodded. "I thought I'd gotten him calmed down later that night, that he wouldn't strike out at you. If you'd told me about the horse, I would have known—"

"And tried even harder to send me away?"

Her eyes were haunted. "I was so afraid."

He hesitated, then said slowly, "Catherine, when Lucas thought you were his wife, did he ever—"

"Touch me that way?" she finished for him. "No. I was spared that. I suppose it was because of what he remembered. That time he went back to was when he and Mother weren't . . . weren't sleeping together. I was never afraid of him that way. I was just afraid of what he'd do to other people. To you."

"I want you to understand something, Catherine," Tyrone said quietly. "None of it was your fault. Tommy, the animals, my ship—you aren't responsible."

"If I had—"

He touched her lips with his fingertips, stopping her. "No ifs. You did everything you could have, my love. Christ, you did more than anyone should ever have to do. You put yourself though hell, and it's over now."

It isn't over. But she couldn't tell him that. Not now. Not yet. She was so tired.

Tyrone stood easily, still holding her in his arms. His eyes gleamed down at her, and a faint smile curved his lips. "And now, my darling Catherine, I'm going to carry you upstairs and put you into bed. Into *my* bed, where you belong."

Catherine could almost let herself believe it. Almost. She rested her head on his shoulder, telling herself that one night wouldn't hurt, wouldn't matter. It would be a memory she could cherish. She could sleep with him this one time, and pretend it was forever.

He carried her up the dimly lighted stairs and into a bedroom on the second floor, where a lamp already burned and the covers of the wide bed were turned back. He shut the door with one foot and carried her to the bed, lowering her gently to sit on the edge, then knelt and calmly began removing her kid boots.

"You don't have to—"

"Catherine," he said lightly, "shut up."

She could hardly help but smile despite everything. "You've been telling me to do that a great deal lately."

"One of these days," he said, "you might listen to me." Then he was going on in the same easy tone. "I've wanted to take care of you for such a long time, but you wouldn't let me."

"I couldn't," she told him.

"Yes. I know. But now you can." He slipped her stockings off and tossed them toward a chair, then stood and pulled her gently to her feet. He unfastened the dark skirt and let it drop to her feet. The white blouse soon followed, and she stood wearing her thin shift.

Tyrone frowned a little, then turned away briefly to the wardrobe and pulled out one of his shirts. "You can sleep in this," he said, returning to her.

"It's silk," she protested weakly.

"I've always wanted to see you in something made of silk. There were many times in New York I'd pass a shop window and see fancy gowns made of silk and satin. I wanted to buy them for you, but I knew you'd never accept them from me." He tossed the shirt on the bed and grasped the hem of her shift, pulling it gently up over her head. And when she stood naked, Tyrone froze.

Catherine quickly glanced down at herself and winced at the sight. The bruising and swelling over her midsection was worse than she'd expected, far worse than her face. Below her ribs on her stomach and right side, the flesh was mottled an ugly black and blue. It looked horrible.

"Dammit," he said hoarsely, "I should have had Dr. Scott take a look at you—"

"It's all right, Marc." She lifted a hand to briefly touch his face. "Bruises, nothing more. They'll heal—and I'm not in any pain now." It was the truth.

He searched her face intently for a moment, a muscle tightening in his jaw. Finally he threw the shift toward a chair and helped her gently into the white silk shirt. When it was buttoned, he turned away toward the bureau while Catherine tugged her hair free of the shirt collar.

"Heavens," she exclaimed, startled, feeling snarls and tangles and suddenly remembering her wild ride earlier. She was afraid to look in a mirror.

Tyrone chuckled, and she saw that he had gotten a silver-backed hairbrush from the bureau. He guided her to sit on the edge of the bed again, half turned away from him as he sat down and began slowly brushing her hair.

"Still taking care of me?" she asked shakily.

"I want to."

Catherine closed her eyes, feeling the brush and his gentle fingers untangling and smoothing her hair. It was wonderfully soothing, and somehow moved her almost unbearably. Pleasure and pain. "You always took my hair down first thing," she said softly.

"Did I?" The slow, steady brushing continued, and his voice was quiet. "Perhaps because when your hair was neatly braided and pinned up, you were the cool Miss Waltrip. But when I took it down, felt it run like silk through my fingers, then you were my Catherine."

She kept her eyes closed, and couldn't say anything because her throat was tight. It occurred to her only then that he had not once tonight pressed her for a declaration of love, that he hadn't even asked if she loved him. It would have been a natural question, considering that he knew, now, the risks she had dared just to be with him. And he loved her, she knew. But he had never asked if she loved him. He had only asked, when she had refused to marry him, if it was because she *couldn't* love him.

If he had asked tonight, Catherine knew what she would have answered, knew she couldn't have denied it. And perhaps he understood that all her defenses were down, that she was vulnerable as she had never been before. Perhaps he knew only too well that her love, unlike the sound of his name, couldn't be stolen from her, that it had to be offered willingly and without prompting.

It hurts him that I haven't said it, she realized suddenly. That she wanted and needed him was obvious, something she was willing to admit to him. And had. But words of love she had guarded jealously in silence, and because he couldn't know why she was silent, it was hurting him. Hurting him . . . yet he accepted the pain and didn't say word.

She wanted to tell him now, wanted desperately to tell him. But her throat had closed up completely and the pain inside her made her mute.

"You're cold," he said then, seeing her trembling. "Here, my love, get into bed." He tossed the brush aside and pulled her gently to her feet, then drew back the covers and helped her into the bed.

Catherine lay silently and watched as he gathered her discarded clothing, piling it neatly on the chair, then began to undress himself. She watched him move around the room, filling her memory with him, crowding everything into her mind.

When he put out the lamp and slipped into bed beside her, Catherine instantly went into his arms, cuddling close to his hard, warm body. He was holding her with tenderness and possession, stroking her hair, and gradually she stopped trembling. She rested her head on his shoulder.

And wished it could be forever.

Tyrone woke in the silent hours before dawn, woke with the sudden alertness that had been bred into him by years of danger. He knew instantly what had awakened him. Catherine was in the grip of some terrible nightmare, perhaps reliving her father's fiery death, and the soft sounds that escaped her shaking body were like whispers from hell.

He drew her even closer, stroking her body gently, murmuring wordlessly to soothe her.

"Don't leave me," she whispered, clinging to him.

He wasn't sure she was awake, but answered anyway. "I won't. I won't, my sweet."

She finally stopped trembling, and her body slowly

relaxed. And it was a long time later when her voice reached him, a voice that was soft and bittersweet. "I love you, Marc."

It was what he had waited for, longed to hear from her, what he hadn't dared to force from her as he had forced her to say his name. He felt a throb of pain. "I love you too, Catherine." His tone was bleak because he heard the truth in hers. She loved him . . . but it hurt her to love him.

He was still awake when dawn silently arrived.

"Thank you, Sarah."

Catherine forced herself up through the layers of sleep, his voice pulling at her as always. She half sat up, blinking, looking at him as he came away from the door. He was holding a tray. He was also half dressed in trousers, and he had shaved.

She felt immediately conscious of mussed hair and bleary eyes, of wearing only his silk shirt. Her vanity was vaguely outraged.

"Stop frowning at me," he told her as he reached the bed. "If you're wondering, you look beautiful in the morning."

"I wasn't wondering," she lied firmly, resisting an urge to smooth her hair. Since it was obviously expected of her, she banked the pillows behind her and accepted the tray onto her lap, but couldn't resist one rueful shot. "And you know too damned much about the workings of a woman's mind."

He grinned at her, lounging back on an elbow near her knees. Taking one of the coffee cups from the tray, he lifted it in a half salute . "My misspent youth, I'm afraid."

Catherine picked up her own cup, trying to keep from returning his smile and finding it difficult. "A girl in every port?" she asked dryly.

"There was a time," he said. Then, briskly, he added, "Sarah allows no one in this house to go hungry. And since it's nearly noon, she sent up lunch as well as breakfast."

"I'm really not—"

"Catherine," he interrupted warningly.

She glared at him for a moment, then gave in with a smile. Surprisingly enough, she found herself hungry once she began eating, and it occurred to her only then that she hadn't eaten in more than twenty-four hours. Tyrone kept up a light conversation while they ate, entertaining her with his rather pungent descriptions of some of the places he'd been in twenty years of sailing the seas.

She listened with enjoyment, watching his face and absorbing its many expressions. But even though he steered the talk firmly away from any mention of what had happened the day before, she couldn't help but remember. Grief for her father was a dull ache, and something she had prepared herself for during these last difficult years. But she could still feel the shock of watching Marc's ship burn, and that was a deeper ache because she knew he had lost a part of himself.

When the meal was finished and he removed the tray to set it on the floor by the bed, she had to say it. "Marc, I'm so sorry about *The Raven*."

He was still lounging back beside her legs, and shook his head slightly. "I have other ships."

"Not another *Raven*."

Tyrone was too conscious of his own sense of grief to tell her it didn't matter. "Catherine, ships are like people. They live, and they die. It was her time to die."

"Thanks to my father. And me."

"Your father was sick. And you aren't to blame."
He reached over to cover the hands twisting together
in her lap. "I mean that. It's over. Forget it."

"Will you?" she asked unsteadily.

His smile twisted a little. "If I can have you instead, yes."

She looked down at his strong hand, felt a pang
shoot through her. "I can't replace *The Raven*. She
was so much a part of your life."

"My past. You're my future."

I can't be. She looked around his bedroom, thinking almost sadly how different it was from his cabin
on the ship. There was luxury here in gleaming woods
and fine fabrics, but this was the taste of a man who
had earned his wealth over years of hard work and
danger, a man whose memories of being cold and
hungry were few and fleeting now. There was no
ornate bed, no satin draperies, no vividly bright and
luxurious colors.

"Catherine?"

She moved away from him suddenly, throwing back
the covers and sliding from the bed. She felt stiff,
and didn't know if it was a physical or an emotional
thing. Both, probably. Her entire body felt sore, and
her heart felt numb.

"I left dinner ready at home last night," she said
vaguely. "And all the lamps in the house burning.
There are things to do. I have to—"

"You aren't going back there." He had stood as
well, and now faced her near the foot of the bed. His
hands lifted to hold her shoulders so she couldn't
move away from him. "Sarah and Reuben can close
up the house and bring back what you need."

She looked up at him, seeing steady eyes and determination. "I have to go back there sometime."

"There's no hurry." His voice lightened. "Now that I've got you in my house, I'll not let you go."

"Marc—"

"I'll speak to the vicar," he said in the same deliberately easy tone, "and find out how soon he can marry us."

Catherine held her voice steady. "I'll live with you if you like," she said. "But I won't marry you, Marc."

His lean face tautened, but there was no surprise in his eyes. "Why not, Catherine?" His voice roughened, and his grasp on her shoulders tightened. "This time you can't run away without answering."

She knew that. It was what she had been dreading. In her mind she heard the detached, clinical voice of the doctor she had gone to about her father, heard him offer a warning that had altered her life. *Madness often runs in families, Miss Waltrip. If it was passed on to your father through one of his parents, it may also be passed to you, in time. Something to consider.*

Oh, God, how she had considered it . . .

"Catherine?"

In a deadened voice she said, "My father wasn't much older than I am now when he . . . when he began to get sick. There's a chance—Marc, it could happen to me. I could go mad one day."

Tyrone pulled her into his arms suddenly, holding her tightly against him. Her answer had occurred to him in the cold dawn hours while she slept; it was the only thing that made sense. He had thought of her living with a lunatic, protecting him as best she could. And knowing, always knowing and dreading that it could happen to her.

"I'll risk it," he said huskily into her soft hair. "I love you, Catherine. I want you to be my wife."

"No. I won't be a burden." But her arms went around his waist as if she couldn't help herself.

"You could never be a burden to me." He made her look at him, framing her face in his hands. "The only burden would be not having you in my life."

"I—"

"Catherine." His voice was steady, and he held her darkened eyes with his own. "You told me something in the night. Was it true?"

She felt the hot pressure of tears, and thought distantly how odd it was that after years of not being able to cry, now she couldn't seem to stop. And she couldn't lie to him. "Yes. I—I fell in love with you that day by the stream. When you smiled at me."

He bent his head and kissed her gently. "Then nothing else matters."

"No, Marc, I can't." It was so hard to protest what she wanted with all her heart, and her voice broke.

"Yes, you can. And will." He might have said something else, but a soft knock at the door interrupted them. He hugged her tightly, then went over to see who it was.

"Dr. Scott's downstairs," Sarah told him. "He says it's very important that he talk to you and Miss Waltrip."

"All right. Tell him we'll be down in a few minutes."

Sarah nodded and went away.

Tyrone came back to Catherine. Calmly he said, "We'll have to get dressed and go talk to him, I suppose."

"Marc—"

"It's a pity though. You look very fetching in my shirt. However, since I don't intend that anyone but me should enjoy the sight . . ."

She felt a ridiculous impulse to laugh despite everything. Since it had honestly not occurred to her that he would still want to marry her after learning the whole truth, she was at something of a loss. "Marc, you *can't* want to marry me!"

"I will marry you," he said, "by Friday." He was getting a clean shirt out of the wardrobe, and paused in the act to send her a very calm look of utter determination. He smiled gently. "At the latest."

She started automatically to unbutton the shirt she wore. "It's impossible, you must see that." Her voice sounded weak to her own ears, and she thought again that it was too difficult, protesting what she wanted.

What she wanted with everything inside her.

"On the contrary, it's quite possible." He shrugged into his shirt as she shrugged out of hers, and he paused a moment to enjoy the sight of her. "You must heal fast," he said absently. "The bruises are already fading. By the way, have I told you lately how beautiful you are?"

Catherine pulled her shift over her head and gave him a look that was a bewildering mixture of frustration, pain, laughter, and pleasure. She didn't know what she was feeling, and it was very unsettling. He simply wasn't reacting to this the way she had expected him to, and having prepared herself as much as possible for tearing pain, she was somewhat adrift. "Don't say that, dammit, I'm trying to—"

"What you're trying to do, my darling Catherine, is useless." He buttoned his shirt, tucked in the tail. "Do I need a coat for the doctor? No, I don't think so."

"You won't listen to me!" She was half laughing and half crying.

Tyrone lifted her chin with one finger and kissed her lightly, then began helpfully buttoning the cuffs of her blouse. "No, I won't. I learned a very long time ago how to fight for what I want."

Abruptly bemused, she said, "Are you going to keep dressing and undressing me?"

He grinned down at her. "I like it. No, don't braid your hair— it's beautiful just the way it is. I may let you put it up for parties, but nothing else."

She eyed him somewhat warily. "You've gotten very bossy all of a sudden."

"It's your own fault, and you'll have to take the awful consequences from now on," he said to her in a very polite voice.

"The consequences of what?"

"I believe it's called the pendulum effect." He looked thoughtful. "The pendulum swang one way when you wouldn't let me take care of you for so long; now it's swinging drastically the other way since I can."

Catherine shook off fascination, realizing they'd gotten off on a tangent. "Marc, I can't marry you!"

"Of course you can, darling."

11

A quarter of an hour later, when she walked beside him down the wide stairs to talk to Dr. Scott, Catherine had stopped protesting. She felt very peculiar, caught somewhere between giddy happiness and echoes of pain and fear. She couldn't forget the threat hanging over her head, but she loved Marc too much to be able to fight against his determination to marry her.

If this was a dream, she never wanted to wake up.

Dr. Scott was pacing restlessly in the study when they came through the doorway, and turned to look intently at them both.

"Good morning, Doctor," Tyrone said calmly.

Dr. Scott's mouth twitched in a smile. "Good morning." His gaze moved to Catherine's face, no longer so pale, and wearing a bemused little smile.

"You wanted to talk to us?" Tyrone asked, guiding Catherine to the long couch and waiting for the doctor to take a chair before he sat.

Dryly Dr. Scott said, "You'll forgive the intrusion, I think. Am I correct in assuming, by the way, that you've persuaded Miss Catherine to marry you?"

"Certainly I have." Tyrone smiled suddenly. "I had the devil's own work of it though."

'I can imagine.'' Dr. Scott sobered then and looked very gravely at Catherine. ''You don't have to be afraid of going mad, child,'' he said firmly.

In the darkness of her eyes a light stirred, and she glanced at Tyrone before looking back at the doctor. ''I don't?'' Her voice trembled, revealing how afraid she was to hope.

''You knew I'd written to colleagues in London?'' He waited for her nod, then went on. ''The packet from England came in this morning, and the answers we wanted as well.''

''What are the answers?'' Tyrone asked. The cold fear for her that he hadn't allowed her to see was beginning to ease.

''Confirmation from the doctors who treated Catherine's mother, and a bit of research into Lucas's family, particularly his parents. They died sane, by the way, and of natural causes. No history of brain disorder. There was only one answer left, only one possibility given the facts. Syphilis,'' Dr. Scott said. ''It's what drove Lucas mad, and it's what killed his wife.''

Tyrone, who had seen some of the ravages of the disease in different parts of the world, took Catherine's hand and looked steadily at the doctor. ''Is she in any danger?''

''No. When I realized what it must have been, my major question was, of course, when he could have contracted the disease. Lucas wouldn't talk to me about it, so I was dependent on Catherine's memories of the years before her mother died. There are so many forms of madness, you see, and I couldn't be sure it wasn't something he was born with, something that developed slowly over his entire life. But, since Catherine's mother had died of what was clearly a terrible illness and one her father seemed guilt-ridden about, I had to consider the possibility that he blamed himself for what killed her."

"Father said that." Catherine's voice was soft. "When he was ill with that cold. He said he'd killed her."

Gently Dr Scott said, "He did, child. I'm sorry. If it's any comfort, he had no way of knowing it would happen."

"Are you sure about this?" Tyrone asked.

"Yes. It fits the pattern perfectly. Lucas contracted the disease from the prostitute he went to when Catherine was a child. A few weeks, perhaps a couple of months later, he became ill. Catherine remembered. Her mother mentioned a slight rash, said that her father was feverish. Then it passed gradually. At some point then or during the following years, he gave the disease to his wife. She suffered two miscarriages, the second of which strongly affected her health. Another sign."

"The arguments," Catherine said. "Their fighting."

Dr. Scott nodded. "One of her doctors remembers suggesting to her that she was infected with syphilis. She knew she could have gotten it only from him. His single lapse of fidelity cost them both a great deal."

"And Catherine," Tyrone said.

The doctor, watching Catherine's face, nodded. "And Catherine. But you don't have to be afraid any longer, child. Your parents' disease never infected you."

She drew a deep breath, feeling a tremendous weight slide from her shoulders. "Thank you," she whispered, blinking back tears. "Then, I can—" She stole a glance at Tyrone.

Scott chuckled quietly. "You can marry this man, certainly. Not that I imagine he would have taken no for an answer in any case. And you can have no fear of harming any child the two of you may have."

Tyrone swore suddenly, realizing. "So that was it!"

Ridiculously, Catherine found herself blushing. Idiotic, she thought, since she'd never blushed at anything Tyrone had said or done. And God knew she had never been able to afford embarrassment around the doctor.

Scott was chuckling again. "That was it," he said. "If it bothered you that Catherine confided in me to the extent of learning how to prevent a pregnancy, now you know why. It wasn't because of moral shame, but out of very real fear."

Ignoring her hot face, Catherine said to the doctor, "You weren't supposed to know who I was seeing though."

Wryly he said, "I've spent my entire life observing people, my dear. The two of you were very good at hiding your feelings, I'll give you that; all I had to go on was a hunch. Until recently, at any rate, when the captain began rather obviously wearing his heart on his sleeve."

Unabashed by the comment, Tyrone smiled crookedly. "You're very good at keeping secrets," he told the doctor dryly, thinking of all Dr. Scott could have told him about Catherine.

"You should know." Dr. Scott looked suddenly at Catherine, then lifted a brow at Tyrone.

"No, she doesn't know about your other patient yet. It's time she did, however. Since you're here, why don't you go up and see him?"

"I'll do that." Dr. Scott rose to his feet, waving Tyrone back when the younger man would have stood. "I think you two have things to discuss. I'll say good-bye on my way out." He left the room, heading for the stairs.

Tyrone lifted Catherine's hand to his lips and said huskily, "Another risk you took for me. I was a blind, selfish bastard, Catherine."

"You couldn't have known. I made sure of that." Her smile was gentle.

He shook his head. "I deserve everything I felt when you told me so flatly that there wouldn't be a child."

She looked at him searchingly. "I didn't mean to hurt you, Marc. You caught me off guard asking about it."

"All I could think in that moment was that you must have really hated the way I could make you feel. You were so damned determined there wouldn't be any ties between us."

She heard his voice in her mind suddenly, remembering what he had said to her then. *God, don't look like that! You can't hate it that much, what I make you feel. You can't hate it that much, Catherine!*

Her arms went up around his neck, and she pressed herself close to him. "What I hated," she said unsteadily, "was that I couldn't love you the way I wanted to. I never hated you, Marc, and I never hated the way you made me feel."

Tyrone's arms held her tightly, until she drew back abruptly with a startled sound. "What?" he asked, smoothing a strand of dark hair from her face.

She stared at him, then smiled a bit hesitantly. "Well, it would be a miracle after ... after everything that happened later, but there's a chance—Marc, when I left the ship yesterday, I had a lot on my mind."

"I remember," he said dryly.

"Yes. I went back to the house and I didn't—well, I didn't do what I always do after we've been together. So it's just possible . . ."

He slowly began to smile. "In that sultan's bed of mine?"

"Oh, I hope so!" she said.

Tyrone kissed her. "So do I, my sweet."

They sat that way in peaceful silence for a few moments, and then Catherine lifted her head from his shoulder. "You said that Dr. Scott had another patient? Upstairs?"

"Those secret dark rooms we talked about yesterday," he said quietly. "I have them too, remember."

She remembered something else then. "The man you said was on his way here with questions?"

"Yes. And the answer is upstairs. I'll take you up to meet him later this afternoon. He'll be tired after Dr. Scott sees him, and he'll need to rest for a while."

"I wanted to ask you then," she said. "But there were so many secrets of my own, it didn't seem right to ask about yours."

"I know. It's all right." He smiled at her. "Everything's all right now." And if he thought of the determined man with questions still to be faced, he pushed that into the back of his mind.

Dr. Scott left sometime later with a brief statement to Tyrone. "It won't be long now. Tonight, perhaps."

Catherine agreed to allow Sarah and Reuben to close up the house she had shared with her father, and bring her what she needed, partly because she knew Tyrone would go with her if she insisted on doing it herself; she didn't want him to have to look at a harbor empty of his *Raven*, or, worse, see the charred remains of a mast jutting up out of the water. There would be time for that painful sight later.

They spent the early afternoon quietly, never more than an arm's reach apart. With so much behind them, and so much pain too recent in their memories, it was a time of peace rather than laughter. The only wryly humorous moment came when Sarah and Reuben returned from their errand bearing a gift.

From Mrs. Symington.

Tyrone was strongly inclined to dispatch the tremendous basket of fruit immediately back to its sender with a blistering note, but Catherine pointed out gravely that it had been sent to her rather than to him.

"She's feeling guilty, and she should be," Tyrone said. "Let her suffer awhile."

Catherine smiled. "She—all of them—treated me the way I treated them. Coldly. I won't say it didn't hurt, but I certainly can't blame them."

"I can."

"Marc."

His jaw hardened stubbornly. "If I speak a civil word to any of them, it'll be a miracle!"

"If you snap at the vicar," she said, "he won't marry us."

"Then I'll—" Tyrone stopped, realizing. "Hell. The place is a damned island."

She nodded solemnly. "Dr. Scott said the packet had already left. And sometimes it's months between them. If you go around being uncivil to everyone, we're not going to have a very easy time of it."

He frowned at her.

"Make peace," she suggested. "It's the best way."

"So I don't send the fruit back?" he asked wryly.

"No. And I write a thank-you note to Lettia."

Tyrone sighed. "I hope you're with me the next time I see her—for her sake. You can keep me from choking her."

Catherine laughed and went to write the note.

Later that afternoon Tyrone took Catherine upstairs to meet Dr. Scott's "other patient." He hadn't explained anything to her. And, once she saw, he didn't have to.

Not really.

The bedroom was dimly lighted, since a single lamp burned by the bed and the curtains were drawn. There was a fire in the hearth, and the small room was very warm, but there were many thick blankets and quilts on the bed. All around, on shelves and scattered on the floor, was a myriad of toys and games and storybooks. Childish drawings in chalk and charcoal were pinned to the walls.

Tyrone quietly introduced Catherine to Mrs. Tully, who then folded up her knitting and left the bedroom. He guided Catherine to sit in a chair by the bed, and spoke softly and gently to the man who had opened his eyes to watch them.

"I've brought someone to meet you. This is Catherine."

He didn't say the man's name. He didn't have to.

Catherine accepted the big, knobby hand that was held shakily out to her, holding it for a moment in both hers. She felt her throat close up, and smiled at the gaunt face.

"You're pretty," he murmured in a weak voice, childlike eyes fixed on her face.

"Why, thank you." Her voice was gentle, hushed.

The man's eyes wandered to Tyrone where he stood behind Catherine's chair, and a smile curved his lips. "Marc thinks so too."

"You're both very kind." Catherine tucked his big hand back underneath the covers because she could feel it was getting cold. "Would you like me to read to you?" she asked, seeing the book lying nearby on the nightstand.

His eyes brightened "Yes, please."

So Catherine picked up the book and read to the man in the bed. Her voice was soft and slow, and seemed to please the man. His smile remained even after his eyes had gradually closed and he slipped easily into sleep. Catherine went on reading quietly until the story was finished, and then laid the book aside, knowing it wouldn't be read to the man again. It was clear that he was failing fast.

She sat for a moment in silence, gazing at the man and conscious of Marc's presence behind her chair. It made sense now, she thought—why he had come here; why he had built a home on this remote island and chosen the most isolated spot on it for the house; his polite but firm warnings against casual visitors; his regular visits over the years and long before she had met him.

Secrets . . . dear God.

She rose finally, and went with him out of the bedroom. She didn't realize she was crying until he pulled her into his arms with a soft sound. And she clung to him, thinking of a strong man holding answers that were secrets, quietly caring for a sick, broken man whose very presence must have haunted him unbearably . . . especially because Marc Tyrone may have helped break the man.

They made love that night in his house for the first time, and it had never been so sweet between them. Desire welled slowly, a yearning that escaped in soft words and murmurs that were like the slow shattering of glass. They were utterly close now, tied together in love, the bond between them tested in pain and fear—and fire. Two separate, lonely, secret beings had found each other and had clung with unacknowledged need, wary and prickly, pretending to be strangers.

Neither was alone any longer.

Catherine woke sometime near dawn, conscious that Marc wasn't in bed beside her. She sat up, her searching eyes finding him easily in the dimness of the room. He was standing by the window, gazing out at what she knew was a perfect view of the ocean.

She wondered if the sea was whispering to him.

"Marc?"

He turned immediately, returning to the bed, and her. Gathering her into his arms, he said, "Did I wake you? I'm sorry."

"You weren't here," she answered simply, cuddling close to him. "What woke you?"

"I don't know." His voice was low. After a moment he went on in a musing tone. "During the war I sometimes felt an impulse to change whatever plan I'd made. To alter the destination of the ship, or just to change course. Always, I found that by doing that I avoided some danger I couldn't have known about."

"Is that what you're feeling now?" she asked softly, respecting the instincts his life had given him.

"I think so. I looked out now, and I felt as if . . . as if something dark were moving toward me."

Catherine felt a chill. "That man with the questions?" She knew the whole story now, knew what a threat to them those questions could prove to be.

"No," Tyrone said slowly. "Not him. Not Delaney. This is something else."

"What could it be?"

"Something . . . I didn't see. Something I missed." He shook his head slightly. "I don't know."

"If I lost you now, I couldn't bear it," she whispered.

His arms tightened around her. "You won't lose me, love. A man with as much to live for as I have isn't an easy man to kill. I plan to grow old with you."

"Promise?"

"I promise."

Lulled by the steady beat of his heart, by the comfort of his arms, she drifted back into sleep. And if nameless fears crept through her dreams on cat feet, they were silent shadows and left only faint tracks behind.

In the morning Mrs. Tully told them that the man had slipped away just before dawn, without waking.

Catherine and Tyrone stood together behind the house late that morning. They were near the edge of the cliffs that bordered that end of the island, and stood gazing out to sea.

"I thought I caught a glimpse of sails a little while ago," Tyrone said absently, looking toward the harbor that wasn't visible from the clifftop path behind his house.

"Another packet?" she asked, having seen nothing herself but trusting his captain's gaze.

"No. A clipper, perhaps. Too far away to know for sure."

They could both hear the distant thuds of a hammer in the stables, where Reuben was building a coffin, and Tyrone's mouth twisted as he listened to it. "I think I hate this more than anything. Putting him in an unmarked grave."

"It isn't that," Catherine said quietly. "Not really. He's buried far away, we both know."

"His name is. And his memory."

"Aren't those the important things? His name and his memory. In the end that's all that matters for any of us."

'   Tyrone lifted her hand to his lips and kissed it, smiling down at her. "You're right."

"Stop blaming yourself, Marc. I can see now why you said the war wasn't over for you, why it couldn't be. You've lived with it every day since. But you can't go back and change anything."

"I don't even know if I would, given the chance." He sighed a little roughly. "And it isn't just my own part in the war. There's the rest. I keep asking myself if I could have prevented some of what happened later. So many died for that damned gold, suffered because of it."

"You did what you thought best. No one could have asked more than that of you."

Tyrone slipped her hand through his arm and they resumed their walk along the cliff top path, moving more swiftly away from the house and stables, away from the sounds of a coffin being made.

"You're throwing my own words back at me," he said.

Catherine laughed, remembering that he had said much the same thing to her about her own guilts. "Well, it was good advice. We *can't* change anything, Marc. We don't have the luxury or even the right. And what if things had been different? If you hadn't been a blockade runner, you wouldn't have been in a position to take care of a sick man who had no one else. You certainly couldn't have brought him here, kept him safe and as happy as possible all these years."

Accepting what she said, Tyrone spoke in a deliberately light tone. "I knew there was a reason I loved you."

"Yes, why don't you tell me about that?" she prompted him smiling. "I've been wondering."

"Blue eyes," he said quickly, a gleam in his own eyes. "I've always had a weakness for them."

"And dark hair, no doubt."

"That too. Of course, a neatly turned ankle always did catch my eye."

"Oh, of course. Perfectly natural."

"And you were wearing a hat with feathers that day I first saw you."

"I was not!"

"I remember it distinctly. A little blue hat with feathers. You were wearing blue gloves, too, and a blue gingham dress."

Catherine started to laugh. "I bowled you over, in fact?"

He stopped them and turned her to face him. His hands were holding her shoulders, and though he was smiling, there was a serious look in his gray eyes. "You did that. I didn't recognize it for far too long, but that's what happened. I never felt the slightest interest in another woman after I met you."

Catherine, looking up at him, felt her heart lurch. But before she could say anything, a vicious, ringing shout came from several feet behind Marc.

"*Tyrone!*"

He stiffened, his face tightening and gray eyes going hard with a silver glitter. "Of course," he murmured to himself in a slow voice of realization. "I should have known."

"Tyrone, you bastard, turn around!"

"Marc?" She whispered the question.

"Don't move, Catherine." His voice was low, calm. He lifted one hand, touched her cheek lightly. "Don't move."

She wanted to cry out suddenly in an instinctive protest against something she saw in his eyes. But her throat had closed up, and she stood stiff and silent when he slowly turned and took two steps away from her. Then she saw the other man.

He didn't seem much of a threat at first glance. A man of late middle age, short and thin. Dressed in clothing that looked as if he had worn it for days. His thinning brown hair stood up like spikes in the breeze. With his aggressive stance and mussed appearance, he could have cut a comical figure.

Except that he didn't.

In his eye was the wild gleam of panic and rage, his pale face twitching nervously. But the hand holding the gun that was aimed squarely at Tyrone was very, very steady.

"Sheridan," Tyrone said in a flat, dry voice. He had deliberately moved away from Catherine to keep Sheridan's attention fixed on himself, hoping desperately to safeguard her. But when he saw the other man's eyes, a sick feeling grew in his chest. Sheridan was in a blind panic, and was all too obviously in no state to think things through.

"You wrote down our names, you son of a bitch," Sheridan said thickly. "Left them for Delaney to find. And he's hot on your trail, determined to get his damned answers."

Tyrone wasn't armed, and he was one step too far

from Sheridan; he couldn't hope to disarm the other man without taking at least one bullet for his effort. Still, he felt his body tensing, felt muscles gathering. Holding his voice calm and steady, he said, "I should have known it was you."

Sheridan twitched. "You're wrong. You don't know what you're talking about."

"Oh, yes. You were impatient even then, always apt to act without thinking it through. I should have realized." He was intent only on getting Sheridan off guard somehow to give himself the seconds he needed.

"No! It was the others—"

Tyrone shook his head slowly, never taking his eyes from Sheridan's face. "Not them. I wasn't sure at the time, but I am now. Of those five men you were the only one who could have planned such a clumsy attempt."

Sheridan's mouth dropped open suddenly. *"Attempt?"*

Knowing he might well be making a terrible mistake, Tyrone nonetheless followed his instincts. "That's right—attempt. It failed, Sheridan. I lied to you and the others when I returned and told you he was dead."

The senator gasped. "He was! He died!"

"No. But I knew at least one of you had planned the attack, and I couldn't risk another attempt on his life. So I lied. I kept him safely on my ship, hid him, and then I brought him here."

"You wouldn't have," Sheridan protested numbly. "You didn't give a damn about any of it."

"He was my *friend.*" Tyrone heard his own harsh voice, and fought to keep calm, steady. "He was a sick, pitiful man who was no threat to your grand plans."

"He *was* a threat. As long as he was alive." Sheridan had stopped denying. "And so are you. I can't allow you to tell Delaney about it. I *can't!* Leon says that Delaney could go either way, could take it public. I can't let that happen. I have too much to lose, too much I've built. My *life* will be destroyed if the world knows what happened!"

"You aren't thinking, Sheridan," Tyrone said softly. "Do you really believe I kept him alone in my house all these years? That others don't know about him?"

"Years?" Sheridan whispered. "He lived years? I don't believe it! You would have tried to blackmail us if that were true; you would have held it over us!"

"Why?" Tyrone made his voice flat. "None of you had anything I wanted, Sheridan."

Sheridan's eyes were darting about, his face twitching more violently. But the gun hand was steady. "He's dead, isn't he? He's dead now?"

"Yes. He's dead now. You can't hurt him."

"But you can hurt me," Sheridan said thickly. "You'll tell Delaney the whole story. And then he'll tell the world."

"You can't know that."

'I can't take the risk, don't you see?" Sheridan laughed wildly. "I can't! If we'd all done it—if all of them had planned to kill him—then we'd stand together. But they weren't part of that. And they won't hang, not them. They'll say it was my doing, and you'd back them up. I'd be the one swinging, just me!"

Catherine, standing in frozen fear behind and to one side of Tyrone, felt rather than saw him gather himself. Sheridan was so dangerously close to the edge of the cliff. Catherine knew then with an awful, tearing certainty that he would leap at the man with the gun, that he meant to carry the man with him over the cliff.

"No . . ." But it was a whisper, barely escaping her lips. From the corner of her eye she caught a glimpse of movement, but all her attention was fixed on what was happening before her.

"I won't let my life be ruined," Sheridan was saying hoarsely. "I can't. I have to stop you from telling Delaney."

"What about the others in the house?" Tyrone asked. "What about the doctor here that I brought him to? What about his nurse and the housekeeper and her husband? Will you kill them all, too, Sheridan?"

But Senator James Sheridan was beyond considering the futility of what he meant to do. He saw only a mortal threat to his safety before him, and reacted, as always, without thinking it through. With a grimace contorting his face, he cocked the pistol in his hand.

Tyrone began to leap toward him, but a shot rang out from the right, knocking Sheridan's gun from his hand before he could fire it. The impact swung him around—and he was too close to the cliff.

With a shriek he toppled over the edge.

"Marc!"

He caught Catherine in his arms and held her shaking body close, even as he half turned to see who had fired the shot. And, somehow, he wasn't surprised to see Jesse Beaumont, his sister, Victoria—and Falcon Delaney.

Delaney had fired the shot.

Conscious of relief, of easing muscles, Tyrone held Catherine tight as they approached. Conscious that at long last it was almost over. He looked particularly at Delaney, and felt a sudden amusement. Saved by his nemesis. There was, he decided, an appropriate irony in that.

"Thanks," he told Delaney in a dry tone.

The other man holstered his gun. "You're welcome." If there was any irony in his voice, it wasn't obvious. "Not that I intended to kill him. I didn't realize he was so close to the edge of the cliff."

"It's a fifty-foot drop here," Tyrone said. "And rocks below. He's gone."

Jesse, who had taken a quick look over the edge and then swiftly retreated, nodded agreement. "I'll say. The tide's about to get him." He looked at Tyrone, remembering suddenly. "And that's not all the tide's getting. *The Raven*'s mast is sticking up out of the harbor, and the rest of her's charred driftwood. What the hell happened, Marc?"

"She burned, obviously." Tyrone released Catherine but held her hand firmly as she looked at the others in bewildered interest. "I'll tell you the story later, Jesse." He looked back at Delaney, saying briefly, "You've come to hear another story."

"I think I heard part of it." Delaney glanced toward the cliff, then back. "I'd like to know it all though."

Catherine gazed at them, puzzlement gradually disappearing. The blond man was one of Marc's captains; he had mentioned Jesse Beaumont to her before. The dark man with the hawklike looks and cool green eyes had to be Falcon Delaney and, judging by the way she had slipped her arm through his and by their wedding bands, the lovely blond woman was obviously his wife.

His new wife, she realized, because Marc had also noticed their closeness and commented with some amusement to Jesse.

"I see, Jesse, that you weren't the only one who found her."

Calmly, Victoria Delaney told him, "If I'd had about

three more minutes to talk to you in New York, we might both have saved poor Jesse from Apaches and saddlesores."

"You were called away," he reminded her, smiling, then looked at Jesse with a lifted brow. "Apaches?"

"I don't want to talk about it." Jesse seemed disgusted at the memory. "Give me a ship and the sea any day, and you can forget about dry land and Apaches."

Catherine looked between them all, feeling an absurd impulse to laugh. She'd expected Falcon Delaney to be a threat to Marc and to herself, and yet . . . There was something more here, something that was almost—and very curiously—friendly. When Tyrone introduced her, which he did then, it began to make a bit more sense to her. At least the introductions explained how Marc's supposed enemy arrived at the island aboard Jesse's ship, *The Robyn;* Falcon Delaney, it seemed, was Jesse's new brother-in-law.

It also developed that Jesse had, having unknowingly sent the senator off to try to kill Marc and then been told about the situation by Delaney, pushed his ship to her straining limits in order to get there as soon as possible.

"Almost tore the heart out of her," he said to Tyrone as they began moving toward the house. "But Falcon was convinced the senator meant to kill you, so there was no time to waste."

Tyrone looked at Delaney. "What set the senator off?"

"I did," Falcon told him dryly. "And it's your own damned fault, leaving cryptic lists in ledgers."

"Safely locked in my office," Tyrone murmured.

"You ought to get a better lock."

"It was easy?"

"Too easy. A dangerous temptation to thieves."

Catherine found herself smiling, and noticed that Victoria, too, was smiling. Jesse was indignant.

"Dammit, Falcon, you didn't tell me you'd broken into Marc's office!"

"You didn't ask," his brother-in-law reminded him calmly.

"I was responsible for that office," Jesse said irritably, then looked at Tyrone, wearing an aggrieved expression. "Which reminds me. All your business affairs are in your lawyer's lap, and I hope he robs you blind. If you want to go junketing off again, Marc, you can damn well hire yourself a manager. I'll sail your ships for you, but I absolutely will not ever again sit behind your desk. It's too damned wearing on the nerves. Fire me!" he finished irately.

"All right, Jesse," Tyrone said softly, smiling.

Encouraged by the mild response, Jesse finished airing his grievances. "You can also tell me—finally— what the hell's been going on. One day Falcon's tracking that damned gold, which wasn't where it was supposed to be, and the next day he's saying something about lists and rabid senators and something called Camelot—"

"I'll tell you, Jesse." Tyrone looked at them all and smiled crookedly. "I'll tell all of you. But first I have something to show you."

They followed him into the house.

12

The room upstairs was very quiet. The drapes were drawn, and candles provided soft light. Mrs. Tully had prepared the man for his final journey, and he lay on the bed fully dressed in a suit he hadn't worn for a long time.

Falcon Delaney stepped to the side of the bed and stared down at the man, feeling a chill of shock. He looked at the bony, gaunt face, and at the receding hairline that exposed a broad, high forehead. Disbelieving, he searched the man's features, half hidden behind a neatly trimmed, graying beard. He looked at big, knobby hands folded in silence.

Finally he believed.

"My God," he whispered, turning to look at the silently waiting Tyrone. "It's *Lincoln*."

"He was failing when the war began," Tyrone said, looking at the others. They were all in his study, the three newcomers still in shock. Falcon, Victoria, and Jesse sat on the long couch; Catherine was seated in the chair near the fireplace where Tyrone stood. And Tyrone spoke slowly, hoping all of them would understand how it had been then.

"His health was breaking. The war . . . perhaps that was the final blow. For many years he had suffered bouts of deep melancholy; always he'd been able to pull out of them before they got so debilitating that he couldn't carry out his duty. But that hateful war. It triggered the deepest, most paralyzing melancholia. He wasn't an effective president, and those closest to him saw it. They tried to hide his incapacity, but it became more and more difficult."

"You knew him then?" Falcon asked.

Tyrone smiled with a touch of bitterness. "I'd known him for years. I met him through Morgan Fontaine, when I was one of his captains. None of us expected things to turn out the way they did, with Morgan actively supporting the Confederacy and myself running supplies to the South—and Lincoln doing his best to hold the country together."

Falcon nodded without comment, and Tyrone went on.

"There was a group of men, friends, who saw what was happening to Lincoln, and who knew what his failure could do to the Union. They had already begun running things themselves. But he was growing worse, and his doctor warned them there wouldn't be any improvement. Even his wonderful iron will was beginning to fade. So, they managed, somehow, to find a man who was a virtual double for Lincoln, and they planned to have that man step in as president."

"And Lincoln?" Falcon asked.

"They planned to transport him—secretly, of course —up to New England, to a private house where he'd be well taken care of, and well out of the public eye."

"What about his wife?" Victoria asked slowly. "And his children?"

Tyrone's voice was slow as well. "His wife was still

grieving over the son they'd lost the year before. I was told she had agreed it was best for all concerned. I never spoke to her. There were two sons left; I was given to understand they weren't to be told anything."

After a moment Falcon said, "So the plan to secretly replace Lincoln with a double was Camelot?"

"Yes. They approached me, oddly enough, without realizing I knew Lincoln. Their aim in choosing me, I believe, was to cover themselves; if anything went wrong, my participation would neatly point a finger toward the South." He smiled wryly. "And who in the Union would have taken the word of a blockade-running ship's captain?"

Falcon was watching him intently. "But you were believed to have no loyalties in the war."

"True. I was, however, very openly running guns and supplies into the South. That would have been enough."

Nodding, Falcon asked quietly, "Why did you agree to do it?"

Tyrone was leaning back against the mantle, gazing at nothing. He looked at Falcon, shrugged slightly. But his voice went a little rough. "I saw him. I wasn't willing to accept their verdict on his condition, so they slipped me in to see him one night. I hadn't seen him in four or five years. It took me no more than five minutes to realize they were right. I told them I'd get him safely to New England."

"Did they pay you?" Falcon asked.

Tyrone smiled cynically. "Of course. The second reason they'd chosen me was that I was known to take any risk if the pay was good enough."

The answer didn't surprise Falcon. Still, he had seen the man upstairs, and he knew very well Tyrone hadn't done any of it for the money. "So you got him out of Washington."

"Yes. That part was easy enough; they'd planned well. And Lincoln was dazed, meek. He went along willingly. I got him onto the ship."

"What about your crew?"

Jesse followed Falcon's question immediately with a bewildered one of his own. "What about me?"

Tyrone sent him a rueful smile. "You were a problem through the entire mess, Jesse. Always underfoot."

"I resent that," Jesse said.

"No doubt. Well, the night I took Lincoln onto the ship, I'd given the crew liberty and sent Jesse on an errand. I more or less repeated that when we reached New England, after having kept Lincoln safely in my cabin during the trip."

"And you took him to this private house?"

"I intended to. However, we were attacked on the road before we could get there. Three men, armed with knives and cudgels. It had apparently not occurred to them that I would be armed as well—with pistols. Lincoln was sleeping in the carriage, drugged. I was having a difficult time with the horses. By mistake I killed all three of the men." He sounded almost apologetic.

"By mistake?" Jesse wondered dryly.

Falcon looked at his brother-in-law. "He needed at least one alive. How else could he know who'd sent them?"

"Oh," Jesse murmured.

Tyrone smiled faintly. "Exactly. Unfortunately I was left with something of a dilemma. Five men knew I'd be on that road at roughly that time; any one of them could have planned the attack."

"You didn't suspect more than one?" Falcon asked,

and only Victoria knew that he was more than a little worried that his boss and friend, Leon Hamilton, might have been involved in the attempted assassination.

"No," Tyrone replied with certainty. "As a group, they didn't need my help to kill him. And they were highly organized; the attack was clumsy, but not deliberately so, and that didn't fit. It seemed far more likely that one of them may have decided to take the opportunity on impulse, had hurriedly sent men without thinking it through."

He sighed. "If I'd been thinking clearly, I would have suspected Sheridan. He's always been known to be impatient and prone to act on impulse. In any case, I couldn't have been sure who it was."

"So all you knew," Falcon said, "was that at least one of those men wanted Lincoln dead."

"Yes. I was angry. I decided that there was no need for whoever was responsible to know his plan had failed. I took Lincoln back to the ship and returned to Washington. I told them what had happened, everything except that Lincoln had survived. They all appeared shocked."

"But not," Falcon said slowly, "unduly disappointed?"

"Not unduly disappointed," Tyrone agreed. "Their puppet was safely installed, and we were all aware of how tenuous my position was. I was no threat to them, and they knew it."

"They didn't demand to see the body?"

"I didn't give them a chance. I made it plain I'd been unwilling to travel up and down the coast carrying a body killed under suspicious circumstances. Particularly the body of the president. I could see them shudder at the very thought."

"And then?" Jesse questioned, torn between fascination and horror.

"I left. And I brought Lincoln directly here."

"Why here?" Falcon asked.

"I'd been here before, and knew the community was small and that there was land available at this end of the island. I also knew that Dr. Charles Scott, highly respected as one of the most knowledgeable brain-disorder specialists in the world, had retired here some years before. I got in touch with Dr. Scott, and he took Lincoln secretly into his house until I could arrange something more permanent."

He looked at Falcon steadily, and said, "All this transpired, by the way, in March of 'Sixty-three."

Falcon's eyes narrowed. "The ledger entry with the list of names was dated April."

"Yes. It was."

Falcon pulled out a long, thin cigar and lit it, frowning. "Dammit," he muttered.

Jesse was bewildered, and looked from one to the other. "What?" he asked.

"Bait," Falcon said somewhat bitterly. "And I took it."

Jesse blinked, looked at Tyrone. "You knew he'd break into your office and find that list?"

"Let's just say I had learned to respect his ... tenacity."

"You *wanted* him to come after you here?"

Tyrone shrugged abruptly. "I wanted it to be over. Lincoln was dying, and I had thoughts of a future on my mind." He sent a glance at Catherine, returning her smile. Then he looked steadily at Falcon. "I'd realized you wouldn't give up, no matter what. However, I didn't expect you to set Sheridan on me."

Falcon smiled suddenly, a gleam of honest amusement in his green eyes. "You think I may have questioned him so bluntly that he took fright and bolted down here?"

"It does seem unlike you," Tyrone said. "I had the impression your methods were more subtle."

"I like to think so. In fact, I never spoke to him at all."

Tyrone's gaze narrowed. After a moment he said slowly, "Some connection to one of the men on that list?"

Falcon nodded. "Leon Hamilton. He's been my boss since the first years of the war."

"Treasury?"

"Yes."

Shaking his head slightly, Tyrone said, "That's what I missed. He isn't publicly linked with Treasury. Naturally, when you found that list while looking for some trace of the missing gold, you confronted him with it."

"Naturally."

"And he warned you off?"

"He certainly did. He wouldn't tell me anything at all about Camelot, said that it couldn't possibly be connected to the gold. Coincidence, he said."

"And you, of course, believed him."

"Oh, of course," Falcon said dryly.

Tyrone smiled just a little. "I imagine he went directly to the others to warn them that you were hell-bent to find me and ask some uncomfortable questions."

"Which," Falcon observed, "is no doubt what sent Sheridan tearing off down here. Leon must have impressed on them that I wouldn't stop until I knew the entire story."

Remembering suddenly, Tyrone said, "Yes, he said

something about that out on the cliff. And more, what probably panicked him the most, that Hamilton thought it was possible you could take the story public."

Jesse looked at Falcon. "Will you take the story public?" he asked.

Falcon didn't answer. Instead, gazing steadily at Tyrone, he said, "Tell me about the gold."

Tyrone nodded. "Much of that story you already know," he said. "I was offered a commission, in Morgan Fontaine's name, to transport goods into Charleston." He hesitated, then said, "At that point I was trying to earn all I could, and I wasn't too particular about what I carried."

Falcon nodded.

"I wasn't a fool, however," Tyrone went on wryly. "When one of the chests broke open at sea, and I realized I was carrying Union gold, I wasn't very happy."

"That's an understatement," Jesse added.

Tyrone ignored the interpolation. "We made Charleston before dawn, and I went ashore to confront Morgan. He wasn't, however, the man who had come to accept the delivery."

"Read Talbot," Falcon said.

"Yes. Whatever happened to him, by the way?"

"He's dead," Falcon told him.

"I see." Tyrone frowned a little. "Jesse's telegram to me reported that Morgan was dead. How—"

It was Victoria who answered quietly. "Read Talbot and two other men tortured Morgan to death. They were trying to find out about the gold. Where it was hidden."

Tyrone looked at her, his face very still. "He was your husband then, wasn't he?"

"Yes."

"I'm sorry."

She looked at him curiously. "You say that as if you were somehow responsible for his death."

"I was."

Jesse interrupted. "But Morgan took the gold."

Tyrone hesitated, then resumed the story. "I managed to choke the truth out of Talbot. When he told me the gold had been stolen to finance an assassination attempt on the president, I couldn't believe Morgan would have sanctioned it. And even though I knew the man in Washington wasn't Lincoln, it was what everyone else believed that mattered."

"So you went to Morgan?" Falcon asked.

"Yes. He was, as I'd expected, furious. He was also defeated. He knew the South was dying. He said that his last gift to the South would be to make certain those men never got their hands on the gold."

Quietly Falcon asked, "Is that when you told him about Lincoln?"

Tyrone looked at him a moment, then nodded. "He had suggested I keep the gold; I'd told him I didn't fancy hanging. Then I told him about Lincoln. I had realized by then how difficult—and expensive—any long-range solution would be. It would take a great deal of money to ensure total safety and secrecy, money I didn't have at that time. Morgan immediately said it would be poetic justice to take the money meant to assassinate Lincoln and use it to make his last years safe and happy ones."

"And you agreed."

"At the time it seemed the only solution."

"But Morgan got the gold," Jesse repeated. "I delivered it to him."

"The gold never left *The Raven*, Jesse," Tyrone said quietly.

"The chests!"

"Yes, you delivered the chests. Filled with bricks. They were heavy enough so that you wouldn't suspect anything."

Jesse was frowning. "Wait. Morgan gave me some of the coins. He opened one of the chests—and there were gold coins."

Tyrone looked at Falcon. "When Morgan and I talked, I told him about the three-dollar gold pieces. Of all the coins they were the only ones that could have been traced. Morgan said he'd take that chest, empty it out later, and bury the coins apart from the other chests. He probably never thought twice about giving Jesse a bag of the coins."

"All these years," Falcon said, "and that puzzled me most of all, that so few of those specially minted coins ever turned up. But it makes sense now. It was only the one bag that Talbot stole from Jesse."

"I left some with Tory," Jesse said, "before Talbot jumped me."

Victoria nodded. "Yes, he said he'd gone back to Regret later and found the bag where I'd hidden it."

Tyrone looked at her curiously. "You spoke to him?"

She returned his look, smiled faintly. "I'm the one who killed him."

"Revenge?" he asked after a moment.

"Justice."

Tyrone nodded, then sighed. "Morgan and I both believed we'd covered our tracks. None of those men knew anything at all about him, where he was from. He said since I was right out in the open, the trail couldn't lead toward me. So we faked the delivery, and Morgan vanished out west."

Victoria looked at her husband. "Illusion. Sleight-of-hand. Being led to believe something that wasn't so. You were very close."

Tyrone spoke before Falcon could respond. "Was he? I rather thought he might be."

"Is that why you left the ledger for me to find?" Falcon asked him.

"One of the reasons, I suppose. I had begun to realize you wouldn't give up, as I said. But it was more than that." Tyrone looked weary for the first time. He moved to Catherine's chair and sat down on the arm, resting a hand on her shoulder. "Things were happening," he said slowly. "People were crossing paths suddenly after all these years, people who knew parts of the story. Of both stories."

He looked at Falcon. "I saw Victoria at that ball, and thought she might have been Jesse's sister, whom he believed had been killed years before. I had no thought of the gold then, not until she introduced herself as Victoria Fontaine. Still, that was possible, given Morgan's nature; he could have taken care of her, thinking Jesse was dead. But you were with her, and I had good reason to know the gold was rarely out of your mind."

"It was that night," Falcon murmured, remembering.

Tyrone smiled but went on. "You had come to my office a few days before that, and from the things you so casually let slip, I realized you were beginning to piece it together." He shrugged. "There isn't much more to tell. When I received Jesse's wire, I decided to come back here. I was reasonably sure you'd find the ledger, but even if you didn't, with Morgan dead the trail of the gold could lead only to me." He looked at Victoria. "I am sorry he was killed."

She shook her head. "It wasn't your fault. I knew

Morgan very well, and I know he would have preferred the trail to lead to him if it had to lead
anywhere."

Then Jesse said, "What now?" He was looking at
Falcon as he spoke.

Catherine, who had sat in silence listening, spoke,
her gaze also on Falcon. "Port Elizabeth is under
English jurisdiction; you have no authority here."

"He knows that," Tyrone said quietly.

And they both knew something else. Gray eyes met
green, the knowledge clear in both. They each knew
that Tyrone had a fleet of ships, including the fast
clipper *Robyn* now in the harbor. They both knew he
could sail away in that ship, and that Falcon would
find it very nearly impossible to catch him.

They both knew the chase could continue for years.

They both knew it wouldn't, that it would end at
that moment.

"Dammit, Falcon," Jesse exploded, "say something!"

Slowly Falcon said, "A country should be obli-
gated to care for its commander in chief. I'd say that
gold was justly used."

Tyrone wasn't really surprised. He smiled faintly. "Is
that what you'll report to your superiors?"

"You forget." Falcon smiled as well. "My superior
is Leon Hamilton. I believe he'll be quite happy to
accept any report I give him."

"Particularly when the dead remained buried?"

"Exactly." Falcon hesitated, then said, "Ironic, isn't
it? They went to all that trouble—and the man they
had so carefully picked to replace the president was
assassinated two years later anyway."

Jesse asked about *The Raven*, and Tyrone explained
briefly. Falcon told Tyrone the details of what had

happened in New Mexico and Texas, filling in the rest of the story.

With a touch of rueful amusement Tyrone invited them to remain a few days. He thought it odd that after so many years of him and Falcon warily circling each other, they should at last have reached a point that appeared to be the cautious beginning of friendship. He was pleased when they accepted the invitation to stay in his house.

Later, as they were all cleaning up before lunch, Tyrone and Catherine had their first moment alone since the confrontation out on the cliff.

In the bedroom they shared, Catherine said fiercely, "You were going to throw yourself at Sheridan, weren't you?"

"It wasn't," Tyrone said in a wry tone, "an option I was entirely happy with."

"But you would have done it?"

He eyed her somewhat warily. After all she had gone through these last days, Catherine had been far more subdued than he was accustomed to seeing her; it seemed, however, that she was now rapidly regaining her more normal stubborn, sharp-tongued assurance.

She stood facing him squarely, slender hands on her hips, blue eyes gleaming. Her dark hair fell about her shoulders like a silky curtain, and the simple white blouse and dark skirt she wore made her look delicate and feminine.

He thought she was beautiful.

"Marc—"

Tyrone cleared his throat. "It didn't come to that, after all."

She stepped toward him and lifted her chin high. "If I had wanted a lapdog," she said, her voice losing none of its fierceness for being soft, "I certainly wouldn't have fallen in love with you. *However*—"

"However?" he asked.

"You promised to grow old with me."

He smiled slowly. "Yes, I did."

"And I'm going to hold you to that promise. So I expect you to stop being so infernally reckless."

"I'm never reckless."

"Marc . . ."

Chuckling, he pulled her into his arms. "I told you before, darling. A man with as much to live for as I have isn't an easy man to kill."

She melted against him. "You just make sure of that, dammit," she said. "I intend to wed only once."

"I'll make very sure of that," he promised, and kissed her.

Victoria watched as Falcon found his journal in the bags they had brought from the ship. "An end to the story?" she asked.

He carried the leather-bound journal to the small secretary in their bedroom and sat down, looking at it thoughtfully. Then his gaze lifted to his wife. "It's a private journal," he said slowly. "And all the damaging information is in my own code. The chances of anyone else understanding or even reading what I've written in it are slim."

She smiled. "And it isn't really ended until you write it all down?"

"And old habit," he had apologized.

"What will you do with the journal?"

He shrugged. "Take it back to Killara, I expect. There are a few journals from various members of the family stored there. Mine will join them." He smiled crookedly. "To molder away into dust through the years."

On impulse, Victoria gave him the assurance he was looking for. "Then make the entry. You won't be really content until the entire story is there, questions answered. The search for the gold was a large part of your life—and mine. It's too important not to finish in every way."

Falcon nodded and picked up a pen.

Later that afternoon Tyrone asked Jesse about another of his ships. "Is *The Ladyhawke* back in New York yet?"

Jesse shook his head. "Probably on the return journey from San Francisco by now. Why? You want me to send her down here?"

"If you wouldn't mind," Tyrone said in a polite tone. "I hesitate to ask after your explosion—"

Jesse made a rude noise. "The ships don't bother me. It's the damned paperwork I hate. So you'll be staying on here for a few months?"

"Yes, I think so. Whether we spend most of our time here or in New York is up to Catherine, so—"

"What's up to me?" Catherine asked, coming into the room.

"The decision about where we'll live," he told her.

Calmly she said, "No, it's up to you."

He eyed her."Why?"

"You have a shipping business to think of."

"I may hire that manager Jesse recommended," Tyrone said thoughtfully. "I'd like to show you the world."

"Will you show me that house in Spain?"

He started laughing. "No!"

"They wouldn't let me in?" she asked curiously.

"They wouldn't let you *out*, more likely."

Jesse was bewildered. "What house in Spain?"

"Never mind," both Catherine and Tyrone said repressively, and Jesse retired, crushed, to wonder about houses in Spain.

Late that afternoon, as the sun was setting, they buried Abraham Lincoln on a bluff overlooking the sea. The grave was unmarked and in time would become a part of the wild landscape behind Tyrone's big stone house. The blue sky would become a headstone, and ivy would grow a protective layer over the ground. The sound of the ocean was steady and constant there, the eternal rhythm of the earth's heartbeat.

No words were said over the grave.

When Reuben, Sarah, and Mrs. Tully had gone back to the house, the others stood in silence for a while.

Of all those involved, they were the five whose lives had been most intertwined with a stolen shipment of Union gold and a deception the world would never know about. They had each played a vital role in history that clearly had also enormously altered their own lives.

Catherine thought of what her life would have been if Tyrone had not built his secret home on Port Elizabeth, thought of the emptiness she would have suffered without him. Of them all, she had been least hurt by the secrets.

She became aware, gradually, that Falcon, Victoria, and Jesse had quietly gone, leaving her and Tyrone alone. She looked up at him as they stood close together, and asked the final question.

"It's over?"

He looked at her, and his lips curved in the smile that had changed her life forever. "It's over, Catherine. The past is buried for good now."

Then he put his arm around her, and walked with her back to the house.

Epilogue

The final entry in Falcon Delaney's journal was dated less than a year later. It was brief, uncoded, and occupied a single page alone.

Under the date of August 1872 were the words:

Born to Marcus and Catherine Tyrone this month, a son.

Named Abraham.

My Dear Maureen,

I know it's been several months since you've heard from me, but as you can see from the heading of this letter, I've been traveling again. I'm writing you from Mr. Shane Marston's Thoroughbred farm here in Kentucky; you should remember he's the husband of Miss Addie Delaney of the Australian branch of our family. Miss Addie was the only one of the three girls who decided to live here in America, and I must say I'm glad to have at least one of them "nearby."

If you're wondering why I'm here, it's because none of my dear boys would hear of me going off to Australia just now, especially since Miss Cara is due within the month. Mr. Burke said firmly he'd have me for *his* firstborn, just like his brothers did. Isn't that nice!

Anyway, since I had a hankering to see Miss Addie's little girl, Mr. Burke sent me out here for a couple of weeks, but made me promise I'd come home the instant he called—as if there was any doubt of that!

Oh, Maureen, you should see Miss Addie's little girl! She's a toddler now—Katie they call her—and she's a love. A tiny redhead, with big dark eyes like her mother and the sweetest smile I've ever seen. Already, she has everyone around scrambling to please her, and it's fair magic the way that child has with animals. Why, Miss Addie's koala, that Sebastian, just follows her around like a puppy—even though I'd swear that creature was asleep most of the time.

Miss Addie's the same as Katie, with that soft voice and sweet smile. You can see that the people around here, friends and employees, just dote on her. As for her husband, why Mr. Shane looks at her with such a glow in his eyes it brings tears to your own. And that little Katie can wrap her father around her tiny finger any time she pleases. It's a good thing that child is so sweet-natured; she'd be spoiled rotten otherwise! Mr. Shane swears they're both enchanted, and I think he's right. My Delaney family is special—I've always said so.

We had visitors here from Australia a few days ago. The pretty lady who used to valet Miss Addie when she was racing came here with her new husband. Her name is Storm, and her husband's name is Tate Justin. They're a fiery pair and no mistake! One minute they're standing toe to toe snapping at each other, and the next they're cooing like turtledoves. They must be Irish!

I've been here a week now, and have had a fine time. Kentucky is quite a change from Arizona, being so green and shady, almost like Ireland. It's a lovely place, but I suppose I've been too long in Arizona to feel a kinship with such a climate. I find myself missing the browns and golds and hot dry air of my beloved Southwest. I think Miss Addie and Mr. Shane know I've been homesick, for it's so kind they've been. Nothing would do but for Mr. Shane to tease me until I made a batch of my gingerbread for him. He pronounced it grand, and he must have meant it because later I saw him feeding some to Sebastian.

I believe I'll finish this letter back at Killara. I know you'll want to know about Miss Cara's babies, and since I'm going home next week . . .

More later.

Tuesday evening
Killara

Maureen—

The babies are here, fine and healthy, and Miss Cara is doing wonderfully. They've named my darlings Brianne and Patrick, after two others of the family who lived long ago, and Mr. Burke is so happy he can't stop smiling.

This family is so blessed! I'm looking forward to seeing to the babies and watching the next generation grow up strong and healthy, just as my boys did.

I was right in what I told you before, Maureen— the years I've spent at Killara and Shamrock have been full of love, and these people, these wonderful Delaneys, do indeed have a grand richness of spirit.

How blessed *I* am!

Love,
Kathleen

P.S. One last thing I wanted to tell you, and thinking of how little Brianne and Patrick are named for long-ago Delaneys made me remember. I know I mentioned to you about all those dusty old journals Mr. Rafe is so crazy about? Well, when he and Miss Maggie came to see the twins, I heard them talking to the others.

It seems there's one special journal, Falcon Delaney's it is, and it's written very oddly—code, Mr. Rafe says. Anyway, Miss Maggie has talked Mr. Rafe into sending the journal off to be deciphered. She thinks it's bound to have exciting things in it, bits of history and all.

Just between you and me—and I'd never breathe a word to Mr. Rafe or Miss Maggie—I think they'll be disappointed. I mean to say, what could have happened that would have been so exciting?

                                                    Kathleen

NEW!
Handsome Book Covers Specially Designed To Fit Loveswept Books

Our new French Calf Vinyl book covers come in a set of three great colors— royal blue, scarlet red and kachina green.

Each 7" × 9½" book cover has two deep vertical pockets, a handy sewn-in bookmark, and is soil and scratch resistant.

To order your set, use the form below.

THE LATEST BOOKS IN THE BANTAM BESTSELLING TRADITION

BANTAM
SHOP-AT-HOME
C·A·T·A·L·O·G

Special Offer
Buy a Bantam Book
for only 50¢.

Now you can have Bantam's catalog filled with hundreds of titles plus take advantage of our unique and exciting bonus book offer. A special offer which gives you the opportunity to purchase a Bantam book for only 50¢. Here's how!

By ordering any five books at the regular price per order, you can also choose any other single book listed (up to a $5.95 value) for just 50¢. Some restrictions do apply, but for further details why not send for Bantam's catalog of titles today!

Just send us your name and address and we will send you a catalog!
